Praise for the first book H

"Debate on global warming helps produce a brisk seller."
New York Times

"A readable book ... remarkably well written ... Not only is the story gripping, it reminds the reader how easily something similar could actually happen, and what the steps to chaos would be. Many of us could use such a warning ... Tushingham is as brave as any of his characters to issue such a warning. And he does it very well."
Charlottetown Guardian

"The deadly events come as rapid fire as, and more unremitting than, in a James Bond movie with no suave hero to save the world. In common with Carson's classic [Silent Spring], this book sends a chill right down one's spine."
Gallon Environment Letter

"A fast-paced novel which seems just ahead of tomorrow's head-lines on the effects of global warming ... Hotter than Hell is an important book because it is a warning ... One hopes the right people will read it."
New Brunswick Telegraph-Journal

"A bullet."
Toronto Star

To Karen and Mike,
I hope you enjoy
my second book.
Mark

HELL
ON EARTH

Sequel to HOTTER THAN HELL

by

MARK TUSHINGHAM

DREAMCATCHER PUBLISHING
Saint John ● New Brunswick ● Canada

TITLE: Hell On Earth

DreamCatcher Publishing acknowledges the support of the Province of New Brunswick.

ISBN 978-0-9784179-1-8

PS8639.U82H45 2008

C81316   C2008-901946-6

Printed and Bound in Canada

Typesetting: J. Gorman

Cover Design: DougBelding.com

DREAMCATCHER PUBLISHING INC.
55 Canterbury St, Suite 8
Saint John, NB, E2L 2C6
Canada
Tel: (506) 632-4008
Fax: (506) 632-4009

"To David,
may your future world be wholly different."

The Lake Ontario Region
of Northern New York and Southern Ontario

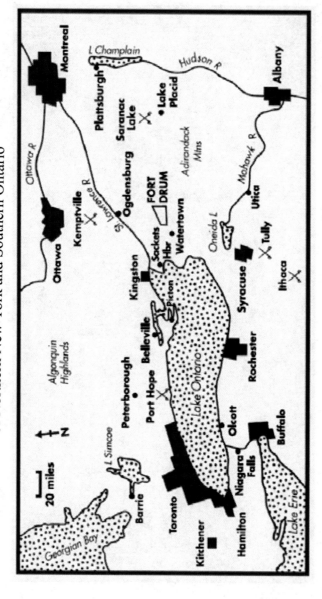

The only Hell we are ever likely to live in is the one we create. I know because I helped create it.

– Lieutenant General Walter J. Eastland
Commanding General, III Corps

Prologue – A Possible Future

Panic took reign as the climate deteriorated. As the world warmed, the energy in the atmosphere grew rapidly and our planet was forced out of balance. The excess energy had to be dissipated somehow; a new balance had to be achieved. As this energy spread through the natural systems of our planet, it caused droughts, floods and hurricanes. It changed patterns of rain and increased evaporation from the soil. Our farmlands dried out. From grain fields to rice paddies, food production struggled, then faltered, and finally failed. Starvation and disease descended on our civilization, and despair was all a generation knew. There were too many fighting for too little.

Governments were overwhelmed by civil strife. For a time, some struggled against the anarchy that spread from country to country, but eventually only I was left to fight on. I was the commander of III Corps, the last organized military force in North America and possibly the world. My army was the last symbol of order in a land destroyed by environmental catastrophes which we, in our greed and ignorance, had brought forth.

But nothing lasted in this hellish world. III Corps finally succumbed to chaos. It tore itself apart in a bloody civil war—a war I lost and fled from. Of my army, only I remained—alone but unbowed.

Death was stalking me and it was close. My enemies had found me.

They're coming.

I'm ready …

Part I

Hell Resurrected

For where we are is Hell and where Hell is, there must we ever be.

– Christopher Marlowe

– Chapter 1 –

Algonquin Highlands

Fear surged through me when I heard the sound of the approaching helicopter, but I fought to master it. I recalled a doctrine my father taught me: control is all, fear is nothing. The doctrine helped. I was a soldier, an officer and a general, who had lived a long and distinguished career with many outstanding achievements. Why should I fear death? I had faced it before and had seen far too much of it. Death held no terrors for me.

My many medals hung against my chest—decorations given to me by an army now destroyed, for heroic acts in the service of a country now gone. Last night when I suspected my capture was imminent I had shined my medals, and now they sparkled in the late morning sun. Major General Hollis Cottick III had taken everything else from me in his coup but I would deny him my dignity. He would find me resolute and defiant.

I tossed my cane beside my tent and walked, with only a hint of a limp, on to a large rock at the tip of the island. My leg, damaged by a splinter bomb many years ago, felt better in the past two weeks than it had in years. I was determined to be found standing proudly, and not leaning on a cane like some pathetic cripple. Lifting my cap I ran my fingers through my thick, gray hair. I combed it the best I could and then replaced my cap. I was ready.

My hideout, a small island amidst the charred forests and dying lakes of the Algonquin Highlands in central Canada, had been discovered. Two weeks ago, Cottick's rebel forces had defeated the last of my army and I had fled. My command survived longer than any other in North America. With it I had imposed order on the civilians in upstate New York and southern Ontario. My iron-fisted rule had saved them from the environmental and social chaos that had consumed the world outside my control, but in the end a civil war had destroyed my command. For years General Cottick, the ambitious commander of the most powerful division within my corps, had planned my overthrow—at first secretly and then in open warfare. His grab for power had succeeded but I had managed to escape from his net. I had been hiding for over two weeks, but his forces had now found me.

The battered helicopter appeared above the tops of the trees and descended to skim just above the surface of the lake. It headed directly for me and quickly reached the island. While it hovered above, the pilot rotated the helicopter so that its left side faced me. The main door slid open and a soldier trained the side machine gun directly at me. The downward blast of air from the rotors blew off my cap, but I made no attempt to retrieve it. With a .50-caliber machine gun pointing at me, I made no movement whatsoever. I kept my arms rigidly by my side. I wouldn't raise them as a sign of surrender, but neither would I offer any resistance or other excuse for them to kill me. Lieutenant General Walter James Eastland, commander of III Corps and once Cottick's superior, would be delivered to Cottick alive.

From the far door, drop-ropes unrolled to the ground and three soldiers descended. They lined up in front of me and leveled their rifles at my chest. No one moved and no one said anything. The helicopter backed away and hovered above the surface of the water. A captain and another soldier jumped off and waded through shallow water towards the others.

The captain, who I recognized but couldn't place a name to, approached. "Lieutenant General Walter Eastland," he said with an unpleasant edge in his voice, "you are under arrest for treason, crimes against the state, crimes against humanity and the murder of two thousand soldiers."

I must have raised an eyebrow at this last charge because one of the soldiers hit me in the chest with the butt of his rifle. I staggered but remained on my feet.

The captain glared at me and then turned away to aid the two soldiers who were ransacking my campsite. While the remaining two soldiers guarded me in silence, the captain and others loaded everything in my campsite into the helicopter. My tent, my cane, my field-stove, my spoon, my spare socks—everything. I flinched as one of the guards suddenly reached out and ripped the medals from my uniform. He slipped them into his pocket while the other guard was busy watching the search of my camp.

I studied the two soldiers who guarded me. I didn't like what I saw or smelled. They were unwashed and reeked and their uniforms were threadbare, but these were common enough. What I found offensive was that they had defaced their uniforms with graffiti. To me the uniform was sacrosanct and to be honored, but these men had desecrated theirs. I had seen this type of graffiti before on the uniforms of prisoners brought before me, but here in the wilderness, and finding myself alone with these men, these graffiti became disconcerting and threatening. There were crude pictures of human skulls, heads of horned demons and other satanic visions, depictions of various weapons, images of rape and murder, and morbid, quasi-religious phrases. One soldier had the words 'Salvation Thru Blood' written across the front of his uniform, although the tattooist had spelled 'Salvation' wrong, putting 'son' instead of 'tion'. The other soldier, a burly, muscular corporal, had his uniform open to his belt. On his powerful chest, I could see a poorly-drawn tattoo of a skull breathing fire with the word 'Death' written above it. On his forearm he had an image of a knife with blood dripping off it. This tattoo appeared fresh and barely healed.

"Put him in the chopper," the captain ordered.

The two soldiers grabbed an arm each and pushed me towards the waiting helicopter. I waded through the warm shallow water, and as I climbed onboard I stole one last glance at my hideout. My stay here was over—a short respite at the end of a difficult and eventful life. I was returning to Hell.

A soldier pushed me into one of the rear fold-down seats. The captain sat on one side of me and the corporal on the other. Facing me, the three privates stared at me menacingly. There were two others onboard: the pilot and the machine gunner. I studied the gunner carefully but discretely. He was very young, fifteen or perhaps even fourteen, and had a nasty scar beneath one eye, possibly from a blow from a fist. The graffiti on the teenager's uniform were sparse compared to those of the other soldiers and I sensed they weren't drawn with the same enthusiasm.

So this was how Cottick had built up his army: he was using children to do his fighting.

I wasn't restrained in any way in the helicopter, probably because of my continuing lack of resistance and the fact that I had nowhere to go, and no one spoke to me. About an hour into the uneventful flight, the soldiers facing me became bored and started to argue about something. I couldn't make out what they were saying over the whine of the helicopter's engine. The two privates began to shove one another and then one punched the other viciously in the side of the head. The two started to brawl. The captain and the corporal seemed to be enjoying the in-flight entertainment, laughing as blood flew from the mouth of one of the combatants. It wasn't until a knife was drawn that the captain and the corporal stood up and intervened.

The corporal soon stopped the fight. It was obvious to me that all onboard, including the captain, were afraid of him. The corporal hit the knife-carrying private hard in the jaw. He grabbed the knife and threatened the private with it. The private made the mistake of arguing and the corporal slashed him across the forehead. Blood from the shallow wound flowed into the private's eyes. The captain held out his hand for the knife, but the corporal ignored him and stuffed it though his belt. The captain withdrew his hand and meekly returned to his seat beside me.

On the island, when first confronted by these soldiers from Cottick's army, I had suspected that discipline within his army had begun to disintegrate; now I knew that for a fact. There might be an opportunity for me if Cottick's command was crumbling—assuming of course that Cottick didn't execute me, his defeated foe, immediately upon my arrival. Much had changed since I last met Cottick over a year ago. The civil war between us had changed everything. III Corps had been destroyed and my troops were scattered, captured or dead. True, I had lost, but now I saw firsthand what the war had cost Cottick. To win, he had resorted to commanding by fear and terror, and because of that he might have destroyed his own army in the process. I commanded by loyalty, duty and order. Cottick hadn't tapped into his soldiers' higher instincts, as I had done, but their baser ones. Those instincts, once unleashed, would be difficult to contain.

I tried to imagine what Cottick's army may have devolved into and what horrors it might be inflicting on the remnants of my command. My imagination, developed in my childhood during the peaceful and prosperous early decades of the twenty-first century, was wholly inadequate to the task.

– Chapter 2 –

Fort Drum

The pilot landed the helicopter. Remarkably smoothly, I thought, considering its dilapidated condition.

We had arrived at Fort Drum near Watertown, New York, home of my beloved Tenth Mountain Division, a division in which I had served for many years and then had the honor to command. More recently, the army base had served as my command center for III Corps. My corps was one of four created to provide American assistance to rebel Canadian generals when they attempted a coup against their government. The generals had offered the United States government unlimited access to Canadian water, and that was an opportunity we could not miss.

The corporal slid open the helicopter's main door and jumped out. The captain started to follow, but seeing my cap on the floor, he bent down and picked it up. He handed it to me without a word and climbed off the helicopter. As soon as I placed the cap on my head, a private put a hand against my back and shoved me out.

I jumped off the helicopter's deck and on to the base's helipad. Pain shot through my bad leg. I paused for a moment to let the pain dissipate. A powerful down-blast whipped about me and I had to keep one hand on my cap to stop it being blown away. The captain pushed me towards a large assemblage of people in the distance. I limped forward, with my guards following close behind. I kept my eyes focused ahead and didn't look around at the soldiers lining the edges of the parade field.

As I neared the assemblage, I at once recognized Major General Hollis Cottick III, commander of the Third Infantry Division and leader of the victorious rebel army. His large, muscular frame was unmistakable. He was almost the same age as me, but he had shaved off his thinning hair to give himself a younger and meaner look. He wore a long, olive-green military jacket open at the front, exposing his powerful, hairless chest. Unlike his soldiers, Cottick had not despoiled his uniform and there were no tattoos on his skin.

Behind me, one of my guards put a hand on my shoulder and shoved me down on to my knees. I instinctively resisted for an instant, but my good sense prevailed and I decided to comply. Kneeling, I looked up into Cottick's eyes: they were wide and bright. He was smiling like a cat about to pounce on a trapped mouse.

Cottick studied me in silence and then suddenly reached out his brawny hand and lifted my cap from my head. He studied it for a moment.

"Private, put this in the trophy room," he ordered a nearby soldier. Cottick then reached down and ripped my general stars from my shoulders. "These too," he added.

He quickly scanned my uniform. "Where are his medals?"

None of Cottick's soldiers moved and no one said a word.

"Captain, where are his medals?"

The captain fidgeted awkwardly. "He was wearing them when we captured him."

"Search them," Cottick shouted.

Soldiers searched the captain and my guards. The medals were found in one of the soldiers' pockets. He was led away under guard. The fear in his eyes told me he knew he was a dead man.

19

My medals were handed to General Cottick, who examined them in his palm for a minute and then placed them in his pocket. He looked at me and smiled malevolently. A shiver ran through my body, and Cottick's smile broadened when he saw this.

"General Eastland," Cottick said in an artificially friendly manner, "welcome to my command. You'll be my guest for the rest of your life." Cottick found this statement funny.

He barked out an order and the row of soldiers behind him parted, revealing three seated figures. Before me, tied to metal chairs and gagged, were Major Generals Donald Tuckhoe and Samuel Price, two of my loyal division commanders, and Major General Eva Micklebridge, my deputy and a close friend and trusted confidant. They had been tortured and were barely conscious. Their faces were badly bruised and their wrists had been rubbed raw by their binding ropes. Every insignia, badge and medal had been torn from their uniforms.

I looked from the tortured faces of my loyal officers and glared at Cottick. Anger surged through me.

I rose to my feet and shouted at him: "Cottick, what have you done? These are fellow officers who surrendered honorably to you. They deserved to be treated properly. For God's sake, they were once your friends! Why did you do this?"

Cottick frowned. "You will address me as General. And you will salute me. I have promoted myself to a full four-star general. I am now your superior."

After the collapse of the United States Army, I had never once considered changing my rank. The Army had made me a three-star lieutenant general and I was proud to have that rank. Obviously, Cottick had not placed such a restriction on himself. His real rank of two-star major general was inferior to mine and I understood Cottick's need to promote himself—but it did not sit right with me.

Cottick smiled oddly at me and his voice changed to a

friendly tone. "I could overlook your outburst but that would set a bad precedent for the men. You need a lesson. We've shared great responsibilities, you and I, so you of all people should understand what has to be done."

I glared at him, and he glared back with eyes that shone with a wild, crazed look.

One of Cottick's soldiers tried to force me back to my knees, but I resisted. Cottick waved the soldier away.

"Soon, Eastland, you'll want to be on your knees before me. You'll acknowledge me as your superior."

"Hollis, you're not well. Turn over your command to me and you'll be well looked after. I promise you'll receive the best medical attention. You have my word as a fellow officer."

I didn't expect a reply from Cottick, but I said this for the benefit of the soldiers that stood nearby. Surely, they couldn't all be blind to what Cottick had become. I had to create internal dissent if I was to survive and reclaim my command. His soldiers had to know that they had another option. I hoped some would rise up—if not now then later.

Cottick ignored what I said. "Lesson One," he shouted.

In a flash, Cottick drew his pistol and placed it against General Price's forehead. Price was too far gone to realize what was happening.

"For God's sake, Hollis. Put the gun down. You've made your point."

A single shot shattered the silence of the parade field. Its echo reverberated for several seconds. I couldn't avert my eyes from the slumped body of General Price.

Cottick grabbed the back of the chair and pushed it over. The limp body of General Price, still tied to the chair, fell over backwards.

"Lesson One is complete. Now, Eastland, on your knees. Beg for my forgiveness."

"Cottick, you'll pay for that!" I attempted to rush at Cottick, but his soldiers held me back.

Cottick watched his soldiers struggle to regain control over me. He smiled as he slowly shook his head in mock disappointment.

"Lesson Two." He moved beside General Tuckhoe and placed the pistol against Tuckhoe's head. Tuckhoe was alert enough to realize what was happening and struggled against his bindings.

"No, Cottick. No! This isn't necessary." I fell to my knees.

Cottick squeezed the trigger and a second shot shattered the silence. He pushed Tuckhoe's body over with his foot.

"You didn't address me as General." He stepped over to General Micklebridge. "Time for Lesson Three, I think. Ask for my forgiveness."

Eva squirmed and mumbled something through her gag. She looked terrified.

"I'm sorry, General Cottick, sir," I groveled. "Please forgive me."

"For what?" he demanded.

This took question took me by surprise and I struggled to invent an acceptable response.

"General Cottick, sir. … Forgive me for challenging your authority … your rightful authority. … I won't do it again, sir. Please don't shoot Eva."

"A good start, Eastland, but you lacked sincerity."

Cottick lowered his gun and shot Eva in the leg. She let out a muffled scream.

"Eva!" I cried out.

She looked at me with pleading eyes and mumbled something but, because of her gag, I couldn't understand what.

"Beg for her life," Cottick demanded.

Rage flooded through me. I didn't trust myself to speak

so I simply shook my head. I realized that we were all going to die regardless of what I said or did. What was the use of abasing myself any further?

He pointed the pistol at Eva's chest, but after looking back at me, he lowered the gun a few degrees. He stared into my eyes, searching for fear, I suppose, but I glared back defiantly. Without looking at his victim Cottick shot Eva in the stomach. Eva writhed in agony.

"Now, Eastland. Beg."

Cottick had done this to my close friend—a friend that had been at my side through many difficult times. He knew what he was doing: a stomach wound would be agonizing and usually resulted in a long, painful death. I couldn't bear to see Eva be tortured like this. My defiance evaporated.

"Please stop, General, sir," I whimpered.

Cottick looked at me and grinned.

"Please stop. She's a good officer. She doesn't deserve this."

Cottick waited patiently.

There was nothing left for me but unconditional surrender. "General Cottick, sir, please let me help Eva. Please."

"Good, Eastland. You've made some progress, but you still resist and make demands upon me. Your training continues. You will now thank me for what I have taught you."

I watched in horror as Cottick put a second bullet into Eva's stomach.

Eva was silent.

Was she dead? How could she still be alive? But then I noticed her hands struggling feebly against the ropes that held her in place.

I clasped my hands together in prayer and said to Cottick, "Thank you, General Cottick, sir. Thank you."

"Louder."

"Yes, sir. Thank you, sir," I shouted for all to hear.

"Again."

I complied.

Finally satisfied, Cottick waved a hand to the soldiers behind me. They lifted me off my knees and then released me.

Freed, I rushed over to Eva before my guards could intervene. I knelt down before her and grasped her hand. I felt a feeble response. Her battered face sagged and life seeped from her eyes. The hand I was holding went limp. Eva Micklebridge, a dear friend and trusted comrade, was dead. I whispered a private goodbye. In my anguish, I attempted to console myself with the fact that she had died in the presence of a friend; I didn't hold out the same hope for myself.

The soldiers pulled me away from Eva and pushed me once again down on to my knees in front of Cottick.

"Very satisfactory," Cottick gloated.

I glared with hate at Cottick. I had never hated anyone so much as I did Cottick at that moment.

"You're stark-raving mad!" I shouted. "For what you have done, I'll make you suffer!"

Cottick looked bored. "Take him to the prison," he ordered as he turned and walked away.

I was escorted to Fort Drum's prison. My mind went numb from the horror I had just witnessed.

* * *

Fort Drum's prison was once home to a large number of military prisoners. When I took command of Fort Drum and the Tenth Mountain Division many years ago, I pardoned most of the prison's inmates on condition that they agree to be integrated into the division. It was an expedient decision, because I hadn't the resources to guard and care for them and I needed soldiers. The final few inmates, dangerous psychopaths who would have endangered my soldiers, had been executed on my orders.

The more intelligent ex-prisoners were placed in a new unit called the 1st Special Support Unit, which later proved to be an effective tool for me. The SSU, as it became known, helped me to control the civilians in upstate New York and southern Ontario. It also provided me with superb intelligence on the world of the urban gangs which existed when I first took command of III Corps. Unfortunately, the commander of the SSU betrayed me and joined General Cottick, and the soldiers of the SSU followed his lead. Since returning to Fort Drum, I had recognized many SSU men among Cottick's soldiers. I had freed them from prison and given them a purpose, and this is how they repaid me.

The cell in which I found myself was a standard one on the ground floor of the prison's main building. It was an interior cell with no window, although there was a window in the cell opposite mine. I could see nothing of interest through its small opening. There was no bed or other furniture, and neither the toilet nor sink functioned. Urine and other unpleasant odors lingered in the air. No one else was imprisoned on the ground floor, but occasionally I heard screams from the floors above.

I was trapped in my cell for three days without seeing anyone, save one guard. He was clearly one of Cottick's fanatics, judging from the amount of graffiti on his uniform and his elaborate tattoos. The guard never said a word to me throughout those first three days. Once a day, he handcuffed me to the bars at the front of the cell, and then he proceeded to clean out the cell. Without a functioning toilet, I had to relieve myself in the corner. Yes, I had descended to that level. The cell, and no doubt my body, smelled awful.

Once the guard had swilled the worst out of the cell, he placed a plastic tray on the ground with my daily rations of food and water. The rations were at starvation level. I suspected that the guard was helping himself to my food before he entered. The guard then unlocked my handcuffs and left. That was it— my daily routine.

On the fourth morning of my imprisonment I awoke with a start. Stiff from my night on the cold floor, I dragged myself up and sat with my back against a wall. I had had a nightmare—about what I could not recall. Something frightening but intangible. In my dream I had screamed, and that was when I awoke.

I was starving for food, but even more for news of what was happening outside my prison cell. No news could be had, and I heard nothing except the screams of my fellow inmates on the floors above. Every once in a while, I spied shadows on the window of the empty cell opposite, sometimes of one person passing by and other times of many. I spent the day alone, fed up and depressed.

That evening, about an hour before the sun set, my boredom abruptly ended. A tall, thin soldier with a feral face, who I recognized as an ex-SSU man, came to my cell, flanked by two other soldiers. The SSU man stated that I was to have an audience with Cottick. The way he said it implied that I was greatly honored to be granted such a rare privilege. I followed the SSU man, with the two guards trailing behind us. Together we left the prison and walked across the base towards the main command center.

I entered the building and was led down into the basement. I was told to stop in front of the door to a room which held the base's supply of maps. The SSU man knocked on the door and waited. After a moment or two, the door opened and another soldier came into view.

I was shoved through the door, which was then closed behind me. The Map Room was a series of large interconnected chambers where once thousands of maps had been stored. There were no maps here anymore for someone had removed them all. Instead, the room was full of officers' caps, insignias, nametags, battle decorations, medals and other military paraphernalia. These had been meticulously placed on tables or on the floor or nailed upon the walls. A soldier pushed me forward into a smaller chamber. Inside, Cottick waited, flanked by two guards.

"Welcome to my trophy room, Eastland," Cottick stated with pride. "You may look around at my collection. Impressive, isn't it?"

Before I could move or say anything, I was kicked hard in the back of my legs. My knees buckled and I fell to the floor. Pain shocked through my bad leg like a jolt of electricity. A gasp escaped my mouth.

"Impressive, isn't it?" he repeated as I struggled to my feet.

"Yes, General Cottick, sir. Very impressive." After what happened to Eva, I had no dignity or defiance left in me.

Pleased with my reply, Cottick bid me towards his trophies. I walked up to the first table and noticed my cap and general stars displayed prominently. Other generals' stars were nearby. There were medals galore including, I noticed, my own. The soldiers of III Corps had been brave men and women and were highly decorated. I was proud to have led them. My training at West Point all those decades ago had taught me that it was a commander's duty to care for the soldiers under his command. How completely I had failed them. I felt ashamed.

I came to a display of nametags. This was the worst yet. I read some of the names: Micklebridge, Tuckhoe and Price were there. The memory of how they died drained me. My eyes watered and I could barely read the next few names. I then saw a name that I didn't expect. There was a nametag belonging to a brigadier general in Cottick's own Third Division, one who I had believed to be particularly devoted to Cottick. Why was his name tag on display?

I noticed Cottick standing beside me, and as if he could read my mind Cottick stated: "He was disloyal and he questioned my methods. To be frank, Eastland, I'm becoming distrustful of other generals in my command. I know they want to take my command away from me. They're all plotting to get power. I just can't trust anyone, particularly not other generals. One day, Eastland, there will be no other generals but me—none at all."

He paused and looked thoughtfully at the ground.

"But of course, you're a general, aren't you, Eastland? And that won't do. Fortunately, I can quickly remedy that."

I thought I was going to be killed then and there, but Cottick's mad solution saved me. He reached over to the display of my cap and stars. He picked them up and beckoned me to follow. We walked out of the building and towards a nearby latrine—apparently none of the base's toilets functioned under Cottick's thoughtful management. Cottick casually threw my cap and stars into the dung-filled hole. The insignias of my rank, which I had sacrificed so much to obtain, disappeared into its murky depths.

"There," Cottick announced with finality. "You're no longer a general." He strolled away without saying another word.

I was escorted back to my cell. My second meeting with Cottick was mercifully over and I still lived. As long as I did, there was a chance that I could avenge my men.

– Chapter 3 –

Prison

Over the next few weeks my routine remained unchanged. Life in my small cell was uncomfortable, but I was still alive. The weather outside oscillated between muggy heat and damp cold. Winter was coming, but summer wouldn't relinquish its fierce grip without a fight. It was suffocating in my cell in the hot weather, but at least then my cell was dry. During the cold spells, my cell was damp from the condensation which formed on the concrete walls. The old wound in my leg ached badly and I suspected that I had arthritis in my knee.

Whenever the mood took him, Cottick visited me and in his presence I was subjected to one form of humiliation or another. Occasionally I suffered physical torture, but that wasn't the rule. Cottick preferred to see me groveling before him. Because I wanted to live, I abased myself without shame.

With the exception of Cottick's visits, the boredom of my prison life was crushing. All my life, I had been used to activity and making important decisions, but now all I could do was stare at the walls and think. I didn't want to dwell on the past but in spite of my resolve I did anyway.

In the prosperous and predictable world to which I was born sixty-four years ago, I would have retired by now after a distinguished military career. I would have had a cabin in the mountains, where I would write my memoirs and entertain old colleagues. We would sit on the veranda and reminisce about our careers, basking in our achievements and romanticizing about our hardships. Perhaps I would have gone skiing in the winter. I was a good skier in my youth. My father, an expert, encouraged me in the sport, pushing me to ever greater challenges. He would fly down the slope and I had to push myself to my limit just to keep him in sight.

Skiing—that was a laugh. Snow was virtually unknown now. On occasion, once every few winters, it did get cold enough for snow to fall, but it never lasted on the ground for more than a day or two. Short, cool, wet winters were followed by long, scorching, dry summers.

At school, I remember being taught all about how we were changing the world's climate and what the future would bring. The concepts were abstract and remote. Neither I, a child who would inherit the world, nor the adults, who had the power to stop the change, truly believed the world could change so drastically. The world was comfortable and fertile, and it would always remain so. Our civilization was rich and complacent.

When I was a child, we could have stopped the impending disaster, or at least slowed its approach and better prepared ourselves for its impacts. But no. That would have required acknowledgement of the real scale of the impacts and the enactment of painful and unpopular solutions. As it was, little was done until the climate disaster was evident to all.

I was there at the place and at the time when the disaster could no longer be ignored. Twenty years ago, when I was a major, the event that opened the world's eyes occurred: the Los Angeles Water Riot. A searing heat-wave and a prolonged drought in Los Angeles forced the government to issue draconian water rationing laws, and these led inexorably to a devastating riot by the thirst-crazed residents of Los Angeles. The riot left nearly one hundred thousand dead, including the leaders of the California government, who were attending a political convention in the city. There were over one million wounded and the hospitals of California and the neighboring states were overwhelmed. The fires set by the rioters during their battles against the Army engulfed the city and left eight million homeless. I was there, and I barely escaped with my life.

After the Los Angeles Water Riot, governments around the world panicked. Faced with an impending global disaster, crushing environmental laws were enacted. It was too late. There was no time for the global economy to adjust and it collapsed. Our civilization's wealth evaporated almost overnight and billions starved. It was too late to stop the change to the climate; the damage had been done and the change was irreversible and unstoppable. Nature had won the race. Droughts led to famines, famines caused disease, disease resulted in social disintegration, and social disintegration meant war.

War was endemic. Country fought country for dwindling resources. The defeated populations were ruthlessly destroyed, and the victorious countries turned on themselves. Civil war and warlords became the rule. I should know because I was the first American warlord. My command, III Corps, was the first to declare its independence from a ruined United States government. Other Army units followed my example and the United States of America was no more.

My command, which covered northern New York and southern Ontario, was the largest of the independent commands and it lasted longer than all the others. Then like a wounded animal maddened by pain, it, too, turned upon itself. Led by General Cottick, rebel units of III Corps fought my loyal units. Cottick's forces won and my army was destroyed. My friends and colleagues were dead and Cottick had me prisoner.

But why did I dwell on the past? I had too much time to think in my tiny cell, and that did no good at all. It was better to focus on survival.

* * *

One afternoon in early December, Cottick visited me in my cell. The weather was unusually humid and the warm air made me lethargic. I lay on the floor dozing and didn't notice Cottick arrive.

"Eastland!"

My eyes opened immediately and I struggled to rise. With my old leg wound and my arthritis, it was difficult to get up. Cottick knew this and enjoyed watching me in pain. I got on my knees before him. Cottick's goons had trained me well as to the position I had to assume when I was in his presence.

Cottick was seated on a fold-up metal chair on the other side of the cell-bars. He was alone, which was unusual—in fact it was unique. Cottick had never come to my cell alone. At a minimum he had his goons, but usually there were other soldiers as well and occasionally even civilians. Cottick liked an audience to witness my humiliation.

Furtively, I scanned either side of Cottick. We were indeed alone.

There was a distant crack of thunder. Cottick turned and looked behind him through the window of the cell opposite mine.

I remained on my knees in silence. Outside I could hear the wind whistling.

At length, Cottick turned back and faced me. "There's a storm coming. A big one," he said in a conversational tone.

"Yes, sir, General Cottick, sir," I groveled.

"Enough of that, Walter. You're not as broken as you pretend. You can stop the act. It has been amusing to watch but today isn't the day for it."

Walter?

What was going on?

There was another crack of thunder, closer this time.

Cottick waited for the rumble to subside, and when it had he said calmly, almost benevolently: "I'm planning your execution. It's long overdue, Walter. Long overdue." He slowly shook his head as if he was chastising himself for overlooking such an important task.

Over the past weeks, Cottick had often claimed that my execution was imminent, but this time I truly believed him. Perhaps it was the way he was talking to me, or perhaps it was because this time he was alone and had no audience to perform to.

"Christmas will be ideal. I'll have plenty of time to make the arrangements and my men will welcome the entertainment. It will be memorable, Walter."

As if on cue, a blinding flash of lightning appeared in the window behind Cottick, followed immediately by a prolonged and deafening blast of thunder which shook the walls. After the thunder stopped, I could hear the roar of the wind and the pellets of rain hitting the window. Such violent storms were common enough, but rare for December.

"Hmm. It looks like the heavens have opened up," Cottick said. "I don't want to go out in that, so I'll have to remain here with you. We can talk about old times."

I remained on my knees and silent.

"Come on, Walter, off your knees. We shouldn't waste this opportunity to have a chat. There aren't many of us left who can remember the good old days."

I didn't move for I was wary of being tricked and wanted to avoid the pain that would inevitably follow.

"Please, Walter." He waved his hand as a sign for me to rise.

Cautiously, I struggled to my feet, and with no reaction from Cottick I walked over to the far wall and sat on the floor facing Cottick.

"Walter, do you remember Vegas? Now there was a place you could have fun. The gambling and the shows, and of course the women! They always showed you a good time. There was one. She was good—really good … What was her name?" Cottick sighed. "I can't remember. It's been thirty years since

I was there last. What a shame they had to close it down."

Had Cottick's insanity overwhelmed him or was this a rare lucid moment? Or was it all an act? One moment Cottick was planning my execution and the next he wanted to reminisce about Las Vegas. Where would this lead? Was this friendly Cottick more or less dangerous than the other Cottick? I decided to take the plunge without knowing how deep the water was.

"I remember Las Vegas," I said, "especially the lights. In fact, I was there when they were turned on for the last time."

"Were you?" Cottick seemed genuinely interested.

I nodded. "I was a captain in charge of a company which was protecting the Army engineers when they shut off the electricity to the city. But before they did, they treated us all to one last display."

"I remember the lights. They were spectacular. Something we won't see again. What a loss. The young will never know what we had."

"Maybe that's for the best."

Cottick mused on my observation for a while and then nodded. "Perhaps you're right."

"Hollis, what's this all about?" My plunge was complete and I was now immersed neck-deep in water.

"Walter, you and I graduated from West Point where we were taught to do our duty. We have commanded men in battle, made great decisions, and done whatever was necessary to win. We're the same, you and I. There is no one else I can talk to."

I could not let that pass.

"We're not the same," I insisted. "My duty was to protect my men from the disasters that befell our country. I wasn't the one who destroyed our corps."

"No, you did far worse. You destroyed the United States Army. You pushed the first domino and then everything I valued collapsed. What I did pales in comparison."

"It's not the same at all. The world was disintegrating, but I managed to maintain order in one small corner. The world needs order, not the chaos you have brought."

"The world needs cleansing. I see my duty clearly. You were content to put up your walls and hold only what you had. Don't you see? We had a larger mission—one which you ignored. We had to save the rest of America, not just a sliver of northern New York. We must advance out from our enclave and go and save the rest. The old world has to be brushed away one way or another, and only then can we start again fresh and renewed. It's my destiny to undertake that task, and no matter how unpleasant it will be I'll do whatever is necessary."

"III Corps was barely strong enough to hold what we had, and you want to throw away our men's lives on some damnable crusade?"

"It has to be done and I will do it. You were in my way."

Cottick was mad and I was arguing with him. What did that make me?

"And what about Eva? And Tuckhoe and Price? You murdered them in front of me. Your colleagues and your friends. You murdered them."

"They disobeyed orders. They wouldn't tell me where you were hiding."

"They didn't know!"

Cottick shrugged.

Another clap of thunder shattered the air, and rain continued to smash against the pain of glass in the window opposite.

After the interruption, Cottick continued: "You needed to be taught a lesson. You had to understand that it was I who now commanded III Corps. My men had to see you obey my orders. And they did."

I lashed out. "You're twisted, Cottick. You should be put down like the mad animal you are."

Cottick smiled. "So, Eastland, you tire of our chat. You

really don't understand, do you? We have a great mission, but you ignored it. Yes, your execution is long overdue."

There was a rumble of thunder, quieter and more distant that the previous ones. The rain slackened noticeably.

"I'm going to miss you, Eastland. You entertain me. Your execution will have to be very special. Unique. I'm looking forward to arranging it."

Cottick left with an air of smugness. He seemed pleased with his afternoon's performance and excited about his plans for my execution.

I remained seated on the floor of my cell, alone with my thoughts and the sound of rain gently tapping against the window.

– Chapter 4 –

Parade Field

Christmas Day, the day of my execution, had arrived. For the past week, Cottick had visited my cell daily to hint at some gruesome plan for my execution. My death was going to be a grand spectacle, complete with hundreds of spectators.

At dawn, I was visited by a major and three guards. The major ordered me to remove my clothes. Once naked, I was hosed down with freezing cold water, while my threadbare clothes were taken away to be washed. Dirt and grime were slowly scrubbed away. It felt good to be clean again. I had long accepted my upcoming death and promised myself to enjoy whatever modicum of pleasure I could take from the day. The cold shower felt invigorating and I focused on that pleasure alone.

After I dried off from the shower, I was provided with a meal. I was still naked as my clothes hadn't yet been returned. I sat on the floor with the plastic tray on my knees and stared at the meal before me. My mouth watered at the sight. The meal contained the largest portions I had seen during my captivity. Mash potatoes, dandelion leaves, a tiny carrot, and some type of fatty meat (God only knows what). I drank hot dandelion tea from a delicate china teacup, and I was even provided with a dessert: a small, thin cake drenched in honey. It was the most delicious meal I had ever tasted and I savored every mouthful.

Some time after I finished my meal, my clothes were returned. I was saddened to see that someone had drawn graffiti on my uniform depicting numerous skulls and demons surrounding a central stick-figure, which I assumed represented me. I loathed putting on my defaced uniform but I had little choice. Once I was dressed, the major returned and placed a chair in the middle of my cell and sat down. He commenced reading a long list of charges which had been brought against me and a tirade of justifications for my impending execution. I didn't even pretend to be interested, and I sensed that the major was only going through the motions.

My mind wandered and I thought of my mother. I had not thought of her in years. Why should I think of her now? Perhaps all condemned prisoners think of their mother just prior to their execution. I could barely remember mine, just images of a thin, tired-looking woman from old photographs and a few flashes of disjointed childhood memories. My most vivid memory of her was at her funeral when, as a child of ten, I peered over the edge of the casket and saw her lying there. She looked so peaceful. I started to cry as I reached out to take hold of her hand, but my father seized my hand and stopped me touching her.

In an angry whisper, my father scolded me. "Walter, stop that! You're stronger than her. Your mother did something stupid and doesn't deserve your pity. Be strong."

Be strong. How many times had I heard my father say that to me?

My father pulled me away from the casket and dragged me out of the room. He never spoke of her again. When I was older and could understand such things, I came to believe that he took her suicide as a defect in himself and he could not forgive her for disgracing him so publicly.

I dismissed that unpleasant memory. Today was not the time for such melancholy thoughts. Instead, I focused on a happier time with my mother. She was reading to me at bedtime when I was five or six years old. I can't recall the name of the book but it had talking mice in it. I remember watching her thin, bony fingers pointing to pictures in the book and her telling me all about what the pictures showed. Her voice was quiet and reassuring. My mother had gotten out of her bed just to read to me, and that made me feel special and loved. The warmth of that moment flooded through me and gave me strength for what lay ahead.

The major's speech was agonizingly long, but at last the denunciation mercifully concluded and I was told to stand. The major informed me that it was exactly noon and it was time for my execution. For the first time since I arrived, I was offered the use of my old cane but I refused it. The major placed the cane against the wall of my cell.

The major led the way, followed by me and the three guards who had hosed me down. We walked to the prison's exit. My leg ached badly and I limped, but I wasn't about to change my mind and ask for my cane. Outside we were joined by more guards, their uniforms resplendent with Cottick's gruesome graffiti.

As my guards ushered me towards the base's parade field, snowflakes swirled in the air around us. The fine mist of snow was delicate and ephemeral. Large bonfires had been lit all around the perimeter of the field. The parade field was the one I had marched on as a young second lieutenant just assigned to the Tenth Mountain Division. It was also the same field on which, as a newly-promoted major general, I had assembled my troops when I first took command of the demoralized division. In some way, I felt it fitting that I should die on the field that held so many good memories for me.

In the distance, Cottick was seated in the parade-stands, surrounded by his officers and soldiers and some civilians. In front of the stands, there was a collection of ominous-look contraptions—no doubt designed by Cottick's twisted mind. I shuddered and looked away from the torture devices.

I reached the center of the field. All was quiet. I felt strangely serene.

Suddenly, gunfire shattered the hushed atmosphere.

A bullet ripped through the back of the major's head and two soldiers crumpled to the ground beside me. Another soldier fell. I spun around to face the sound of the shots. I couldn't see who was killing my guards. Another soldier fell and three others fled. The two remaining guards fired wildly at who-knows-what, for I couldn't see any target. First one and then the other was hit in the head. I still didn't have an idea where the sniper was. The sound of the shots echoed off the walls of the various buildings, which made it impossible to locate him. He could be anywhere. This sniper was good.

I found myself momentarily alone in the center of the field. I was unsure what to do or which way to run. Someone had a plan, so I would let him or her come to me. I crouched down and waited. Maybe five seconds or so after the last soldier fell about a dozen horses and riders came out from behind the Junior Officers' Quarters. As they charged towards me, some of the riders fired at the stands while others shot at different targets. The bullets flew wildly and ineffectually, but they forced those in the stands to dive for cover.

Two soldiers stopped near me. One led a large black horse, while the other looked down at me and smiled. I looked up to see the familiar face of Lieutenant Colonel Jan Sheflin, loyal commander of the 317th Cavalry Battalion. Her pretty face beamed, and her shoulder-length blonde hair whipped about in the wind. At that moment, she appeared as though she was an angel.

"Quickly, sir! Get up."

I needed no additional encouragement and I climbed into the saddle, never giving a moment's thought to my bad leg.

While I was commander of the Tenth Mountain Division, I had encouraged Sheflin's efforts to replace the 317th's armored fighting vehicles with horses, and so the battalion once again became an old-fashioned cavalry unit. Due to the never-ending fuel shortages, the reconnaissance battalion had lost its mobility and Sheflin's clever solution was supremely effective. Her petite frame held within it probably the most imaginative officer I had ever commanded—both a visionary and an achiever. Her loose but dynamic and ever-enthusiastic style of command worked well for her, and she was well-liked and respected by the soldiers of the 317th. The unit itself was superb, with the highest morale of any unit under my command. It saddened me when, near the end of the war against Cottick's forces, I was informed that the 317th was cut off on the Isle of Quinte on the northern shore of Lake Ontario. At the time I assumed that the unit had been captured or destroyed.

Sheflin led me and her eleven soldiers towards the southwest perimeter of Fort Drum. I was still too stunned by my sudden and unlooked-for escape from an unpleasant death to worry about mundane problems such as how to get past Cottick's men guarding the base's perimeter fence. Sheflin had solved that problem. I was astounded to see some of Cottick's men standing at attention and saluting me as we charged through a wide gap cut in the fence. I automatically return a salute. Yes indeed, Cottick's command was crumbling. Excellent!

Once we were though the gap, the men at the perimeter fence started firing at us, but this was just for show and no one was hit. Several of Sheflin's men fired back, with an equal lack of effect.

We traveled southwest at a gallop until we reached a deserted village where we joined up with more mounted soldiers from the 317th. In all, Sheflin's force now totaled some sixty cavalrymen. All the soldiers of my rescue party were heavily armed—all that is but one. When we stopped and dismounted for a brief rest, I corrected that situation immediately. I demanded a weapon and was promptly issued with a spare automatic rifle. It felt good to have a weapon back in my hands. I slung the rifle over my shoulder and strode over to Sheflin.

She was talking to her deputy, but when she saw me approach she snapped a salute. I returned the crispest, sharpest salute I had given for years. It was a salute that a West Point cadet would give to his drill sergeant. I then did the most unmilitary act that I had ever done. I grabbed the short woman and gave her a lengthy bear-hug, lifting her off her feet. I was that relieved to be free of Cottick. I recovered myself and released my embrace. Sheflin looked flustered and embarrassed at my surprising act of emotion, and her face reddened.

"Glad to have you safe again, sir," Sheflin said after a brief moment of awkward silence.

"I'm very glad to be safe, Colonel. That was a superb performance. Just superb! You and your men are to be commended."

"I can't believe that we managed to pull it off," Sheflin's deputy said to no one in particular.

"But you did," I exclaimed as I reached out to shake his hand. I turned to Sheflin and her soldiers. "Cavalrymen, I can't praise you enough. It was a thoroughly professional operation. Once again, the cavalry came over the hill at the last moment to complete a daring rescue." I turned to Sheflin and said quietly, "Thank you, Colonel. Well done."

"But now to business, sir. I don't think General Cottick will allow you to escape without a fight."

The brief moment of levity abruptly ended. Sheflin was correct. Cottick would do everything he could to recapture me. I was certain Cottick realized that if I escaped I would eventually return to kill him. However, my escape was not certain. Here I was, just south of Fort Drum. The base contained many elements of his Third Infantry Division, and further to the south, units from his Fifth Guard Division barred the way. Cottick had thousands of soldiers at his command; I had just sixty.

I asked Sheflin for the plan of escape.

"We have a navy, sir," she said with a mischievous grin. She shouted loudly to her men, "We ride to Sackets Harbor. Let's get the General home!"

A cheer went up from the men and everyone remounted.

As we rode west towards Sackets Harbor on the eastern end of Lake Ontario, we heard a helicopter searching for us far away to the south, but otherwise the trip was uneventful. I was concerned that Cottick might place pickets along Interstate 81, but we crossed the disused highway unobserved and without incident.

We reached Sackets Harbor in the late afternoon. A lieutenant and another ten or so men of the 317th greeted us when we arrived. They saluted and I returned the gesture with pleasure. The lieutenant reported that the ship was secure. Sheflin acknowledged the report and then asked me if I would like to inspect my new navy.

She led me over the brow of a hill and there sitting quietly in the small harbor was an old roll-on-roll-off car ferry. It looked ancient. There was barely enough paintwork left on its rusted surface to show that it had once had a black hull and a white superstructure.

"Sir," the lieutenant reported to Colonel Sheflin, "it will take us another fifteen minutes to get the engines working again. We couldn't afford the fuel to keep them going while we awaited your return."

Sheflin nodded in acknowledgement. She then left with the lieutenant to go onboard the ferry to supervise the finicky procedure of starting the antique and worn-out engines.

Sheflin's deputy departed to inspect the outer pickets. So far we hadn't seen any evidence of Cottick's soldiers, but it was best to be safe. I was left alone, with just one soldier for protection. I dismounted and held the reins of my horse. My mount was a large, placid mare with a midnight-black coat, powerful chest muscles and a noble head. I stroked her nose and she whinnied in appreciation. Then and there, I named her Judge, as a reminder of what role I would take the next time I met Cottick: I would be his judge and I would find him guilty.

What happened next happened in agonizing slow-motion

43

and with a dreadful sense of inevitability. We all heard the sound of approaching helicopters at the same time. The distinctive noise of their blades was unmistakable.

I shouted to the soldier next to me: "Did you bring any surface-to-air missiles?"

"I think so, sir. I'll check."

"Hurry! Get a missile ready."

The soldier rushed away to find his sergeant.

I saw a massive helicopter gunship rise over a distant hill and fly down the length of the bay. Behind it followed a smaller scouting helicopter. There was a flash of flame as the helicopter gunship let loose an air-to-surface missile. The flight of the missile took a second, maybe two, to traverse the distance between the gunship and the old ferry. I watched transfixed as the missile slammed into the ferry and exploded. The flash momentarily blinded me and then the blast-wave hit me and flung me backwards on to the soft grass. My horse bolted and pulled the reins out of my hand. I recovered quickly and looked up at the approaching helicopter gunship just as one of our portable surface-to-air missiles slammed into it. The main rotors spun wildly away from the fuselage, and the helicopter fell from the air and crashed into the bay. As it sank, the men of the 317th sprayed the wreckage with bullets. There were no survivors. With the larger helicopter destroyed, the smaller scouting helicopter retreated out of sight.

I rushed over to the ferry. Thick black smoke belched from its side and covered much of the deck. Rescue operations had just started when I arrived. Six men were dead on the deck, and three more were floating face-down in the water nearby. I watched two soldiers dive into the water to drag out a wounded comrade. Ducking low, beneath the choking smoke, I ran along the deck toward the main engine hatchway. A man dragged himself out of the open hatch to the engine room and then staggered and fell. I rushed over to him. His uniform was smoldering and his face and hands were badly burned, but

44

I recognized him as the young lieutenant who had left with Sheflin. He died there in my arms.

I looked up as a sergeant ran through the hatch and climbed down into the engine room. Moments later he emerged with a body draped over his shoulder. He lay the body down beside me; it was the blackened body of Lieutenant Colonel Sheflin. A jagged piece of metal protruded from her cheek and blood and soot covered her face. Blood oozed from her right eye.

Sheflin, my rescuer, was dead. She had risked everything for me. I laid my hand on her charred uniform and said goodbye to my angel. A powerful feeling of injustice overwhelmed me.

I felt her chest rise. I couldn't believe it. She was alive!

"Medic!" I shouted.

The medic knelt beside me and started to work on Sheflin. Occasionally he instructed me to hold a bandage or put pressure on a wound. I did whatever he asked and would not allow anyone else to take over from me.

After what seemed an eternity (but was probably less than two minutes) the medic nodded to me and said that it wasn't as bad as it looked and that Colonel Sheflin should be okay. He carefully washed the blood and black soot from her blistered face. The burns weren't severe but they complicated the removal of the piece of metal. The medic gently tugged at the metal shard and it slowly slid out of the wound. He told me to gently but firmly press a cotton pad on to the wound. The medic swabbed Sheflin's face with the last of the burn-jelly and injected her with irreplaceable drugs.

Slowly his patient opened her good eye. I felt a huge surge of relief flow through me. The beautiful angelic face that had looked down at me on the parade ground only hours before was now grotesquely disfigured, but at least my rescuer was alive.

"How many?" she mumbled.

That was typical of this fine officer. Her first thought was for soldiers under her command.

"Ten," I replied solemnly. "You and another are wounded. But don't worry—I will get you and your men to safety."

"But I was supposed to rescue you."

"You did. And it is now my duty and honor to return the favor."

I stood and rallied the men around me. Colonel Sheflin was their leader and had been for many years. They were stunned by the events of the last few minutes and needed reassuring.

"Your colonel will be fine," I informed the assembled soldiers, "but the escape route she planned is gone. We have to leave now. Load the wounded on the horses and put the bodies into the lake, weighed down with something if you can. We're not leaving anyone to Cottick's mercy—not even the dead. We leave in five minutes."

A quick, unceremonious burial in the bay was the best I could do for soldiers who had given their lives to save me. They deserved more and one day I might be able to give them more, but not today.

We rode south for the remainder of the day. The sound of a helicopter accompanied us for an hour before it faded. I assumed that it had to return to base due to it running low on fuel. That was the last we heard from any of Cottick's forces. When night fell, I turned the men east. I had decided to head for a place which I knew well but Cottick didn't. As a teenager, I had hiked and skied in the Adirondack Mountains, so I didn't need a map to know my way around the hills and valleys and lakes. Once again, I sought refuge in a wilderness, but this time it wasn't to hide and avoid capture: it was to build and organize my forces. When next I confronted Cottick, I would have an army behind me.

– Chapter 5 –

Mount Marcy

Dawn broke. A wonderful pink glow appeared in the sky as the rays of the rising sun caught the bases of some clouds. I wasn't the least bit tired from the night's ride. Life felt sweet and precious to me and I noticed everything around me. Damn, it felt good to be alive.

I led my men into the wilderness of the Adirondack Mountains and navigated a route by memory through the charred tree-trunks that covered the hills. Most of the once-proud forest had been engulfed in a huge fire a few summers ago. The scorching summer temperatures dried out everything in the forest and it needed only a single bolt of lightning to start a raging fire. Grasses and scrub bushes grew here and there, but they were meager and thin. Occasionally, I spied a squirrel scrambling through the undergrowth or a bird flying above. The forest had been destroyed, but a new one was slowly growing back in its place. Life continued, but I wondered how long this new growth would last, given the summer droughts and heat-waves that were now the norm. When would the next great fire sweep through?

I have always enjoyed the raw splendor of wild places, so the sight of such destruction of nature's work would normally have depressed me. Today, however, nothing could get me down. I saw beauty in everything: the pink sky above, the green grass below, even the charred trunks. The ruins of the forest were majestic in their own way.

Behind me I heard the reassuring sounds of a moving column of cavalry: horses snorting, hooves hitting stones, soldiers fidgeting in their saddles. My troops were physically and mentally exhausted from the exploits of yesterday. The adrenaline rush from battle had ebbed and fatigue had taken its place. I, however, was fresh and ready for what the day would bring. I had plans to make, operations to put into motion, and an army to create.

We rode in column formation through an area of the Adirondacks which I knew well from my youth. We skirted the southern shore of a lake, which after the constant summer droughts was just a remnant of its former self. As a teenager I swam in this lake's crystal-clear water, but now I wouldn't want to go near the muddy, algae-filled bog that the lake had become.

We reached a road and traveled along it and into a deserted village on the shore of the lake. The buildings lining the road were dilapidated and slowly decaying. Windows had shattered long ago, roofs were holed or had completely collapsed, and once-manicured lawns were now covered by weeds and shrubs.

I recognized one ruin as a small motel where my father had once taken me for a long weekend away. It was a happy time. That vacation was one of the few times that my father, a hard, morose and sullen man, had laughed (at least around me). He had taken me on an arduous hike into the hills. To build character, he told me. Building my character was a sacred parental duty to my father, and one he took very seriously and spent considerable effort planning. My father was immensely fit and strong, as one would expect from the commander of an elite Special Forces team, and any physical weakness on my part was unacceptable. During the hike, a chipmunk darted out of the undergrowth directly in front of where I was walking and surprised me. I stumbled backwards and tripped over a root, and my canteen flew out of my hand and gracefully arced through the air. It landed directly in my father's hands. He took a long drink from my canteen and then thanked me. Afterwards, he burst out laughing. I wasn't sure if he was laughing at the miraculous trajectory of the canteen or at my clumsiness. I remember sitting there in the grass looking up at him while he laughed. I hardly recognized him and I actually felt quite uncomfortable with this unusual behavior. Remoteness, not levity, was his norm.

I left the lake and my childhood memories behind and continued on. There was no time for such daydreaming now, so I dismissed my ancient memories and resolved not to let them intrude again.

Our column left the road and returned to the dirt paths of the forest. I didn't want to risk detection by Cottick's soldiers, who would put a priority on watching the roads. In the distance, I saw the peak of Mount Marcy, the highest hill in the Adirondacks. In the shadow of that hill, I would rebuild my army.

* * *

It was a new year and a new beginning. I had set up my headquarters on the slopes of Mount Marcy, some fifteen miles south of the old resort town of Lake Placid.

At my first command meeting, I took stock of my situation. I had with me Lieutenant Colonel Sheflin, who was wounded, four other officers, forty-eight soldiers, fifty-seven horses, little in the way of rations, limited ammunition, and no heavy weapons. There was an assortment of light weapons, ranging from army-issue pistols to one light mortar with only four rounds of ammunition. We had used up our supply of portable surface-to-air missiles during the helicopter attack at Sackets Harbor. My communication equipment consisted of three hand-cranked field radio sets, one of which had been damaged in the fight at Sackets Harbor. In any case, I couldn't use the radios without Cottick picking up the signal and triangulating on my position, so for now they were useless. Everyone had an automatic rifle, plus we had seventeen anti-personnel grenades to share out amongst us. Each soldier carried a killing knife, and we each had armored upper-body vests, with three spares taken from those who died at Sackets Harbor. There were tents and sleeping mats for about a third of us, which was adequate because we would sleep in three shifts. As for food, we had barely enough for three days. When I was the commander of the Tenth Mountain Division, I had developed good relations with the local farmers. I hoped that they would remember and supply my food requirements. I sent messages, via couriers on horseback, to a number of trusted farmers to the north of the Adirondacks.

I felt as though I had returned to the Stone Age. My poverty in men and supplies was acute, but nothing worried me. I was once again in command—and that would be more than enough.

Colonel Sheflin insisted on providing me with a report on intelligence which the 317th had gathered during my absence. Rumors would be a more accurate description of what I was listening to. Sheflin had barely recovered from her injuries, but she had refused to stay any longer in our cold, makeshift field hospital under the care of our only medic and his limited medical supplies. Under the circumstances, I couldn't blame her. I insisted that Sheflin take more time to recover from her injuries, but she was adamant that she could return to duty. I let her have her way and treated her as though nothing had happened, which was what she wanted. The wound to her cheek was heavily bandaged and the medic had covered her damaged eye with a patch. He didn't know whether she had permanently lost the vision in that eye.

After the surrender of my forces to General Cottick, a few of my men had managed to slip through Cottick's net and escape into the wilderness of the Adirondack Mountains and regions to the north and east. My first task was to find all these loyal soldiers and rally them to me. I ordered scouts to be sent out immediately.

After I gave my orders, I noticed that Sheflin was fidgeting on her feet. I ran a tighter command than Sheflin, but I never wanted my officers to feel that they couldn't argue their point with me, so long as it was done discretely and not in front of the men. I asked Sheflin to tell me what was bothering her.

"Sir, I'm concerned about sending all these scouts out at once."

"Go on."

"Sir, with so many scouts out, the odds of one of them getting caught increase. If General Cottick finds out where we are, we will quickly find ourselves in trouble. We should take time to build up slowly and secretly. My original plan was to use the ferry to take you back to the Isle of Quinte and build up our forces secure behind our lines."

A sensible plan. When an army is weak it has to rebuild in stealth from the security of a hidden base. If it is discovered prematurely, the enemy commander will have the time to gather intelligence, prepare his larger force, and attack using a well-developed and thoroughly thought-out plan. But I knew Cottick: he would be frantic to get me back. My escape would have shattered whatever remaining confidence his men had in his leadership. As soon as Cottick found out where I was hiding, he would go into a rage and drive his troops to hit my position quickly. His battle-plan would be confused and he would commit too few men. This is what I hoped for. Was it wishful thinking? I had misjudged Cottick before. Would he surprise me again? Doubts assailed me, but I ignored them.

"Colonel, I've spent too long hiding. I want as many people to know about this base's general location as soon as possible. How else will my troops know where to come to join me? They will come and our numbers will swell, Colonel —don't doubt it. I've seen Cottick's army close up. It looks tough and powerful, doesn't it?"

"Yes, sir."

"It isn't. It's brittle—very brittle. It only looks strong from a distance, but once you are near you can see the cracks. At the first strong blow, it will shatter like an eggshell and its insides will ooze out. You'll see. One hard blow and Cottick's army will disintegrate. Do you study history, Colonel?"

"When I have the time, sir."

"Good for you. You can learn a lot from what happened in the past. At West Point, I received an award of merit in military history."

As soon as I said that I felt embarrassed. Why was I trying to impress Sheflin in such a juvenile way?

"Colonel," I continued after an awkward pause, "technology changes, but human nature does not. Humans keep doing the same things over and over again with tedious repetition. If you know what they did in the past, you can predict what they'll do in the future—and the further back you look, the further ahead you can see."

"Oh. I see, sir."

Sheflin was bright and maybe she did understand. She was capable of very imaginative solutions and leading men into battle, but could she get into the mind of the opposing commander? That was the true test of an army commander. I prided myself that I could. I knew—just knew to my core—what Cottick would do when he discovered my whereabouts.

I spent a long time with Sheflin teaching her the various lessons I had learned in life—military ones and others. It was unusual for me to spend so much time musing with an officer under my command, even one that I liked and owed so much to. I felt sorry for her disfigured face and wounded body and I wanted to ensure that she did nothing more stressful than sit and listen to me ramble on. It was important that Sheflin understand and trust me—not just obey, but really trust me. I needed her to anticipate my orders. My old command staff was captured, in hiding, or dead, so all I had to work with was the imaginative and unconventional Lieutenant Colonel Jan Sheflin. I wanted her to know me, and, oddly, I wanted her to like me.

* * *

Over the next few weeks my soldiers returned to me. At first, they came in ones and twos, then in squads, and then in whole companies. All were in bad condition and had terrible stories to tell. The weather didn't help. It was the coldest January in a long time and it actually snowed twice. I hadn't seen snow stay on the ground for years. It made transportation difficult for several days and our food stocks dwindled to nothing. Fortunately, along with the snow came Colonel Marum Omar, the chief supply officer for the Tenth Mountain Division.

I greeted Colonel Omar on the morning of my sixty-fifth birthday—a day which was unmarked by all but me. He trudged through the ankle-deep snow towards me and faithfully reported for duty. Omar explained that he had barely escaped from Fort Drum when Cottick's forces closed in. Since then he had been living quite well on a farm overlooking Lake Champlain. His short body was round and plump—an amazing achievement in those lean days. If he could feed himself, he could feed my growing army. On the spot, I made him my supply officer and he went to work on the troublesome problem of supplies. A week later, after the snow melted and we could use the old roads again, a dozen farm wagons and one truck drove into Lake Placid. I cannot imagine where Omar found the diesel for that truck, but I had learned it was best not to ask him too many questions.

Others came as well. Colonel Holcomb, the Tenth Mountain Division's chief operations officer and a close friend of Omar, arrived. They had escaped from Fort Drum together, only to become separated later. I had worked closely with both of them when I was the commander of the Tenth.

Major Woo, III Corp's energetic deputy intelligence officer, appeared one morning. I had known Woo for sixteen years. He and I were the sole survivors of III Corps's command team; the rest were dead. Woo was calm and detached and a useful man to have in a crisis, although I thought that he became a little too engrossed in details at times and missed the larger picture.

Lieutenant Colonel Hunt, commander of the 132nd Infantry Battalion, arrived with seventy-six of his men. They had swum the freezing water of the Saint Lawrence River and walked south to the Adirondacks. His lean, lanky frame moved with a measured progress that could be infuriatingly slow at times. Hunt had been with me twelve years ago when I had taken the 132nd into Manhattan after Hurricane Nicole hit. During that perilous operation, Hunt led his men with caution and we lost only one man. The men of the 132nd had been my sole companions during those difficult circumstances, so I was pleased so much of the unit had survived.

Colonel Rourke, commander of the 88th Urban Regiment, arrived with twenty-five men but with no armored vehicles or even weapons. I wasn't at all surprised that Rourke had decided not to meekly surrender; he was the definitive fighting man—big, bold, loud and tough.

Lieutenant Colonel Petras, deputy commander of the 41st Guard Regiment, arrived from his hiding place in the Mohawk Valley, along with a hundred-and-forty guardsmen. He was with me nine years ago at the Battle of Kemptville where he had personally led his force that took a key bridge. He should have been at his headquarters but he ignored protocol and led his men from the front of the battle. Brave but reckless — something deep inside the man drove him toward danger.

As my army grew, I moved my headquarters out of the hills and into the town of Lake Placid. I commandeered an old hotel at the top of the main street. Just after this, the best helicopter pilot that I ever knew returned to me. The superb flying of Captain Belinda Bokuk had twice saved my life. She returned with my personal helicopter. Both were warmly welcomed.

During the third week of January, deserters from Cottick's army began to arrive. They came by themselves, with a comrade, or in small groups. A Canadian from the 32nd Security Brigade was the first. The oddest assortment of deserters was a group of eighty women soldiers from Cottick's own Third Infantry Division led by Captain Janice King, a tall, powerfully-built, somewhat masculine woman. Given Cottick's treatment of women, I wasn't surprised that women soldiers were deserting. King's women despised General Cottick. I kept the unit together and confirmed King in command. Some joker called the company 'Ladykillers' and the contrary nickname stuck. The women didn't seem to mind the name and even encouraged it.

In the last week of January, when I had almost one thousand soldiers under my command, the most important reinforcement of all came to me.

I was at my desk, staring out of the window deep in thought, when there was a quiet knock. The door opened and a captain entered followed by two privates guarding a scruffy, dirty individual. A man of medium height and wiry frame was pushed forward. The prisoner was wearing a tattered uniform resplendent with Cottick's graffiti and with its buttons torn open down to the prisoner's navel. A grotesque tattoo of a fire-breathing demon with long blood-covered horns looked back at me from his exposed chest. I leaned back in my chair and laughed. I recognized the man immediately.

The captain was confused by my levity. "We caught him skulking around at the edge of our perimeter. We think he's a spy."

"Oh, he's worse than that, Captain."

"He said he has news he will only give you."

"I'm sure he does."

I got up and came around my desk. I stood in front of this

man and smiled. I offered him my hand but he indicated that he was wearing handcuffs. I ordered them removed. The captain was completely bewildered by now.

"It's so good to see you alive," I said after shaking his hand warmly. "I was certain you would be dead by now."

"Not me, sir. I was more worried about you."

I turned to the captain and put an end to his confusion. "Captain, this is Sergeant Kellerman, sole survivor of my bodyguard detail."

I didn't tell the captain that Staff Sergeant Stephen Kellerman was also my assassin, and that I had made use of Kellerman's unusual talents on numerous occasions. The captain didn't need to know that—no one did. Kellerman was the best kept secret in III Corps. I had saved Kellerman's life when he fell into the raging waters of the Hudson River just after Hurricane Nicole. Kellerman, a cold, unemotional, dangerous man with hidden depths, had served me faithfully and very effectively ever since.

"Captain, please find the sergeant a new uniform, if there are any around, and then burn the one he's wearing." I dismissed the captain and the guards.

"I might be able to replace your uniform," I said to Kellerman, "but it's a shame about that tattoo."

"Sorry, sir, but I'm beginning to like it. It grows on you after a while."

I changed the tone of our meeting to business. "Make your report, Sergeant."

"As ordered, Colonel Khanan is dead, sir."

My eyebrows shot up. "You amaze me, Sergeant." And I was truly amazed. Khanan, the commander of the dreaded SSU and Cottick's deputy, would have been a very heavily guarded target. My last order to Kellerman before I fled into exile was to kill Khanan and Cottick, and at the time I fully expected Kellerman to die in the attempt. I was immensely pleased that one-half of those orders had been completed and that Kellerman had somehow survived.

"How did you do it?"

"Sir, that can wait. Right now, I have news."

Later I would learn that Kellerman slit Khanan's throat while Khanan was dallying with two women. More than that, I would never know. Sergeant Stephen Kellerman was an assassin who took pride in his work, but he kept his methods to himself.

"Go on," I said, eager to hear the news that had prompted Kellerman's return.

"Yes, sir. I infiltrated Fort Drum to gather intelligence. Two days ago I discovered what I was waiting for."

"Which was?"

"Sir, General Cottick is coming for you. He'll be here in three days."

– Chapter 6 –

Lake Placid

I worked with Colonel Holcomb throughout the night and well into the next morning developing a strategy for the battle ahead. We threw out ideas, debated them, and then developed more. Before my defeat by General Cottick's forces, Holcomb had helped General Tuckhoe work miracles with the dwindling forces of the Tenth Mountain Division. It was Holcomb who, in the last desperate acts of the war, had managed to efficiently transfer the Tenth's 1st Brigade from north of the Saint Lawrence River to the front near Syracuse. That logistical masterpiece had bought me an extra week of time. Holcomb was a thorough officer with a complex, academic mind. He would examine every side of a problem before pronouncing judgment. Occasionally, he had an idea that was truly brilliant, but it was up to me to recognize that idea for what it was before he moved on to analyzing his next idea. Holcomb left my office to develop the details of the plan that I had finally decided upon.

Changing tasks, I wrote an order for Major Woo, my new chief of intelligence. I wanted him to develop an intelligence estimate of the forces that we would face. I knew we would be outnumbered, but by how much? And which units would I be facing? What would the men's morale be like? Very low, I hoped. Who would be commanding them? I was fairly certain that Cottick would come for me in person. He wouldn't trust my capture to a subordinate.

Once I had completed writing my orders to Woo, I prepared an order for Colonel Sheflin, instructing her to send out half of her cavalry forces to scout the likely approach routes. However, she was ordered to stay behind and give command of the scouting force to her deputy. Sheflin would therefore be available to discuss the plan for the upcoming battle with me later in the day. I also wished to get a briefing from her on the events leading up to my rescue. I had been so busy building my new army that those events were still a mystery to me.

But first, sleep. I had been working for twenty-eight hours straight. I was exhausted.

I awoke in the middle of the afternoon after five hours of deep sleep. The day was gloomy, but the cold of the preceding week had gone and the air was much warmer. I told my orderly to bring me something to eat and afterwards to ask Colonel Sheflin to report to my office. Sheflin and the meal arrived at the same time.

Colonel Sheflin saluted and I indicated that she should sit in the chair across my desk from me. Between mouthfuls of dry bread and crumbly cheese, I told her that I wanted to know how she managed to rescue me.

"I was wondering when you were going to ask, sir," she said with a small grin—her scarred face wouldn't permit anything more.

I felt uncomfortable looking at her face, which was disfigured by a fresh, jagged scar running across her cheek, blistered skin, and the blood-filled eye. The ruin of her eye was a particularly gruesome sight. Sheflin must have observed my awkwardness, because she reached into her pocket and extracted the eye-patch that the medic had made for her. She put it on and it transformed her face for she now appeared tough and warrior-like. Despite her injured face, Colonel Sheflin was more than capable of retaining her command. I wasn't going to take that from her. Her lively and unconventional mind was invaluable to me. I wondered whether her disfigurement had left a scar on her psyche, but she gave me no evidence of that.

With enthusiasm and no small amount of pride, Sheflin launched into her briefing on the sequence of events that led to me being whisked from the parade field, right from under Cottick's nose.

Sheflin informed me that during the final days of the war, the 317th Cavalry Battalion had been cut off on the north side of the Saint Lawrence River. The battalion was trapped on a large island which juts out from the northern shore of Lake Ontario called the Isle of Quinte. Cottick's army, with its primary objective of capturing me, ignored Sheflin's small, isolated and unimportant force.

After nearly a month of inactivity, Sheflin's soldiers captured a deserter from Cottick's army. The deserter insisted on speaking to their colonel in private. Sheflin's deputy suspected a trap and recommended a guard be present, but Sheflin overruled him. Nevertheless, before she allowed the deserter to enter her office, she ensured her sidearm was loaded and set the safety switch to the off position.

Sheflin told me that she recognized the man as a member of my personal bodyguard. It was Sergeant Kellerman. Sheflin confessed to me that she had always disliked Kellerman (everyone did, except me). She said that there was something cold and terrifying about the man.

I found myself looking intently at Sheflin. My thoughts wandered to what this woman was like under her professional demeanor. I noticed the deep blue of her good eye, but when she looked back I averted my eyes. I forced myself to stop. Such daydreaming was not useful and I was missing Sheflin's report.

After a moment of awkward silence, Sheflin continued her account of my rescue. Kellerman had informed her that he had just escaped from Fort Drum. He had discovered that General Cottick was planning to execute me on Christmas Day. He insisted that Sheflin mount a rescue. Sheflin hadn't even known whether I was alive or not, so Kellerman's news came as quite a shock to her. Kellerman briefed her on all the intelligence that he had gathered. He also offered to act as a sniper during the rescue. Sheflin accepted this without comment.

Kellerman never told me that he had anything to do with my escape. If he wanted it to be a secret, so be it. I wasn't going to press the matter.

Sheflin ordered a meeting of her officers. She informed them that I had been captured and the battalion was going to attempt a rescue. She assigned men to repair two long-disused roll-on-roll-off car ferries which had been abandoned on the southeastern corner of the island.

Sheflin's scouts had found the ferries shortly after arriving on the island. They were of little use to her, as her battalion had nowhere better to go. The ferries had been built in the late twentieth century and hadn't been used in at least twenty years. The ferries had lain rusting in their docks. Nearly identical, each had a flat deck of over 120 feet and could carry about 20 to 30 tons. Sheflin intended to use them to transport a rescue force across Lake Ontario to Sackets Harbor and then ride to Fort Drum. She would rescue me and then return using the same route.

One of the ferries couldn't be made operational, but by salvaging useful parts from it, the other was made ready to sail. Sheflin asked for volunteers for the rescue party. She requested sixty cavalrymen plus another ten men to sail the ferry. I was proud to hear that everyone in the battalion had volunteered.

The ferry got underway under cover of darkness and wasn't detected by the few enemy pickets on the far shore. In the morning, the wind started to blow heavily from the east and three-foot waves developed. The ferry wasn't designed for crossing open water in heavy weather, so the crossing was unpleasant. Most of the soldiers were seasick and half the horses showed signs of distress. The waves didn't diminish until the ferry reached sheltered waters near Sackets Harbor. The rescue party landed unopposed just before midnight on Christmas Eve, six hours behind schedule. Fortunately, no enemy forces were present in the town.

After four hours rest to recover from the arduous voyage, the main force mounted and rode out, leaving ten men to guard the ferry. Sergeant Kellerman met them halfway to Fort Drum. He informed Sheflin that sympathetic elements of Cottick's army would allow them passage through Fort Drum's southern perimeter.

An hour before the scheduled time for my execution, Sheflin, eleven cavalrymen and Sergeant Kellerman departed for Fort Drum, leaving the bulk of Sheflin's force hiding in an abandoned village to await their return. Kellerman led Sheflin's small force to the perimeter fence and the guards there let them pass, just as Kellerman said they would. A mile into the base, Kellerman climbed off his horse and left to find his sniper position. Sheflin brought Kellerman's horse with her as an extra horse for me to escape on. The small rescue party then found a concealed location within sight of the parade field and awaited my appearance.

And that was how I came to be rescued—through the talents of Sergeant Kellerman and the brave actions of Colonel Sheflin and her men.

I stood up and came around my desk to stand in front of Sheflin. I commended her for her actions. "Thank you, Colonel. I owe you my life."

I offered my hand. Sheflin gave me an odd, wistful smile and reached out and held my hand. She brought her other hand and laid it over our clasped hands.

"I would do anything for you, sir," she whispered. "Anything." She moved closer to me.

I looked into her good eye and saw longing. My first

reaction was one of panic. I recognized it to be selfish and ignoble, but I needed this woman to continue to be the superb commander of my most effective unit. This was not the time for romantic involvements. I had much more pressing needs for I had a battle to win. And besides, I was too old for such things. And yet, if I rejected her out of hand, how would her effectiveness as a commander be affected? Would her loyalty to me be diminished? I had always liked Sheflin as a person. She was a good woman with a lively mind and I enjoyed talking to her. She had been attractive in a wholesome way before the fire scarred her face. I saw her as a friend and colleague, but clearly she wanted more. I needed Colonel Sheflin the loyal and effective soldier, not Jan Sheflin the woman. What was I going to do?

Doubt began to appear across her face. I had to say something quickly.

"Thank you … Jan. I will remember that."

I pulled Jan close and gave her a gentle hug. She responded but with more pressure.

I moved away and smiled at her. "Now, Colonel, we have a battle to win and our lives to regain."

"Yes, sir."

Sheflin saluted and left my office.

I let out a sigh. Crisis averted, I hoped, and no promises made.

* * *

I left my office to take a stroll down the streets of Lake Placid. I needed some fresh air and time to reflect on my plan of battle. Had I missed anything?

The winter sun was barely above the hills that towered over the town. On the slopes of those hills, I could see new growth covering the ground around the base of the charred tree-trunks. The vegetation was stunted and would never match the grandeur of the previous forest. However, it would be shrubs, bushes and spindly saplings such as the poor specimens I now regarded which would provide the cover my forces required during the upcoming battle.

I walked along the busy main street of Lake Placid. There was no vehicular traffic, of course, but there was a constant flow of pedestrian traffic. I watched my soldiers resting, playing cards or other gambling games, or bartering with civilians. My soldiers and the local population of this wilderness town mixed affably. I had issued standing orders that all civilians were to be treated with respect and nothing was to be stolen. I had Cottick's army in front of me, so I didn't want hostile civilians behind me.

A corporal and a girl of perhaps sixteen walked down the street toward me. The corporal saluted and I returned the salute automatically. The uniform of this scrawny, young corporal was frayed at the edges and covered with mud. The soldier's rifle was slung casually over his shoulder. The girl wore a dirty coat which was open at the front, revealing a faded pink dress. It was much too large for her and hung poorly on her skeletal frame. I turned and watched the two of them for a moment. The corporal stopped and whispered something in the girl's ear. She smiled and nodded. The corporal took some rations from his pocket. The girl eyed the food greedily. She slipped an arm around the corporal's waist and the two walked away at a faster pace than before.

I realized that this small event encapsulated the difference between my men and those who followed General Cottick. The girl would have been taken by Cottick's men, but with mine she was simply bought.

A horse and rider cantered down the main street towards me. It was one of Sheflin's men. The cavalryman pulled up his horse and dismounted. The horse was thickly lathered and snorting heavily, and the soldier appeared highly agitated. He saluted and made his report.

"General Cottick's forces are on the move. They are

heading towards us along Route 3. They should be here by tomorrow evening."

It had begun.

I was surprised to find myself undisturbed at the news. No, not just undisturbed. I was at peace with myself.

– Chapter 7 –

Route 3

Route 3 connects Fort Drum to Saranac Lake, a village ten miles from Lake Placid. The road goes around hills and lakes and into the heart of the Adirondack Mountains, taking just over one hundred miles to go from the gates at Fort Drum to the center of Saranac Lake. The road's asphalt was cracked and potholes, large and small, were common. Weeds grew in the cracks and were encroaching from the road's shoulders, and the yellow centerline had long since faded away.

It was along this road that Cottick drove his forces forward. There was no finesse to his plan. He just came on in a straightforward frontal attack on what he thought would be a vastly inferior enemy. It was reported to me that he undertook no reconnaissance. Cottick expected to simply drive into Lake Placid and capture me. I had a few surprises awaiting him.

My army had grown to nearly a thousand soldiers, but that was still much less than the three-and-a-half thousand that Cottick was throwing against me. With me I had loyal and experienced soldiers from various units once in III Corps. Some units were well represented, others by just one or two soldiers. I also had deserters from Cottick's Third Division: women who had fled his tyranny and men who remembered better times under my leadership. All were veterans of many battles over the years. All were welcome.

The plan I had developed with the aid of Colonel Holcomb was simple: along the twelve miles of road between the village of Saranac Lake and the deserted hamlet of Coreys to the west, we would turn Route 3 into a deathtrap. I would remain at my headquarters in Lake Placid with a tiny staff to coordinate the attack using old hand-cranked radios. We wouldn't use the radios until the moment when the trap was sprung, and then it would be too late for their use to warn Cottick. My soldiers would block the road before Saranac Lake and stop Cottick's column dead in its tracks. Others would create a roadblock at Coreys once the enemy had passed. When all was ready, we would attack Cottick's exposed flanks along the entire length of his stretched out column. We would cut his column into small, isolated, vulnerable formations and then destroy them piecemeal. The term for this type of battle is a motti attack—a Finnish word, I believe, meaning logs or cutting logs or something like that. It is a particularly effective type of attack in rough and heavily wooded terrain, and it has the potential to completely destroy the enemy down to the last man—provided of course that the necessary surprise can be achieved. That was my plan, and I prayed that it would work. The risk was that if my forces were discovered prematurely, they would be unable to support one another and would be destroyed by Cottick's larger army one by one.

* * *

It was five after two in the afternoon and I was in the communication room in Lake Placid. I couldn't sit on the chair provided for me and instead I paced around the room. I hadn't heard any news from my field commanders and my anxiety was growing exponentially. My pacing was making the communication staff nervous, so I stopped and sat down. My fingers started to drum on the arm of the chair. I stood and resumed my pacing. Why was I not getting any reports of fighting?

I sighed and walked back to my chair. The radio crackled and I froze half way through the act of sitting. The noise from the radio shattered the hush of the room. Everyone strained to listen but there was only static coming from the radio.

My radio operator started to speak into the microphone: "This is Echo-One. Repeat, Echo-One. Identify and report activity. Over."

The old radio squawked and whined.

"This is Echo-One. Message not received. Repeat, not received. Over."

The radio crackled. "This is Romeo-Two," a voice said through the static.

Romeo-Two—that was Rourke's command. I had placed all my anti-tank squads, consisting of twenty two-man teams each armed with portable anti-tank missiles, in and around the village of Saranac Lake. One hundred supporting infantrymen provided protection for the anti-tank squads from enemy infantry. Both forces were under the command of Colonel Rourke.

The voice on the radio continued: "Engaging heavy tanks. Romeo-Two. Out."

Rourke's forces were fighting Cottick's tanks in Saranac Lake. Cottick had placed his heavy tanks at the front of his column to punch through whatever resistance he came across. So far I had guessed right.

I unfroze and started to pace again. Rourke, my toughest commander, had the difficult task of stopping Cottick's tanks. Would his men hold?

Every now and then I stopped pacing and stared at the old windup clock someone had found and mounted on the wall just above the radio. The clock read 2:15.

The minutes crawled by.

2:22.

2:28.

2:31.

"This is Romeo-Two. Taking heavy casualties. Withdrawing to Position Bravo."

My chest tightened. Rourke had been forced to abandon

68

his first line of defense, and was moving to his second line. He had only two lines of defense.

2:33.

2:37.

2:45.

The battle in Saranac Lake had been underway for nearly forty minutes.

2:51.

"This is Romeo-Two." This was a different voice. I recognized it to be that of Colonel Rourke's. "We are—."

The radio whined and static shrieked out of the speaker.

"This is Echo-One. Message not received. Repeat, not received. Over."

Static.

"We are holding. Repeat, we are holding. Recommend Hammer. Over."

"Repeat recommendation. Do you confirm Hammer?"

Static.

"Affirmative. Confirm. Repeat, confirm Hammer."

My heart skipped a beat. Rourke had held Cottick's tanks at his second line of defense. By recommending the commencement of Operation HAMMER, Rourke was giving me the all-clear to close the trap on Cottick's army. With one end of Cottick's column stopped, I now had to close off the other end.

"Contact Colonel Sheflin," I ordered the radioman. "Order her to advance to Position Charlie."

The radioman passed on the message. "Sierra-Seven. This is Echo-One. Advance Position Charlie. Confirm receipt. Over."

My anxiety climbed as the radio remained silent. Colonel Sheflin couldn't be reached. Her command was the furthest unit from my headquarters and there were numerous hills between us. The atmosphere had so much static in it—unusually so, I thought. Reception wasn't good with Rourke's command, which was much closer to me than Sheflin's. This didn't bode well for my contacting Sheflin.

My radioman became increasingly frantic in his efforts to raise Colonel Sheflin. We both sighed with relief when she finally acknowledged.

"This ... Seven ... Acknowledge ... Advance ..."

The trap was sprung. Sheflin and her cavalrymen set up a roadblock on Route 3 at Coreys.

Cottick had his forces stretched along Route 3, and the road had become completely jammed. At one end of the enemy column, Cottick's powerful tanks were engaged against Rourke's anti-tank squads and supporting infantry. At the other end, Sheflin was preparing to hold back any attacks on her roadblock.

The trap was closed. I contacted Colonel Petras, who commanded Papa-Five, my central force south of the road. Moments later Petras reported that his forces had opened fire all along the length of the road. The area around the road was too narrow for Cottick's forces to deploy properly, particularly to the north where numerous small lakes blocked the way.

I finally sat down in my chair and never again moved from it for the remainder of the battle. My forces were committed and I had nothing else to do. The plan had been successfully put into operation and now it was up to the determination and bravery of my soldiers to decide the issue. My role in the battle was finished.

I sat like a statue as I listened to incoming radio reports. Petras reported that the enemy were abandoning their trucks and wagons and retreating to the north side of the road, where more of my soldiers lay in wait. Petras's men struck hardest at the center of the enemy column, and pushed Cottick's soldiers northwards into the waiting arms of an ad hoc collection of soldiers under the command of Colonel Holcomb. His force, along with Captain King's Ladykillers further to the west, cut the retreating men to bits. Holcomb's men captured hundreds of prisoners, but the all-women force under Captain King took no one alive. I decided it prudent not to investigate too closely why that was.

Less than an hour after Petras opened fire, Cottick's forces were in total disarray, except for his tanks which were still fighting in Saranac Lake. Cottick's men, fired upon from the south side of the road and ambushed to the north, began to flee in panic. Many surrendered, others fled back toward Sheflin's roadblock at Coreys, and others became lost and separated in the forest. The enemy tanks in Saranac Lake finally discovered that the infantry behind them had all fled, so they disengaged and withdrew west along the road. A bridge west of the village was blown up by Colonel Hunt and his men of Hotel-Three, thereby trapping the tanks, which stopped in front of the destroyed bridge and wisely surrendered.

As the early darkness of winter fell over the battlefield, two enemy armored personnel carriers and a mob of desperate men forced open Sheflin's roadblock at Coreys and fled back towards Fort Drum. Sheflin's cavalrymen at the roadblock couldn't hold them and had to withdraw into the forest. Later, after the cavalrymen had regrouped, Sheflin led them in a series of quick hit-and-run harassing attacks. Throughout the evening, many more of Cottick's soldiers died.

Just before seven in the evening, Colonel Holcomb called. "Echo-One, this is Hotel-Four. Joined with Papa-Five. Fighting stopped. Many prisoners."

Holcomb's soldiers north of the road and those of Petras's south of the road had met and the enemy had surrendered. It was over.

I sat in the chair next to the radio operator and let out a loud sigh of relief. Against odds of over three to one, Operation HAMMER was a staggering success. I was victorious.

– Chapter 8 –

Saranac Lake

The following morning at first light, I mounted my horse, Judge, and with a small escort rode briskly along the ten miles of road between Lake Placid and the village of Saranac Lake. As soon as I arrived at the village, I hastened to Colonel Rourke's command post. I passed ruined buildings, smoldering tanks, and burial details collecting bodies from alongside the streets of the village. The fighting here in the village was the most intense struggle of all actions during the battle. Rourke's men could be proud of what they had accomplished, but they had suffered many casualties.

I met Rourke in his command post, a ruined building in the center of town. The big man was in a jubilant mood for he knew his men had fought well and his victory had decided the fate of the battle. We left the command post together and traveled along the length of Route 3 from Saranac Lake to the site of the roadblock at Coreys. Along the way, I received reports from my commanders: Hunt, Petras, Holcomb, King and Sheflin. They were tremendously excited about the results of the battle.

My victory was stunning—there was no other word for it. I had captured over two thousand prisoners, five functioning tanks, fifteen trucks, plus ammunition, food, fuel and other supplies. Over four hundred of Cottick's men lay dead along the road and in Saranac Lake, whereas my forces had lost only sixty-two dead and one-hundred-and-seventy wounded or missing. The 1st Brigade of Cottick's Third Infantry Division had been effectively wiped out. Regrettably, Cottick managed to escape when his fleeing soldiers forced open the roadblock at Coreys, but he limped back to Fort Drum with less than a third of the men with which he had left so confidently.

I did, however, have a prize with which to console myself. Among the prisoners Rourke's soldiers had captured in Saranac Lake was one who I was pleased to have my hands on. Brigadier General Daniel Zhang, commander of Cottick's 32nd Security Brigade, had bolted from his burning tank and had taken refuge in a nearby barn. While the tankmen of the 32nd were fighting and dying, their commander hid in a pile of straw. Rourke informed me that Zhang had surrendered without a fight.

Zhang was under tight guard in the barn where he had sought to hide. When he saw me enter, he stood and saluted. I didn't return the gesture. The short oriental Canadian appeared to be frightened of me—as he should.

"I'm glad to have a chance to talk to you, General," he said smoothly. "General Cottick ordered me to lead the attack. It wasn't something I wanted to do. General Cottick should never have started this war. There were other ways to settle this."

Zhang couldn't have found anything else to say that would have made me angrier. Before I entered the barn my anger was cold and grim, but now my anger turned white-hot. Zhang had betrayed me and now he was prepared to betray Cottick. Enough was enough.

I shouted to Rourke: "Colonel, hang him. Now!"

Zhang tried to flee, but Rourke's men held him tight. A rope was found and a soldier tied it around Zhang's neck. The prisoner struggled but the soldiers held him tightly. There was no escape for General Zhang.

"I want it done slowly," I added cruelly. I was in no mood

for mercy.

The rope was looped over a beam. Three of Rourke's men pulled on the rope and Zhang was slowly lifted into the air. He clutched with his unbound hands at the rope.

I watched Zhang's face slowly turn blue. Eventually, his hands relaxed and fell away from the rope. He was dead, but his body continued to twitch for some time. My orders had been carried out: Zhang had indeed died slowly.

"Leave him there to rot," I said to Rourke as I turned and left the barn.

* * *

Two days after my victory and a day after General Zhang's execution, I held a command meeting in the largest house in Saranac Lake. Its occupants had wisely disappeared when Rourke's men had first arrived before the battle. The question of what to do next weighed heavily on my mind. My army had captured over two thousand prisoners and I couldn't afford the men to guard them—not if I was soon to march on Fort Drum, which was my firm intention.

Captain King, who had taken no prisoners during the battle, wanted me to execute all the bastards—her word, not mine. Rourke suggested that only the officers need be executed, and the men could be used to reinforce our depleted army. Sheflin and Holcomb were horrified that I might execute so many— most of whom were just following orders from superior officers.

I listened to my officers argue for some time, and it was true that the captured food supplies would last longer if the prisoners were executed. However, the bottom line was that I needed trained soldiers and even more I needed junior officers to lead them. I still had the war with Cottick to win—and I wasn't going to do that with only one thousand men. I needed Cottick's men. I wasn't happy about it, but I had no choice.

I had vented my rage on General Zhang, and the other

prisoners were the beneficiaries of that release. I showed mercy and gave them a second chance. All officers above the rank of captain were imprisoned, but everyone else was offered the opportunity to join my army. The vast majority decided to join my fight against Cottick. They were weary of the chaos that Cottick's command had become and welcomed the order that I promised. Of those few who didn't join me, the belligerent ones were executed and the others were imprisoned along with the senior officers.

The very next day, my swollen army began its march to Fort Drum. Cottick's command over the old Army base—my base—would soon be over. I made sure that news of my march preceded me. Many deserters from Cottick's army heard the news and joined us during our journey along Route 3. I accepted them into my ranks.

I entered Fort Drum six days after the Battle of Saranac Lake. Cottick's soldiers from the Third's 2nd Brigade, who he left behind at Fort Drum, surrendered to my forces without incident. Half of Cottick's once-powerful division had been destroyed, but Cottick had escaped. He had fled to Kitchener with his hardcore supporters to the safety provided by the remaining two brigades of the Third, which had stayed behind in Kitchener guarding Cottick's headquarters.

I was once again the commander of Fort Drum. At least one thing in this screwed up world was back to the way it was supposed to be.

– Chapter 9 –

Fort Drum

I wandered around the burnt-out wreckage of a helicopter which lay strewn across Fort Drum's extensive helipad area. A medical team struggled out of the wreckage with yet another corpse. Behind them, the charred body of the helicopter's pilot was bent forward over the control panel.

I turned to a captain from the Third's medical battalion and glared at him angrily. "Are you sure Cottick isn't in there?"

"Certain, sir. He was definitely on one of the helicopters which got away."

The doctor looked down at the ground, avoiding eye contact. I was loathe to rely on any officer from the Third, but too few of the medical staff from my loyal units had survived. When Fort Drum fell to Cottick, most of my doctors, nurses and medics had faithfully remained with the wounded, as they felt duty-bound to do. Cottick had them all shot: medical staff, along with the wounded. For that crime alone, Cottick deserved to die. With too few medical personnel of my own, I was compelled to use captured doctors to identify the bodies in the helicopter wreckage.

I strolled over towards the scene of the recent battle. Dead soldiers lay everywhere, killed by bullets or grenades. One soldier had been cut in two by machine-gun fire. All the dead soldiers were from the Third Division. As my army closed in on Fort Drum, some of Cottick's men turned on him and staged an uprising. Dozens on both sides had been killed, but Cottick and a few others managed to escape.

The men of the Third had charged the three fleeing helicopters, only to be mowed down by the helicopters' machine guns. Someone, who was probably dead now, had launched a small surface-to-air missile and brought down one of the helicopters just as it took off, killing all onboard. The two other helicopters had escaped.

I stood in front of one of the dead soldiers who had rebelled against Cottick. He was curled up on his side and looked like he was sleeping. I thought that I recognized him. Using my foot, I gently rolled him over on to his back and studied him. He was a burly man in his mid thirties, with a broad chest and big hands. He had a scar running across his chin. His cropped blonde hair was matted with blood that had oozed from a bullet wound to the top of his head.

"Get Sergeant Kellerman here at once," I ordered.

While I waited for Kellerman to appear, I stood staring at the dead soldier without really seeing him. My mind was locked in a struggle about what to do with the soldiers of the Third. When I marched into Fort Drum, over four thousand of them had surrendered to me without a fight. I had put the officers in the base's prison, except for the medical officers, while the men sat on the parade field under guard.

The soldiers of the Third knew why I had ordered them to sit on that field: it was the place where Cottick had planned to execute me. The prisoners were afraid because they didn't know what I was planning to do to them—and they had every right to be afraid. They had helped Cottick destroy III Corps and kill many of my men. I had already heard the standard excuse: they were only following orders. My hand moved to my holster and rested there. I was furious. To hell with it, I thought, I should have them all shot.

But yet, there were other considerations. Logic and practicality calmed my fury. Some soldiers of the Third had joined me to fight Cottick at the Battle of Saranac Lake, and here at Fort Drum others had died in an attempt to prevent Cottick from escaping. The remaining men of the Third had surrendered peacefully to me as soon as I arrived at Fort Drum. There were no incidents. If I killed them now, how would I differ from Cottick? They were only following orders. Yes, I had heard that refrain so many times in the last few hours. I demanded obedience of my men, and these men were obeying orders from their general. In my career, I had to obey many distasteful orders—but nothing like this. I knew I would have disobeyed Cottick's orders, but I was older and wiser than these men, most of whom were only in their teens or early twenties. I had a lot more experiences to draw upon. Would I have disobeyed a general's orders when I was twenty-one? Yes, given the right circumstances, I would have. In fact, while fighting in Siberia as a fresh second lieutenant four decades ago, I had done just that: I had disobeyed a direct order from a general in order to save the life of a girl. I knew what was the right thing to do, then and now, but the men of the Third did not.

There were practical considerations. I was desperately short of men and particularly trained junior officers and sergeants. If I was to regain control of my territory, I would need these men—if they could be trusted. The medical and engineering units of my loyal divisions had been decimated, and most of the educated and trained technical specialists who remained were from the Third. I had to have access to their knowledge and expertise if I was to rebuild. Furthermore, Cottick had fled to Kitchener and was surrounded by the two remaining brigades of the Third. If I executed the men of the Third who I had taken prisoner, the survivors in Kitchener would have nothing to lose and would fight to the death. I couldn't afford such a bloodbath.

Sergeant Kellerman arrived beside me. I nodded at the body at my feet. "Is this who I think it is?"

Kellerman looked at the body. "Yes, sir. That's the sergeant who let us pass through the base's perimeter."

I thought I recognized the soldier. He had taken an enormous risk on that day on my behalf, and I would have decorated him. Another good man gone. My anger rose again.

I was interrupted in my thoughts. "What is it?" I snapped as I turned to see Colonel Holcomb standing beside Kellerman.

"Sir, there's a private from the Third who has asked to see you."

I nodded in acknowledgement. Moments later a thin, scrawny teenage soldier was ushered before me. He couldn't have been more than fifteen. His uniform had graffiti drawn on it, just like all Cottick's soldiers, but perhaps somewhat sparser.

"Go on, private, make it quick," Colonel Holcomb prompted.

The young private looked nervously from Holcomb to Kellerman and finally to me.

"General, sir, I want to return these to you," he stammered.

"Return what?"

The teenager reached beneath his ill-fitting upper-body armor. In a flash, Holcomb and Kellerman drew their pistols and leveled them at the private's head. The boy froze.

"Slowly," Holcomb ordered.

The private moved his hand slowly out from under his armor. I could see clenched in his fist several pieced of shiny metal and brightly-colored ribbons. He opened his hand and I recognized the pieces of metal as medals. Among the many medals there was a Department of Defense Distinguished Service Medal. This was rare and only given to commanding generals. It could only be mine. In fact, they were all mine. I took them from the private.

"General Cottick ordered me to retrieve your medals from the map room," the private explained. "He wanted to take them with him to Kitchener, but I ran away with them. I've kept them safe for you."

I studied the boy. I recognized him as the machine gunner

on the helicopter that had taken me from my hideout in the Algonquin Highlands.

"Release him, Colonel. At ease, Sergeant. This brave soldier has completed an important mission for me," I said, smiling at the boy. It was the first time I had smiled since I had recaptured the base.

Holcomb and Kellerman cautiously lowered their guns.

"Do you like horses, Private?" I asked the teenager.

Confused by the question, the private simply nodded.

"Colonel Holcomb, this soldier has guarded some important things for me at considerable danger to himself. Take him away, clean him up and feed him. He's to be assigned to the 317th."

"Yes, sir," Holcomb replied.

I turned and walked away with my medals in my hand. I fingered each one in turn, recalling the action for which I was awarded it. The Soldier's Medal of Heroism I had received for my actions during the Los Angeles Water Riot. I was awarded an oak-leaf cluster to that medal for rescuing three men, one of which was Kellerman, from the raging waters of the Hudson River after Hurricane Nicole. The medal was the Army's highest decoration for bravery in non-combat action and I had been awarded it twice. The Department of Defense Distinguish Service Medal was the highest honor a commanding general could receive for leading his men in action, and I was awarded it for leading III Corps into Canada. The Meritorious Service Medal was awarded to me for saving my tank regiment from capture by Libyan forces during the desperate battle for the waters of the Nile. There was also a Purple Heart with bars for the various wounds I had received in the course of my duties, along with other decorations. Circumstances had forced me to become something I was not. Many thought me a warlord and a tyrant, but my medals showed the world what sort of person I really was. My medals were important to me. I needed them to remind me of what I should be. It was so easy to become lost, just like Cottick had.

Once again I became lost in thought on the subject of what to do about the soldiers of the Third. The teenage private and the dead sergeant had both served me well, as had Captain King and her women soldiers, and even the doctor was working for me now. How many other soldiers of the Third would serve me loyally in the future? But, how many would turn on me once again if they had the chance?

I finally decided that I wouldn't decide anything yet. The answer would come eventually.

* * *

Colonel Sheflin asked me to accompany her to a building which had once housed unmarried junior officers and was now a gymnasium. I passed two soldiers guarding the door. As a young lieutenant with the Tenth Mountain Division, I had spent many hours in this gym toning my youthful muscles— and proud of them I was, too. I felt very old when I thought of my sixty-five-year-old aging body, with its gray hair, heavily lined face and damaged leg.

Inside the gym, I was greeted by an odd sight. Half a dozen soldiers from Sheflin's battalion were guarding, and leering at, a collection of about forty women huddled together. None of the women was older than twenty-five and all were very attractive. They were prostitutes from the Third Division's infamous officers' brothel. Cottick, in his haste to escape, had abandoned these women.

It was claimed by many that when Cottick made use of the brothel's prostitutes he treated them roughly. "Like the whores they are," Cottick was rumored to have said. According to Captain King, Cottick's hatred for women came out into the open after he had captured Fort Drum and believed the war was won. Not only did his abuse of the women of the brothel become worse, but he turned on his own female soldiers now that he thought they were no longer needed. He encouraged men under his command to follow his lead. The women were raped and beaten by their previous comrades-in-arms. Captain King explained that after the rape and murder of a young lieutenant under her command she secretly gathered as many women as she could. She led them into the Adirondacks to find me. After King told me her story, I understood why her soldiers hadn't taken any prisoners during the Battle of Saranac Lake.

I looked around the gymnasium. The exercise equipment that I had once used was long since gone. A few of the women were leaning up against the far wall, but most of them were sitting on the floor. None looked happy to be there. Two medics were attending a woman with a bleeding forearm, likely caused by a stray bullet. The superficial wound didn't seem to warrant the attention of two medics. One could have treated her adequately.

A petite woman stood as soon as she noticed I had entered the room and began shouting profanities at me. Her language was foul enough to make a drill sergeant blush. I think she was demanding to be released, although it was not easy to tell what she wanted through all the swear words that she sprinkled liberally into her sentences.

A tall woman who was leaning against the wall shouted at her: "Shut it, Betty! You're not going to get any joy that way. This ain't situation normal. The General's here to help us."

The petite woman flung a few choice words at the other woman and then fell silent.

The second woman came up to me boldly, and attempted a military salute. Although she appeared to be saluting in earnest, the gesture looked playful, even suggestive. This woman had wild jet-black hair, hazelnut-colored eyes and thin-but-smiling lips. She was by far the most attractive woman I had ever met. Curvaceous, voluptuous, beautiful. She was healthy and well-fed, as were the other women of the brothel. Cottick's tastes didn't run to emaciated women. Cottick might beat them, but he did feed them—better than the troops under his command, judging by the appearance of his soldiers who I had captured. This beauty before me was wearing olive-drab military trousers crudely cut into skimpy shorts, and a silky, bright-red blouse. I estimated her age to be twenty or twenty-one. Her skin was perfect, other than a nasty bruise on her forearm where someone had grabbed her, a yellow-and-purple bruise on her cheek, and scars around her wrists and ankles. The top third of her blouse was unbuttoned, revealing impressive cleavage.

I was aroused by what I saw. Maybe I was old but I wasn't quite dead yet. It was with some effort that I focused my attention on her eyes.

"General, sir, we've met before," she said in a soft, seductive voice which was quite different from the aggressive voice she had used with the petite woman.

"Have we?"

"Yes, General. The last time you were in Kitchener it was I who warned you."

I remembered now. Just before the civil war with Cottick started, I had made a surprise visit to his headquarters. During that visit, a woman from the brothel had warned me that all wasn't what it seemed and I had managed to escape. She had saved me from capture and execution.

"Yes, I remember you. I owe you a debt of gratitude. What's your name?"

"Around here I'm known as Vicky the—uh, no, never mind about that," she said, quickly stopping herself. "I think it's time for a new start. I'm Victoria Hewitt. Pleased to meet you again, General."

"Thank you, Miss Hewitt, for your quick thinking that day. You're right. I'm here to help you. A new start is just what you need. Colonel Sheflin, look after Miss Hewitt and the other women. Clean them up, feed them, and find them some decent clothes."

"Yes, sir," Sheflin responded, somewhat coldly I thought.

Here was an interesting contrast. Victoria Hewitt was an experienced seductress, confident of her beauty and the effect she had on men. Lieutenant Colonel Jan Sheflin, on the other hand, was a warrior, a comrade-in-arms with whom I had shared many dangers, and a loyal officer who had bravely rescued me. She had saved my life and been disfigured in the course of doing so. I liked, respected and trusted Jan Sheflin— and I had not forgotten her hint that she wanted us to be more than just friends. How strange it was (or was it just typical?) that I should be so enamored with someone who was a stranger to me. Perhaps it was because Victoria Hewitt represented a beauty which hadn't yet been lost in this ugly world, or perhaps it was because she had been for a time Cottick's woman and so she represented a victory of sorts over him. Either way, she was very desirable.

I shook my head to clear my mind of the distracting Miss Hewitt and then turned and exited the gymnasium.

I left Colonel Sheflin to carry out her orders. I left loyalty to look after beauty.

* * *

The next morning, I descended the stairs into the command center's basement to perform a sacred duty. I pushed open the door to the Map Room and walked in. As I had ordered, no one accompanied me. Cottick's 'trophies' were still on display: medals, decorations, insignias and nametags from the officers and men of my defeated III Corps. Except where the teenage private had shattered the glass of a display case and grabbed my medals, the room hadn't changed since I was last here as Cottick's prisoner.

First, I came to a display of medals taken from the bodies of my brave soldiers. I would later remove the medals and award them to those who had served me well in my new army. I noted a Congressional Medal of Honor in the case. I would give that to Sergeant Kellerman. I wondered if he would wear it or hide it away safely. Probably the latter, I decided. Next, I came to a display of nametags. It was the sight of these nametags that upset me the most. As I read them, I could picture the faces of the men and women to whom the nametags had once belonged. All dead now. I picked up three tags. On them was written the names of my dead colleagues and friends, Micklebridge, Tuckhoe and Price. I placed the tags in my pocket. These tags would be given the proper funeral that my friends were denied.

I came to the display of insignias. Passing by the eagles of the colonels, I stopped in front of the silver stars of the generals. This was the main reason I had come to the Map Room. Except for Cottick and his few subservient brigadier generals, I was the sole surviving general in all of III Corps. Here I was, a three-star lieutenant general, but I had no insignias of rank. Cottick had thrown my stars and my cap into a latrine. I had sacrificed much to get those stars and even more to keep them. It was important to me to replace my missing stars, and it was necessary for me to have a visible sign of my rank for my men. There was a depressingly large collection of stars for me to choose from. Generals from throughout III Corps were represented in Cottick's morbid display. Labels, written in a neat hand, identified to which general the stars belonged. A lieutenant general needed six stars, three for each shoulder. I picked up two stars belonging to Eva Micklebridge, another two belonging to Donald Tuckhoe, and a single star from Samuel Price. Five stars. I needed a sixth—and I knew where I would get it. I would rip it from Cottick's uniform.

I removed my jacket and affixed the stars to the shoulders. Once the task was completed, I put my jacket back on and admired the stars. There were three on my right shoulder and two on my left. I placed them in a particular order: Micklebridge's two were the innermost on either side, Tuckhoe's were the middle ones, and Price's the outer one on the right. The outermost space on the left side remained empty.

My men would notice the missing star, but that was just as I wished. I wanted them to know whose star would fill the void, and in that void they would see a sign of my determination to kill Cottick and finish this destructive and futile civil war.

I removed General Tuckhoe's cap from the wall and placed it on my head. It fitted reasonably well. I had completed here what needed to be done and it was time to go.

I left the Map Room, exited the command center, and walked over to the base's prison. My soldiers were guarding the officers of the Third. As I walked slowly past the cells, I turned to look at the prisoners. Some were sullen and remained sitting while others rose to their feet and saluted. I didn't return their salute.

There was one cell which I had ordered not to be filled: my old cell. A guard pushed open the door and I stood in the doorway and scanned the space. It was untouched from the moment that I was escorted away. Was that less than two months ago? It seemed much longer.

The plastic tray that held my last meal remained on the floor where I had put it. My cane was still propped up against the wall where it had been placed when I refused to use it on my journey to the parade field. I recoiled at the idea of entering the cell, so I ordered a guard to retrieve my cane for me. It had spent longer in this cell than I had and deserved to be liberated. Over the past two months, I had managed well enough without it, but for the first time I welcomed rather than resented the support it offered. My old leg-wound ached badly from my constant activity.

Colonel Holcomb arrived, but remained silent beside me. I turned to him and took a deep breath. I was about to take a big risk.

"It's time, Colonel. Assemble the prisoners in the courtyard."

"Yes, sir."

The colonel left to oversee the activity. I remained staring into my old cell for quite some time.

Finally, Holcomb returned and advised me that all was ready. I followed him to a wall-top walkway which overlooked the courtyard. The eyes of ninety-one prisoners watched my every move. Was it to be life or death for them?

After a sleepless night, I had finally decided what to do with these prisoners.

"Officers of the Third Infantry Division," I began in a firm voice, "General Cottick has deceived you all, and your misplaced loyalty to him has brought you here. Many of my soldiers wish you dead. Comrades of the ones you murdered want revenge."

I paused. There wasn't a sound from the assembled prisoners. The air was absolutely still.

"However, there will be no revenge. I give you the opportunity to serve me once again."

If I was to reconstitute my shattered command and restore the order and peace that I had promised my men, I needed these officers.

Someone cheered weakly but then quickly fell silent.

"Don't deceive yourselves. I offer you a chance to redeem yourself—a chance to regain my trust. If you fail in any way, the consequences will be dire."

I then went on to explain how the world had become a very harsh place and if we were to survive—if any of us were to survive—we would need order. If they were prepared to give me their absolute, unwavering loyalty and help me provide the order that we desperately needed, I was prepared to give them back their honor.

Murmurs came from the assembled crowd.

I waited for silence before continuing. I explained that there would be consequences. Their units were to be disbanded and they would be assigned to other units to replenish their depleted strength. They would be demoted one rank, and more important, they would be required to give me a personal oath of loyalty and obedience. It wasn't much of a punishment, but I had to do something to appease my loyal officers. None of them would like taking orders from an officer from the Third. I expected reprisals, to which I would have to turn a blind eye, at least for a while. The reprisals would rid me of the Third's worst offenders.

To those who didn't wish to give me a personal oath of loyalty and obedience, I offered exile. The officers who chose exile would be instructed to return to their cells, while those who were prepared to make an oath to me were to stay in the courtyard.

"You have five minutes to decide," I concluded.

I left and returned five minutes later. I wasn't surprised to discover that no one had moved. I descended to the courtyard where Colonel Holcomb had set up a small table and chair. He sat down with two sheets of paper before him: one blank and one with a short paragraph written on it. I stood beside him.

"First," he shouted.

Colonel Fajia, the senior officer of the prisoners, made his way to the front. Fajia was Cottick's senior signals officer. I needed him if I was ever to get my communications network functioning again. Fajia looked at me and saluted. There was fear in his eyes.

"I'm sorry, sir. It just happened. How can we ever …?" His voice trailed off.

I remained unmoved and silent.

"Name and rank," Colonel Holcomb said officiously.

Fajia stood to attention. "Fajia, Mamud, Colonel, 3rd Signals Battalion."

"No such unit exists, Lieutenant Colonel," Holcomb stated with emphasis.

Fajia was silent for a moment and then said loudly for all to hear: "Fajia, Mamud, a lieutenant colonel in General Eastland's army."

"Now, Lieutenant Colonel, read this aloud." Holcomb handed Fajia one of the sheets of paper.

Fajia scanned the sheet and then read aloud its contents. "I, Lieutenant Colonel Mamud Fajia, swear complete loyalty to General Eastland, my commander. I will undertake my duties to General Eastland with unwavering obedience. I will not fail him on penalty of death." He placed the paper on the table.

"Sign this," Holcomb commanded.

Fajia took the pen offered and signed the blank sheet of paper at the top. He saluted me and this time I returned the salute. My expression remained inscrutable.

One down, ninety to go.

* * *

I was losing control over some of my soldiers. Reprisals against the men of the Third had to stop. I had made repeated orders prohibiting reprisals, but what did I awake to this morning? More of the same. I had underestimated the fury of my loyal men against the soldiers of the Third, and more so my ability to control that fury. I had to make an example.

During the night, two women of Captain King's unit were discovered stabbing to death a corporal from the Third. They were caught in the act and covered with his blood. There was no question of guilt. I was certain that the corporal deserved it, but what was I going to do? I needed the men of the Third to defeat Cottick. This had to stop. An example was required.

With Colonel Holcomb and Lieutenant Colonel Sheflin seated on either side of me, I called Captain King to my office. As she stood at attention in front of my desk, I informed her that I had decided to make an example of these women. The reprisals against the men of the Third couldn't continue. Her two soldiers would be executed by firing squad. King was prepared for this and mounted a solid defense for her soldiers. I wasn't surprised to learn that the corporal had beaten and raped both of them and killed a comrade. King provided graphic details of the events and the names of the men who helped the corporal.

After listening in silence, I explained that I understood the circumstances and the women's motivation for murdering the corporal. In the past I would have sympathized with them, but I had an army to control. I couldn't have my soldiers murdering one another. I had promised the men of the Third that they could make redemption for their crimes (which no doubt were many) by loyally serving my new army.

"My decision stands. Dismissed, Captain."

King didn't give up. "Sir, these women fought with you at Saranac Lake. They are brave and loyal soldiers—loyal to you."

"Dismissed," I repeated.

"General Eastland, he raped them and—."

"Colonel Sheflin, escort the captain out."

Sheflin stood and moved towards Captain King. King saluted abruptly and left, obviously furious at me. I couldn't blame her.

Holcomb was uncomfortable with my decision and Sheflin clearly didn't agree, but I stood firm. I ordered Holcomb to arrange the firing squad, and he reluctantly complied. He judiciously selected a combination of three men and three women and ordered them to report for the execution detail. The executions were set for eleven o'clock, and I ordered all soldiers who weren't on essential duties to assemble in front of the prison. An unpleasant mood swirled through the troops. The men of the Third wanted the death of the murderers of their comrade, while the rest of my army sympathized with the ill-used women.

Precisely on time, the women were escorted out of the prison and marched to a rusty chain-wire fence that ran nearby. Their guards tied the women to the fence and withdrew. The women were pale and disheveled and were still dressed in their blood-covered uniforms. One sobbed quietly, while the other glared angrily at me. Neither cried out for mercy. They had given none to the corporal and didn't expect any for themselves.

Holcomb marched his firing squad into position, and then turned to face me. "Detail ready, sir," he said after giving me a crisp salute.

"Carry on, Colonel," I ordered.

Holcomb turned sharply towards the firing squad.

"Detail, present."

There was a long pause.

"Aim."

Another pause.

"Fire!"

Six soldiers squeezed the trigger of their rifles and six shots shattered the tense silence.

It took the assembled troops a moment to realize that the two women were unharmed. Could it be that all six soldiers on the firing squad had deliberately missed? Maybe they had, but no one will ever know because I had secretly ordered Holcomb to load the rifles with blank training rounds. Holcomb was enormously relieved when I told him this. He didn't want to execute these soldiers, but he would have obeyed my orders. By permitting these women to live, Colonel Holcomb would reward me with his complete trust. The same was true with Captain King and her soldiers. Now I had to achieve that same level of trust with the rest of my men.

Holcomb turned to me and saluted. "Execution completed as ordered, sir."

I turned my back to the women and faced my soldiers.

"These women, and all of you, and I include myself, are victims of the treachery and misery that General Cottick has spread," I said. "I have shown mercy this once, but only this once. Consider this your final warning. Reprisals end now!"

And so they did. My absolute command over my troops had been reestablished.

Part II

Hell Reclaimed

Let none admire that riches grow in Hell.

— John Milton

– Chapter 10 –

The Army of Threecor

III Corps, my old command, was dead—a sad but inescapable fact. I had to create a new army.

With me at Fort Drum, I had soldiers who had fought with me during the Battle of Saranac Lake and the rehabilitated soldiers from the Third. When I was given the command of III Corps, I had almost ninety thousand troops under my command; now, I had barely eight thousand.

Eight thousand tired and worn-out soldiers weren't enough to defeat Cottick now that he was secure in his headquarters in Kitchener. Cottick commanded the remaining half of the Third Infantry Division, as well as the Fifth Guard Division and two armored brigades. Twenty thousand officers and soldiers, at least.

Twenty thousand versus eight thousand; odds of nearly three to one.

I had to find more soldiers. Those who were left were battle-hardened veterans, but they were exhausted and too few. I needed to recruit new soldiers and train new officers—and quickly.

Cottick had a supreme advantage over me: he had fuel. I had captured the base's fuel tanks, which Cottick had graciously left half-full when he fled, but that was it. Perhaps enough for a month's worth of active operations, perhaps not—and this didn't take into account the fuel I would have to trade with the local farmers to enable them to harvest their crops before the heat of the summer. I had no other source of fuel, but Cottick did. He had been operating the old, almost-depleted oil wells of southwestern Ontario near Petrolia and Oil Springs for many years now—first for III Corps and then for himself. Cottick had probably exhausted his fuel reserves during the battles to defeat me. It would take him some months to replenish them. In that time, I would have to find more fuel or suffer defeat a second time.

On top of my shortages of manpower and fuel, I had to contend with an even larger problem. Napoleon once said that an army marches on its stomach, but my men's stomachs were empty. And it wasn't just the army that needed feeding: civilization too marches forward on its stomach. The fragile food production and distribution system I had imposed before the war against Cottick had collapsed when the fighting started. A food crisis was looming and I had to do something about it quickly. Starving men with guns don't make for a controllable situation.

With the able assistance of Colonel Holcomb, I developed a plan for a complete reorganization of my army and an entirely new command structure. I presented it to my officers at a general meeting in the base's auditorium.

Colonel Holcomb called the meeting to order and provided some background details. He listed our meager assets: from hundreds of bicycles to a single helicopter gunship, from a few civilian automobiles to three heavy battle-tanks and seventeen lighter urban tanks, from hundreds of horses to dozens of army and civilian trucks. He also provided my officers with figures for our reserves of fuel and munitions. I wanted everyone to understand the magnitude of the challenges which lay ahead of us.

When Holcomb finished, I walked on to the platform. Behind me, there was a large map of upstate New York and southern Ontario. The map was the original one that I had used years ago to plan the thrust of III Corps into Ontario. It still had colorful arrows on it indicating initial unit movements. In front of me, there sat over three hundred officers from second lieutenants to full colonels. I waited for the usual coughing, shuffling and muttering to desist before I began.

My speech gave, I would like to believe, a modicum of hope in a troubled world. I commenced by recapping the events of the last few months and then summarizing our current problems. I then launched into my plan for the reorganization of III Corps into the Army of Threecor, as I now called it. My soldiers were already calling not just my old corps but the whole region that I commanded 'Threecor'. They considered it their home. They no longer considered themselves Americans or Canadians, but citizens of this new country—and I was its leader. I liked the name and the continuity it implied, and so, although the original structure of my command of III Corps was gone, the new army I was creating would keep its old name.

My plan had four distinct but connected elements. First, the army was to be organized into six fully-independent battalions. Each battalion would operate as independently as possible, so that it could protect and police its assigned region of Threecor without having to draw upon other more distant battalions (thus saving fuel). Each battalion would have its own artillery, missile, transport, signal, engineering, medical and provost support.

The second element of the plan was the creation of a large quartermaster regiment. This independent regiment would be responsible for the centralized coordination, collection and distribution of supplies, including water, food and fuel. Colonel Omar, the supply officer from the old Tenth Mountain Division, would command the regiment and would report directly to me. He would bring order to the food production and distribution system and increase my supplies.

The third element was the creation, or I should say resurrection, of the military college at Kingston and the Light Fighters Infantry School at Fort Drum. My young officers, non-commissioned officers, and soldiers had to be trained. The youth were our future. We had to pass on our knowledge and experience so that they could carry on when the control of Threecor was placed in their hands. The Canadian Royal Military College at Kingston, abandoned over a decade ago, was to be rebuilt and would become Kingston Military College—our West Point. Graduates from there would lead our children to a brighter future (for how could it get any worse?) The Light Fighters Infantry School at Fort Drum would, for selected soldiers, provide advanced training courses on urban and guerilla warfare. Colonel Holcomb eagerly accepted the post of commandant of these two training facilities when I offered it. I think it appealed to his academic nature. From my point-of-view, I wanted someone I could trust to instruct my newest officers. I wanted him to leave no doubt in their young and impressionable minds who commanded their army.

The fourth and final element was the most radical. My soldiers would protect Threecor; however, everyone who lived in Threecor and benefited from the order I would bring had to assist in that duty. All civilians above the age of thirteen would be drafted into a new militia. Cottick wouldn't be the only one to use children to do the fighting. There would be a militia regiment set up in each of eight militia districts to be established within Threecor. Every civilian had to do his or her duty for their regiment, either in a combat or a supporting role. Each regiment would be commanded, on a rotating basis, by an officer from my regular forces. The training that the militia received would facilitate later recruitment of soldiers into the regular army if the need arose—which I was sure it would.

Initially, there might be resistance by some civilians to this imposed obligation, I told my officers, but this would pass as the civilians saw the benefits of the order and stability that this structure provided. Failing that, a regular army battalion would be posted to any troublesome areas. In short, there would be no more civilians in Threecor. There would be no more us and them; there would only be the Army.

"We will have order," I concluded. "We will have peace. We will have food. And we will have a future—that I promise you. I give you a vision of hope, and now together we will work to realize that vision."

The assembled officers stood and clapped for a long time. I deliberately didn't mention General Cottick during my speech. My men were weary of fighting and needed a rest. The time would come when I would order them to complete the task that we had started at Saranac Lake, but that time wasn't now.

Over the next week, I promoted many officers who had fought with me at Saranac Lake. Sheflin, Petras and Hunt became full colonels. I didn't want to promote my three senior colonels, Rourke, Omar and Holcomb, to brigadier generals. I had had my fill of other generals. I was beginning to believe that Cottick was right in his distaste for them. There could be only one general and I would be that one. However, in lieu of promotion, I gave Holcomb the two military schools to command and Omar the vital Quartermaster Regiment. For Colonel Rourke, my most experienced and fiercest commander, I placed all my armored forces in one battalion and gave him command. These posts were important, and if I couldn't give these loyal officers the ranks they deserved, at least I could give them prestigious commands.

As for Captain King and her soldiers, I kept them together and encouraged other women to join a new all-women battalion, the 200th. I foresaw that there might be problems recruiting women, and I thought that such a battalion might encourage other women to volunteer for my army.

It had become a very hard life for women, even more so than for men. The technologies that made advances for women possible were gone. Birth control was largely not available. Pregnancies were common and often unwanted. Back-room abortions were dangerous and often deadly, but that did not stop the growing demand for the quack practitioners. Even when a woman wanted to bring a child into this troubled word, miscarriages and deaths during labor were frequent among the poorly-fed populace. Infant mortality was high. I remember when I was a young man it was unheard of for a baby to die; now one in three died during birth or from disease or starvation within the first year. Unwanted babies were abandoned or drowned. Just the other day, when I was inspecting Watertown, I saw a tiny corpse floating in a creek. I had my escort fish the baby boy out of the creek and bury him. If a child survived, the mother was trapped. If she was lucky, the father helped raise the child. The stress of survival took its toll on relationships. Marriages were rare; beatings were common. Yes, if there were levels to Hell, women had been condemned to the deepest one. They had lost the most when our civilization collapsed from the environmental catastrophes we had unleashed. I told myself that my all-women battalion would at least give some an option for a better life.

I raised King three levels to the rank of full Colonel. Such a promotion was unprecedented, but she proved at Saranac Lake that she was ready for it, and I was short of trustworthy officers. Since I had spared her two soldiers from the firing squad, King had become fanatically loyal to me—and that was more important than anything else.

I confirmed Petras, Hunt and Sheflin in command of their battalions; they certainly deserved it. I also created a new battalion, the 15th, which was made up entirely of men from the Third Division. I gave the command to Colonel Juan Flores, a quiet, unassuming and rather old officer from the Third. He had deserted Cottick and had joined me prior to the Battle of Saranac Lake. He had fought well alongside Colonel Rourke on that day and had led his men in the destruction of one of Cottick's heavy battle-tanks and the capture of a second. As for the remaining soldiers of the Third (and there were many of them), I dispersed them throughout my army in order to bring all my battalions up to full strength.

In a moment of inspiration, I assigned a lively outgoing officer, Major Bors Barovscu, to create for me a small navy, consisting of old Coast Guard patrol-craft and civilian yachts and sailboats. This would enable me to control the eastern end of Lake Ontario, to patrol the Saint Lawrence River between Kingston and Ogdensburg, and, most important, to reduce my need for land transport, thus reducing my fuel needs.

I made Captain Andrew Woo my intelligence chief and promoted him to the rank of lieutenant colonel. I had known Woo for many years, ever since he was under my command at the World-Watch Operations Center in Fayetteville. He approached every problem as an intellectual exercise for his nimble mind. I had every confidence that he would make a superb intelligence chief.

Finally, the most important command, that of my personal security detail, I gave to Captain Belinda Bokuk. For that post, I needed someone who I could trust without question. Bokuk had been my personal pilot and would continue in that role. She was the last soldier, except for Kellerman, to stay with me after Cottick had captured Fort Drum. She was the best helicopter pilot I had ever known, and by her superb piloting abilities she had twice saved my life. I promoted her to a major and also gave her command of my meager air assets. The ability to fly rapidly between places had become a significant strategic advantage and one I wanted under my direct control. I hadn't forgotten that Cottick had escaped by helicopter, and prior to that, so had I.

Sergeant Kellerman would continue to secretly and effectively do for me what he had always done. I didn't offer him a promotion, and he wouldn't have accepted if I had. I did, however, insist that he accept the Congressional Medal of Honor that I had found in Cottick's display case. Kellerman deserved the medal for his services and, although he didn't show it, I think he was proud of it because it represented praise from me. As I expected, he told no one of the medal and hid it away among his few personal effects.

I still had to find commanders for the militia regiments, but that would come in time. First, however, I had to persuade, or coerce, the civilians in Threecor to become part of the new militia. I didn't delude myself that the task would be easy or quick, but I was determined to make it happen.

– Chapter 11 –

Montreal

The preparations for my departure were almost complete. I had just one more item to attend to before I headed northeast to Montreal. I ordered Kellerman to report to my office. He entered only moments later. In addition to his secret duties, he was a member of my personal guard and therefore always nearby. I motioned for him to close the door.

"I have a task for you," I said.

Kellerman's expression didn't change, but I knew him well enough by now to know he was eager to undertake any mission that required his particular talents. He was bored with life around Fort Drum and missed the freedom and the danger that he could only get on a mission.

I explained that I wanted intelligence on what Cottick was up to in Kitchener. "But," I emphasized, "I don't want him assassinated. This is an intelligence-gathering mission only. No risk-taking. Is that clearly understood?"

"Yes, sir."

Kellerman was disappointed. He wanted to finish the assignment that I gave him before my capture. It was unfinished business for him—and Kellerman was a tidy man who didn't like to leave loose ends. However, I couldn't risk the life of my assassin on an attempt to kill Cottick, who would be extremely well guarded. I might need Kellerman for other missions. That was one reason, but it wasn't the primary reason for my prohibition—not by a long shot. The simple fact was that I wanted to reserve the satisfaction of killing Cottick for myself. I wanted to watch as life left his eyes. Cottick would die slowly, painfully, and by my hand. I wouldn't permit Kellerman or anyone else to take that pleasure from me. I dismissed Kellerman to start his preparations for his mission.

Alone in my office, I looked around for anything else I needed to bring with me on my trip to Montreal. I satisfied myself that there was nothing more. All was ready. I took my pistol out of its holster and checked that it was fully loaded. I strode out of my office and crossed the base to where Major Bokuk and my personal guards had assembled. They were all mounted, save one who was holding the reins of Judge. There was someone else standing beside my horse: the woman from the brothel, Victoria Hewitt. She was less provocatively clothed this time—and I was bemused by my disappointment.

"General, sir," she said.

I mounted Judge before I nodded an acknowledgement.

"General, I just want to thank you for all you have done for me and the other women."

I had done very little. I had simply disbanded the brothel and permitted the women to choose how they would like to assist my army. Some went to work in the laundries and kitchens on the base, while others helped out in low-level administrative duties. I believe one or two enlisted with Colonel King's all-women battalion. I suspected that more than a few still plied their old profession, but that was their choice now.

"And how have you fared, Miss Hewitt?"

"I'm helping out in the kitchens, General, sir. I like to cook."

I already knew she was working in the kitchens. Despite my better judgment, I had kept a discreet interest in the life of Victoria Hewitt.

There was a long pause.

"Perhaps, one day, I might sample your treats."

Miss Hewitt smiled demurely.

"Of your cooking," I stammered hastily. I swear I truly meant the pleasures of her cooking. But now the idea of what other pleasures Victoria Hewitt might bestow was in my head and I couldn't get it out.

"I would love to, General. I have a special dessert, which I'm told is unforgettable."

I had never married and had sacrificed much for my military career, but I knew quite well what she was implying. She was over forty years my junior, but why not? After what I had been through, I needed some pleasant experiences for once. I deserved it.

I smiled at her and then tugged at Judge's reins and rode away. My guards trailed after me. Major Bokuk rode up beside me in silence. She kept her eyes focused ahead, but I noticed a restrained grin.

* * *

I rode at a leisurely pace northeast along the southern shore of the Saint Lawrence River. I was taking my time getting to Montreal; there was no hurry. The spring weather was perfect. The sky was a deep blue with delicate white clouds drifting lazily along. The temperature was only in the low eighties and there was no humidity to speak of. The fine weather matched my buoyant mood.

Along the way I visited Ogdensburg to see how the development of my militia was progressing in the Seaway District. Over the years, I had had many dealings with the citizens of this region and they knew me and my ways. They trusted me. I wasn't surprised that recruitment to the militia was going well.

Before me, a platoon of militiamen was completing a parade drill. They were consistently out of step but they showed promise. Beside me, the militia colonel, a young and energetic captain reassigned from the 41st, was explaining how he had instituted a rotating training scheme: three days of basic training, then three days of working on the farms (or attending school for some of the younger militiamen), followed by one-day leave.

I must have looked unconvinced, because he was at pains to explain that the leave-day was very good for morale. I couldn't afford to take a day off, so why should my militiamen? However, I didn't want to dampen the colonel's enthusiasm by criticizing his methods. His results were good, so I let it be.

"What about weapons?" I asked, changing the subject.

"No problem there, sir. Almost everyone has a gun, whether it is a hunting rifle or a hand-gun. We even have a few semi-automatics and one .50-caliber machine gun. Many of them have been handed down through generations. We are awash with guns."

"And ammunition?"

"Registered. We have just enough. Unregistered. I think that the civilians around here—militiamen, I mean—have boxes and boxes of ammunition hidden away. As long as we have enough for weapon practice, I'm not going to push the issue. If we ever got into a fight, I'm sure the ammunition would miraculously appear."

I wasn't surprised that the civilians were hoarding their weapons and ammunition. Given the chaos that we had all endured for decades, they knew they had to protect themselves. They had to be ready to fight off thieves, raiders and worse, but then so did my army.

"Hmm. Very well, Colonel. Work it as you see fit. But, if I need this regiment to fight, make sure it can. Understood?"

"Yes, sir."

The colonel invited me to inspect Ogdensburg, which I agreed to do. One of my bodyguards provided him with a mount. The colonel looked uncomfortable on horseback. He was an infantryman through and through. If the animal hadn't been well-trained, the colonel would have gotten into trouble on our ride through the town.

I rode Judge along the main street. There was an odd mixture of well-maintained homes and businesses alongside abandoned and ruined buildings. The numerous potholes in the road had been filled with dirt and leveled smooth. The citizens of Ogdensburg stopped when I passed. Some waved, others saluted. All seemed pleased to see me. And why not? I had given stability and order to this region for years. Naturally, these people were grateful.

At the eastern edge of the town I turned down towards the river front. In the distance I could see the ruins of the bridge over the Saint Lawrence River to Canada. The southern span rested in the river, but the northern half stood proudly erect, as if saying to the world: "Here I am and here I remain. I will not give up." I felt the same.

I stopped Judge and turned her around. I looked back at the town and was satisfied with what I saw. The colonel was doing a good job and his militia regiment was taking shape. These militiamen would fight when I called for them.

* * *

After Ogdensburg, I continued northeast and eventually crossed the old border to Canada—a meaningless line marked only by a derelict customs building and a faded sign welcoming visitors in both English and French. There was less than sixty miles to go to before we reached Montreal.

My purpose in going to Montreal was to observe the Quartermaster Regiment in action. I had sent over three-quarters of the regiment into the city, along with the 41st Battalion, to provide protection. I was hoping to locate supplies, but I didn't know what I would find there. Years ago, Montreal had seen the most severe fighting during our assistance to the Canadian military when they attempted a coup. The situation for civilians in the city at that time was horrific, and I wondered how they had survived. I prayed that my entry into Montreal wouldn't be a repetition of my last expedition to Toronto when my troops were attacked by a starving mob.

I traveled through deserted suburbs southwest of Montreal and finally reached the Saint Lawrence River. On the far shore lay the vast island city of Montreal. All the bridges over the main channel of the Saint Lawrence River had been destroyed in the fighting all those years ago. Off to my left I could see the ruins of a bridge which once connected the southwest suburbs to downtown Montreal.

Engineers from the Quartermaster Regiment had constructed a make-shift ferry, but it could carry only six horses and riders across at a time. After three quick trips my guards and I were across. Colonel Omar, the commander of the regiment, had left word that he was operating in the east end of Montreal at a place called Pointe-aux-Trembles. The lieutenant commanding the ferry engineers provided me with an old, torn map and directions on the best route to travel. I set out at once with my bodyguard detail in tow.

We stayed close to the river and didn't venture into the heart of the city. We saw no one; the streets were deserted. Where had everyone gone? Montreal was once a metropolis of nearly four million, but now no one remained. It had become a necropolis of none. The people had either fled or died in the fighting or during the famine that followed. To the north, the tall towers of downtown Montreal stood like tombstones over the decaying corpse of the city. We reached Rue Notre-Dame, the road that I was instructed to follow. Save for the annoying flying insects, I saw no animal life until I passed what was once a large waterfront park. There, I noticed a flock of mallard ducks bobbing about on the river. They were oblivious to the ruins around them.

We finally arrived at Pointe-aux-Trembles, a large industrial part of the city. I could see burnt-out distillation towers of an extensive petroleum and petrochemical complex. The climatic catastrophe came upon our world so quickly that we had no time to wean ourselves off petroleum—a fact which I often lamented. If only I had another source of energy to operate my army's vehicles. I required gasoline, aviation fuel and above all diesel.

A private with the Quartermaster Regiment's A Company, the unit that specialized in the recovery of fuel supplies, gave me directions to Colonel Omar's command post. I rode over and dismounted my horse. After patting Judge on her neck, I gave the reins to one of my bodyguards and entered a small house which Omar was using for his command post. It was once someone's beloved home, but now it was just an empty, weather-beaten shell. As I crossed the threshold, Omar rushed out, almost knocking me down. His short, rotund body carried quite a bit of weight. Clearly, he knew how to find food in these lean times.

"General, you've arrived!" Omar panted. He was clearly excited. "We've just had a major find. Follow me."

Caught up in Omar's excitement without knowing the reason, I limped after him as he led me to the shoreline.

"See that?" he asked as he pointed to a large, squat fuel storage tank.

I became very excited at the prospect of Omar telling me he had found a large quantity of fuel in that tank.

"It's empty, but—" Omar said.

"Empty?" I interrupted. "Is that all, Colonel?" My hopes were dashed.

"No, sir, you don't understand. The tank is empty, but it is intact. It doesn't have any holes and isn't burned to the ground like the other tanks around here."

"An empty tank isn't much use to me."

"This one is, sir, because it can be used to hold fuel."

"What fuel?"

"The fuel in there." Omar pointed to a large tanker ship

moored at the end of a long pier.

The rusted ship was listing at an angle of about twenty degrees and it appeared to be resting on the river bottom. Omar excitedly informed me that six of the eight holds on the ship were full to the brim with high-quality diesel. This was a find of utmost strategic importance. My fuel-strapped army would be mobile again. I was ecstatic.

I immediately gave orders to Fort Drum, via my hand-cranked radio set, to send a convoy of fuel trucks to Pointe-aux-Trembles by tomorrow, with some urban tanks from Rourke's 88th Armor Battalion for protection. I also ordered my engineers to bring bridge-laying equipment. I had to find a route to get the fuel trucks across the river. The tiny makeshift ferry that my bodyguards and I had used couldn't take the weight of a truck.

Colonel Omar and I watched as the engineers from A Company ran a fuel hose from the tanker to a small, barely-adequate pump, powered by a portable generator. The pump and the generator had been brought by wagon from Fort Drum, but the black hose had been found here. It had become brittle with disuse over the years and was barely flexible. The men had trouble manhandling it into place. Bits of the hose's protective covering flaked off in their hands. They persevered and finally manhandled the hose into place. Because of the risk of being overwhelmed by diesel fumes, the soldier who fed the hose into the first hold of the tanker had to wear a breathing mask supplied with air from a portable compressor. A second fuel hose ran from the pump to the top of the intact fuel tank. The two hoses weren't adequate for the task but they were all we had. The makeshift operation would work, but it was going to take ages to empty just one of the six holds. I was impatient to have my fuel.

The engineers of A Company were doing what they had been trained to do. The first transfer of diesel from the tanker to the storage tank was now underway, so I left Colonel Omar to supervise the next of many such transfers. I assembled my bodyguards and a few engineers and departed to scout the river to find a crossing for the fuel trucks.

After hours of fruitless search to the east, I retraced my journey westward towards the ferry that I had taken in the morning. At the place where I had seen the flock of mallard ducks, the river narrowed as it flowed around a series of small islands that were once a park. The bridge connecting the northern shore to the islands had collapsed, leaving its rusting metal frame protruding from the river. I had a small patrol swim across the narrow channel. The current was surprisingly strong and the men of the patrol nearly didn't make it. An hour later, the patrol returned with good news: a small bridge over the central channel was intact, as was yet another bridge over the southern channel. These two small bridges had been overlooked during the fighting. The roads on the islands were narrow and windy but perfectly serviceable. If I could just bridge the northern channel, I could get my fuel trucks into Montreal and then to the fuel depot.

At noon the next day, the convoy from Fort Drum arrived on the central island via the bridges from the southern shore. The bridge-laying engineers immediately set to work constructing a pontoon bridge over the northern channel.

The first step was to unload the dozens of fiberglass hulls that would form the floating base of the bridge. The fiberglass hulls, molded decades ago, were becoming brittle with age, but they would stand up to the load. They would have to. Each hull was winched into place and anchored. Because of the fast-flowing current in the narrow channel, the anchors wouldn't be sufficient, so ropes and metal cables were used to connect the hulls with the shore upstream. Once the hulls were in place, metal platforms were placed on top. Many of the platforms had been twisted and otherwise damaged during the attack on Fort Drum by Cottick's forces the previous autumn. Lesser damage was repaired, but those platforms that were too badly damaged to be laid down on the hulls were used on-shore as braces and anchors. Fortunately, we had more than enough supplies for the narrow span that had to be crossed.

Little by little the bridge took shape. Building it was a huge task, stretching the limits of my engineers' capabilities, but by nightfall the next day we had finished. When the last platform was laid the commander of the bridging detail and I walked across the span and inspected the work. It was the ugliest bridge I had ever seen, with wires going every which way, but at the same time it was the most handsome. With so much destruction all around us, my men and I had created something—something positive. We all felt a huge sense of pride in our accomplishment. Trucks could now cross and my fuel could be collected and returned to fill empty storage tanks at Fort Drum.

I climbed aboard the lead truck and sat beside the driver. We inched on to the narrow bridge and slowly drove across. I heard every creak and twang of each metal platform as the weight of the truck pressed down. The driver looked pale and nervous, but I did not share his fear. The bridge held, as I knew it would, for I had confidence in the abilities of my engineers.

The truck exited the bridge and accelerated away. I directed the driver to the fuel depot several miles to the east. When we arrived the men of the A Company were waiting, and the fuel transfer from the storage tank to the fuel truck commenced immediately. Colonel Omar, who oversaw the operation, informed me that even with all the fuel trucks filled to the brim, we had only just touched the vast quantity of fuel that we had found. Many more such convoys between Pointe-aux-Trembles and Fort Drum would be need. My army was mobile again. I was overjoyed.

– Chapter 12 –

Saint-Hubert

I remained in Pointe-aux-Trembles supervising the transfer of diesel fuel. There was nowhere else more important for me to be than this place. However, on the fourth day of the fuel convoys, Colonel Omar reported that his men had located something which he insisted needed my unique talents.

With my bodyguards and a guide, I rode Judge over the pontoon bridge and headed southeast to a Montreal suburb called Saint-Hubert. My guide, a corporal from B Company, led me to a long, low, concrete building, with a rotunda nestled in the crux of its two wings. The building sat well away from others in the area. One wing appeared to have taken several missile strikes and had partially collapsed. The glass from the rotunda had long-since shattered and covered the path below. The vast parking lots at the front of the building were covered by a mat of weeds.

A captain from B Company met me at the entrance. "General, welcome to the Chapman Space Center," he said. "It was once the Canadian equivalent of Houston."

The captain led me through the smashed doorway of the rotunda, along a dark corridor, and down several flights of stairs. With no batteries to power a flashlight, he had to use a flaming torch to light the way. Here I was using a medieval method of illumination in a Space Age institution. How absurd was that?

We arrived at a room located three stories below ground. At

the entrance stood a large, thick, steel door with a complicated access panel nearby. The door was ajar so we simply squeezed through. Computer equipment was placed in rows facing a large wall-mounted screen. Although covered by a thick layer of white dust, everything appeared untouched and undamaged.

"Sir," the captain said, "I believe this is where the Canadians ran their satellites from. I have taken a look around and I think I could get the system to work if we had some power. The radio dish on the roof is intact, although I will need to repair some of the connecting wires."

I walked around the room, deep in thought. I now understood why Colonel Omar had said that my unique talents were needed. During my career, I had completed two tours of duty with the World-Watch Operations Center in Fayetteville. During my last tour, I was in command of the Asia Department. I had extensive experience with satellite monitoring hardware and software, and, more important, I had knowledge of satellite codes—if I could remember them from that long ago.

I congratulated the captain on his find and ordered him to make whatever repairs were necessary. He could make use of as many men as could be spared from the refueling operation. Colonel Omar was ordered to send a portable generator and a truck-load of diesel to power it.

For the next two days, I spent my time with my head in electrical access panels and computer control cabinets. I enjoyed the hands-on work. When at last we were ready, I ordered the captain to start the generator and throw the main fuse switch. Electricity flowed through circuits for the first time in over a decade. A relay promptly blew from a short caused by the ever-present dust. After a day of cleaning relays, fuses and contacts, we were ready again. This time it worked. The lights flickered on and the computers came to life.

I sat in front of what I believed to be the primary operational interface for communicating with satellites. With the captain and his small team peering over my shoulder, I waited for the computer to reboot. Finally, the screen displayed the words 'Bienvenue' and 'Welcome' and two icons labeled 'Français' and 'English'. I slipped my hand inside the interface glove and moved the cursor over the 'English' icon. The screen changed to the primary command page and I selected 'Utilities'. I entered the software creation program and began assembling the necessary modules of software. I had no idea what encryption codes the Canadians had used, but I knew the codes for the American satellites. The first order of business was to see what satellites were still transmitting. The program instructed the radio dish on the roof to scan the sky.

There! Almost immediately, the signal from an old weather satellite registered itself on the system. A weather satellite could be useful.

Moments later, a few communications satellites responded, but who could I communicate with? Who would be listening? They were useless sentinels watching over a troubled planet.

I waited. There were no more signals. All the other satellites had been damaged, or had run out of power, or their orbits had decayed.

Then an old friend appeared and said hello. The last military surveillance satellite ever launched by the United States of America appeared over the horizon. It was launched into orbit a long time ago when we had the resources to build such marvelous machines. It was on this particular spy satellite, during my last tour of duty at the World-Watch Operations Center, that I had watched as troops from Indonesia invaded Australia. The Indonesian theocracy had chosen this desperate course as a bid to distract its disgruntled citizens from the famine and misrule which plagued their country,

The satellite was telling me it had data to download, but I couldn't reply until I remembered the necessary decryption codes. There were multiple levels of access and I had to remember the code to each one. Some codes I remembered straight away; others I had to try a number of combinations until I got the right one. I cheered when the satellite finally signaled that it was ready for instructions. Through the interface I ordered the satellite to download the contents of its memory buffers. The buffers could hold only thirty day's worth of data, but that was enough for me to see what was left of our world.

While the data was being downloaded, I climbed out of the basement and returned to the surface for a bite to eat and a breath of fresh air. The midday sun felt good on my face.

I ordered my radio operator to contact Fort Drum. There was one other person who knew satellite systems, and now the system was working I wanted him here to take over from me. Lieutenant Colonel Woo, now my intelligence chief, had served under me as a captain during my last tour of duty at the World-Watch Operations Center. I was informed that Woo was far to the west with Sheflin's 317th Cavalry Battalion. He was scouting the area to the east of Toronto to ensure that Cottick wasn't making any moves against my northwest flank. I didn't want to rush Woo's important work, so I asked that he come to Saint-Hubert only when he had finished.

After a last deep breath of fresh air, I descended the stairs and reentered the computer room. I worked all day and well into the night analyzing the retrieved data. The technical task wasn't appropriate work for a lieutenant general, but there was no one else who knew the system. The satellite informed me that it had no fuel left for its maneuvering thrusters. This was disappointing news, but its orbit was stable and given time it would cover almost every part of the planet. One of its solar panels wasn't functioning, but the other was working at one-hundred percent efficiency. Because this was a military satellite, there were enough redundancies built into the power system to compensate, but only barely. I would have to be prudent in my use of the satellite. Most important, however, the optical systems were functioning perfectly, both in the visible and infra-red spectra.

While I worked busily at analyzing the data, I also trained

the captain and his men. This wasn't an easy task, as the younger soldiers hadn't seen a computer operating before. I was disturbed when one teenage private confessed that he couldn't even read. I would have to do something about literacy in my army, but that was for another time. At the moment, I had more important things to do.

I explained the workings of the satellite interface to the men while I unloaded numerous continental-level images from the satellite's memory buffers. The first nighttime image of the world was deeply disturbing. The coordinates informed me that I was over northern China, Korea and Japan. The last time I had seen such an image, I could make out the landmasses from the lights of the many cities. Beijing, Seoul and four main islands of Japan had been aglow with artificial light. Now there was nothing—just darkness. Without the satellite's infra-red imaging, it would have been impossible to tell where the land ended and where the oceans began.

Over the next many hours we reviewed the data and searched for signs that some fragments of civilization had survived. The lights of Threecor shone brightly in the void. Nearby, Kitchener and other towns in southwestern Ontario and western New York illuminated Cottick's command. He was still out there. It was just the two of us fighting amongst the ruins.

Two hours later the captain brought me an image that showed the lights of Westport on the south island of New Zealand. The New Zealanders' investment in geothermal power was paying dividends for some of its surviving citizens. Soon afterward, we discovered the lights of Trondheim in central Norway, Reykjavik in Iceland, and Inuvik in Arctic Canada. I had given up hope of finding any more when the captain noticed intermittent lights coming from Barrow, Alaska. These isolated northern communities, with nearby sources of energy and sheltered from the heat further south, had somehow survived the cataclysm.

There were other lights as well, but these weren't of civilization; rather, they marked its end. These lights were orange glows from huge fires that covered most of the Congo basin in Africa and the Steppes of southern Russia. I had seen this many years before, when the last of the Amazon jungle burned during my first tour at the World-Watch Operations Center.

The daytime images were no less depressing. Parts of Florida, Holland and Bangladesh were underwater, and sand dunes covered much of Beijing and Cairo. Newly exposed bedrock in southern Greenland was visible. The Southern Ocean was full of icebergs from the West Antarctic ice sheet, which was calving at a frantic rate after the southern summer.

I examined a series of images which a young lieutenant had proudly processed. They showed a large hurricane with a sharply defined eye, category six at least, maybe even a seven, slamming into the Yucatan Peninsula. I wondered if there was anyone left there to be affected by it.

I had seen enough for one day. I stood and walked away from the desk.

"Hell has no fury like a planet scorned," I mumbled.

"Sorry, sir, what did you say?" asked the lieutenant as I walked past him.

"Oh nothing, Lieutenant. I'm just misquoting someone."

– Chapter 13 –

Plattsburgh

My gloom over the satellite images was offset by the knowledge that I alone in the whole world had access to a functioning spy satellite. Its images would be of supreme strategic importance to me in my war against Cottick. I could safely watch his every move. It was now impossible for my forces to be caught by surprise. Even better, Cottick wasn't aware of my advantage. All I needed now was time to rebuild and re-supply my army.

I gave orders for all the satellite control equipment, including the roof dish, to be disassembled, loaded on trucks and moved back to Fort Drum. The system had to be removed from its current vulnerable site and reassembled in a secure location. I wanted it safe and nearby.

One day after the dismantling work began, I received an urgent communication from Colonel Flores of the 15th Battalion. He requested my presence in Plattsburgh, a town on the west side of Lake Champlain some sixty miles south of Montreal. Colonel Flores and most of his battalion were operating in Plattsburgh and the surrounding region. The citizens weren't accepting their obligation to my new militia organization. Flores was convinced that only I could talk sense into the troublesome residents of the town.

Only a few months before, Flores was an officer in Cottick's Third Infantry Division. He was an older officer, diligent and hardworking, but hadn't received promotion to

117

brigadier general when due—something about looking after a sick wife, now dead. After abandoning his comrades to join my forces, he now commanded many of the same men. He had kept his rank, while those under his command had been demoted. His new responsibilities weren't easy. He was also reporting directly to me for the first time, but he didn't yet know my ways sufficiently. He wasn't able to anticipate my orders and I suspected that he was unsure of himself. I would be patient and understanding, but only for a short time.

I would have preferred to continue supervising the dismantling of the satellite equipment, but in the end I decided that others were capable of the purely technical task and I didn't need to be present. I informed Major Bokuk that we would be traveling south to Plattsburgh and that she should make the necessary arrangements.

After an uneventful trip under a gray, overcast sky, I arrived at Colonel Flores's command post on the northern edge of Plattsburgh. Flores had set himself up in a cube-shaped, three-storey, glass-covered building which once held the offices for a software company. The building was easily defended, but it was some distance from the center of town. I was surprised how many of the glass panels remained unbroken. Plattsburgh had avoided the worst of what we had all lived through.

Flores met me at the main doors and led me up to his office on the second floor. Outside the window, the sky had turned dark and ominous. There was a blinding flash of lightning, followed seconds later by a boom of thunder.

I stood before a full floor-to-ceiling window in Flores's office and watched as a torrential downpour began. The road outside soon resembled a river. Such violent deluges were increasingly common but fortunately they rarely lasted very long. The sun would soon return to evaporate all the water the clouds had poured down, leaving little to irrigate our crops.

Without turning around, I ordered Flores to report on the situation.

"Sir, the citizens of Plattsburgh don't want to belong to our militia. The mayor says that Plattsburgh has its own defense committee and they are busy farming and rebuilding their town. He says his citizens are pleased to trade with us, but they won't join any army."

"Who is this mayor?"

"A man called Keese. He seems to run everything around here. The people follow him without question. Apparently, Keese led them through all the various catastrophes which have hit us. They are grateful—more than grateful."

"I want to meet him. Bring him here."

Flores didn't respond. I turned around and repeated my order. Flores appeared uncomfortable.

"Sir, it may be better for us to go to him."

"Why?"

"I doubt he would come here. I always go to City Hall."

With that, I flew into a rage. In no uncertain terms, I reminded Flores that he was the commander of this region—my representative here. People came to him, not the other way round. He was the colonel of one of my battalions and he had better start acting like one if he wanted to remain in command. Flores paled and withered under my verbal attack. Perhaps it was the oppressive weather, perhaps it was the remnants of pent-up anger which hadn't been released since I was Cottick's prisoner, or perhaps it was simply the throbbing pain in my leg (my old wound always ached when it rained), but whatever the reason Flores received a violent harangue.

Afterwards, I turned back to the window and watched as the deluge weakened to a drizzle. I took a deep breath and calmed down.

Behind me Flores cleared his throat and said, "Sir, I'll order my men to bring Mayor Keese here immediately."

I felt something of an apology was owed to Flores. I didn't like to lose control like that. Nevertheless, the verbal whipping had probably done him some good.

"Colonel Flores, you fought with me at Saranac Lake. You joined me when few others did. For that, I'm grateful and gave you command of the 15th. Your men were once Cottick's soldiers. They have shown themselves to be tough fighters who need strong leadership. Don't let them—or me—down. They need to know their commander is just as tough as they are."

"Yes, sir. I understand."

Perhaps Flores did understand. He was an older officer who, like me, graduated from West Point and held command in the once-proud United States Army. He lived most of his life within the rules of that great institution, but like me he had adapted to the new order and like me he had survived. Time would tell if he truly comprehended what was ahead of him.

I turned back to Flores.

"Now to business, Colonel. Call Major Bokuk and your company commanders in here. We have some plans to make. One last time we will go to Mayor Keese."

* * *

With Flores, Bokuk and my bodyguards, I rode down the main street of Plattsburgh towards the old city hall. The ancient brick building was built near the beginning of the twentieth century—an era of promise. The town appeared well maintained and the people, who stared sullenly at me as I rode by, were reasonably well fed. It was an incredible contrast to the deserted streets and decaying buildings of Montreal. Plattsburgh reminded me of Watertown, near Fort Drum, before Cottick brought his war to the town and razed many of its buildings.

It was just after nine o'clock in the morning when I stopped Judge outside the entrance to City Hall. A large crowd had assembled in front of the building. At the center of the crowd, there stood a large man—tall and broad, with a thick mane of brown hair, and wearing a long gold chain around his neck.

Keese, I assumed. Around him, twenty or so men stood guard with rifles.

Keese wanted our first meeting to be public, and that was fine with me.

"You're not wanted here, General Eastland," Keese said in a booming voice. "Unless you want to do some trading," he added as an afterthought.

I ignored him and addressed the crowd. "People of Plattsburgh, I have given orders that, for our mutual protection in these dangerous times, you're all to become part of my army's militia. You'll be trained to protect your home and—."

"We have no need of your militia or your training," Keese interrupted. "We can protect our town. Leave now or we'll force you out."

The crowd murmured in agreement. I studied their faces. It was clear that Keese held sway over them.

What was I to do with such a man? I could buy him or kill him. I doubted I could coerce him. His town was well maintained and his people were healthy and obviously devoted to him. Begrudgingly, I admired Keese. He had done in this one town what I had tried to do for all of Threecor. I decided that I would attempt the first option: I would try to buy him.

"Mister Keese, mayor of this fine town, I have ordered that everyone join the militia—and my orders are always carried out. However ..." I allowed my pause to hang there for a few moments. "However, I'm looking for someone to command this district's militia. You've cared for the welfare of the citizens of this town and are respected by them. I'll place you in command of the Champlain Militia Regiment and give you the rank of militia colonel. You'll report only to me and Colonel Flores."

This was a huge concession on my part. My original plan was to have my own officers commanding the militia. I knew they could train an effective militia, and, more important, I could trust them. Now, I was about to give this command to a civilian and a stranger. This would have repercussions in other districts, but I was prepared to deal with that. I admired Keese and what he had accomplished in this small corner of my domain.

Unfortunately for everyone, Keese would have no part of my generous offer.

"General Eastland, take your soldiers and go. We want nothing to do with your army. We've looked after ourselves in the past and will continue to do so in the future. We don't want you here."

Keese nodded to his men. Twenty rifles were raised and pointed at me and my bodyguards. Damn! I couldn't buy the man.

So be it.

I turned to Colonel Flores and said loudly so all could hear, "Colonel, this man has disobeyed an order. You will arrest him immediately."

"Yes, sir." Colonel Flores raised his arm and soldiers from the 15th appeared on the roof-tops of buildings across the street from City Hall.

Keese and his riflemen were unsure what to do. Flores dismounted his horse and walked though the crowd to face Keese. The riflemen aimed their rifles at Flores.

"You're under arrest," Flores said loudly as he placed a hand on Keese's shoulder. A brave man—this would go a long way towards Flores gaining the respect of the soldiers under his command.

No one moved.

Finally, one of the riflemen bent down and placed his rifle on the ground. The others quickly followed. Keese looked bewildered. That was the difference between us: Keese's men would kill for him, but my men would die for me.

I dismounted Judge and walked through the crowd towards

Flores and Keese.

"Colonel, you'll escort your prisoner into this building. His court-martial will commence in half-an-hour."

* * *

One of the large meeting rooms in City Hall was quickly rearranged into a trial room. Eighteen of Colonel Flores's soldiers lined the room and six more guarded the door. About fifty of Keese's fellow citizens sat in the room. They were nervous and agitated but quiet. They were both witnesses and hostages.

Because by my order everyone was in the militia, this was to be a court martial and not a civilian trial. I convened a tribunal of five, including myself, as senior officer present. I had decided that I would vote only if there was a tie between the other members of the tribunal. The other members were Colonel Flores and Major Bokuk and the rifleman who was the first to put his weapon down. For the fifth member, I chose a nervous-looking woman from the crowd. The rifleman and the woman were sworn in as captains in the militia. I wanted Keese condemned by his own people.

I called the court to order. A sergeant read out the charges of disobeying a direct order in a time of martial law and threatening officers of the regular forces of the Army of Threecor.

I asked Keese how he pled to the charges.

"This isn't a real trial," he shouted. "You have no authority here. Let me go!"

"Let the record show that the defendant pled not guilty."

The court then examined six witnesses. They were each asked the same two questions: Did the defendant reject the orders of General Eastland to command the Champlain militia regiment? Did the defendant order his men to aim their rifles at Colonel Flores and General Eastland? The witnesses weren't allowed to make any reply to the questions other than yes or no. They all said yes to both questions.

I asked the tribunal members to give their verdict. Flores and Bokuk did their duty and confirmed Keese's guilt. The rifleman reluctantly agreed that Keese was guilty of the charges. He then bent his head down and stared at his hands, which were clasped on the desk in front of him. The woman merely nodded and then started to sob.

"Anything to say before sentence is read?" I asked Keese.

"Sorry, General Eastland, sir. I didn't mean to. I would be honored to command your militia." Keese had been doing some quick reevaluating of the position in which he now found himself, but it was far too late for that.

"You've been found guilty on both charges. During this time of emergency, all of Threecor is under martial law. As such, the offences are severe, as is the punishment. This court hereby sentences you to be executed immediately. Colonel Flores, see to it."

Keese looked on in disbelief. It had happened so fast. He was stunned at how quickly his long-held power had been stripped from him.

I stood and left the room and headed into a small adjoining office. The room contained an ancient ornate desk and a well-used wooden chair. I sat and waited. On the opposite wall there was an oil painting of an old man dressed in nineteenth century clothing. There was a large tear in the center of the canvas, scarring the man's face. Overall, the image was dark and foreboding. I looked away, sighing.

What a shame. I could have used a man such as Keese, but the distasteful deed had to be done. Order had to be imposed on this town. I required the citizens of the Plattsburgh region to guard the eastern flank of Threecor. I couldn't have a threat in the east when I moved westward on Cottick's army.

My bad leg hurt, so I gently massaged it. My fingers moved my thigh muscle back and forth. It did no good; my leg still ached.

I remained seated rubbing my muscle for some minutes before a single shot rang out. I stopped my massage. After a brief pause I got up from the chair and limped out of the room.

– Chapter 14 –

Oneida Lake

After the unpleasant but necessary events at Plattsburgh, I continued on what had unintentionally become an inspection tour of my rebuilt command. I visited Colonel King at her new headquarters in Utica, a small town in the Mohawk Valley. All was going well and the soldiers of the 200th Battalion were in fine spirits. I was very pleased with my experiment to create an all-women battalion. It gave women another option to the dreary and demeaning life that had become the lot for most. With no birth control, teenage pregnancies were the rule, not the exception as they were when I was young; and with hunger and poverty rampant and families under stress, abuse was common. The women in the 200th escaped that fate. Under King's leadership, they formed a warrior sisterhood which was effective in guarding Threecor and would be ruthless in battle. And most importantly, they were utterly loyal to me.

Next, I headed west to Syracuse to visit Colonel Hunt and the 132nd Battalion. I had known Hunt for many years, and he knew me and my ways. Hunt was with me when I led the 132nd into Manhattan after Hurricane Nicole devastated the city. He was a cautious and methodical officer—not imaginative but reliable and loyal. I knew him to be diplomatic and a good listener—two traits which were crucial for his new command. Syracuse was the largest city in Threecor (the necropolises of Toronto and Montreal didn't count), and Hunt was the perfect choice to coax and cajole its citizens into the militia. Whereas I could crush dissent in a small town like Plattsburgh, controlling Syracuse would be much more challenging and would require finesse.

After two days of inspections and long meetings with Colonel Hunt, I was ready to return to Fort Drum. Hunt commented that I looked exhausted and after a month on the move I was. He offered me the use of a fine house on the shores of Oneida Lake, just north of Syracuse. I accepted. Leave was just what I needed to rejuvenate myself for the battles to come. It was important for me to be thinking with a clear, refreshed mind.

A young lieutenant from the 132nd acted as my guide. In his company and surrounded by my bodyguard detail, I rode north at a leisurely pace. We arrived at a large, once-luxurious mansion which backed on to the lake. The house had survived the battle between my First Guard Division and Cottick's forces last September. Major General Price had surrendered far too quickly for much damage to be done to Syracuse and the surrounding area.

I left the lieutenant to stable Judge in an empty garage while I made my way upstairs to the master bedroom. Without bothering to undress, I flopped down on the bed and fell asleep. My last conscious thought was of the familiar and oddly reassuring smell of delousing powder which covered my pillow and sheets. I slept like the dead for fourteen blissful hours.

I woke just as dawn was breaking. I was famished, so I wandered downstairs to find something to eat. As it was early in the morning, only a single corporal was on duty inside the house. Major Bokuk had posted guards but they patrolled outside. The corporal informed me that Colonel Hunt had sent some provisions. With the help of the corporal, I prepared a substantial breakfast with a pile of fried potatoes and two sausages, boiled carrots, an apple drenched in cream, and real coffee! Hunt was spoiling me: coffee was exceedingly rare and the packet was from an ancient supply, probably Hunt's own. It was a much larger meal than I had eaten in some time. I invited the corporal to join me (although not for the coffee). He was nervous about sharing breakfast with me but his hunger decided for him.

As we lingered over breakfast, I asked the corporal about his own circumstances. To begin with, he told me what he thought I wanted to hear, but after a while he opened up and revealed more interesting details of his life. He had been posted to the 132nd just after Hurricane Nicole and so had missed the battalion's adventures in Manhattan. His infant son had died from the Adepi virus, which swept through the population and killed at least one in twenty. His wife was killed during the fall of Syracuse, and his eight-year-old daughter had simply disappeared afterwards. Dead, or worse—he didn't know. He stopped talking and the silence of sorrow ended our conversation.

After breakfast, I walked down to an old dock which was part of the property. The concrete structure was slowly disintegrating and the wooden pier had collapsed. I climbed off the dock and down to the rocky beach. The water level was so low that I had to walk nearly two hundred yards to reach the shoreline. I stood by the water, gazing at the far shore. A morning breeze stirred gentle ripples on the surface of the lake.

Ten minutes or an hour later (I couldn't tell which), Major Bokuk approached and informed me that I had a guest. The major seemed quite amused by this development.

I returned to the house and was greeted by a welcome sight. Victoria Hewitt rose from her chair and greeted me with a smile and a playful salute. Her wild, raven hair had been tamed into long, gentle waves, and she wore a pale green dress with see-through sleeves. How such a delicate piece of clothing had survived, I had no idea. The dress was short, revealing her long, tanned, youthful legs, and was cut in a way that made the most of her cleavage. A thin, silver necklace came around her neck and disappeared between her breasts. The necklace led my eyes where, no doubt, she wanted them to go. After a furtive glance, I looked up into her rich brown eyes.

"Miss Hewitt, what brings you here?" I asked with as much formality as I could muster.

"Why you do, General," she replied with a mischievous smile. "I heard you were here and I thought I could help. I could cook for you." She added coyly, "Last time we met I promised you a taste of my famous dessert."

I suddenly became acutely aware of my bodyguards behind me and dismissed them with a terse order.

"Miss Hewitt—."

"Victoria, please. And when we are alone like this, may I call you Walter?"

I was a formal person and permitted very few people to call me by my first name. Yet here I was, excited at the prospect of this woman I hardly knew, and over forty years my junior, calling me Walter.

Victoria must have noticed my long pause, because she politely apologized. "I'm sorry for being so forward. It's just my nature. I won't do it again, General."

I suddenly—and surprisingly—realized that I didn't like her formality and the distance between us that my rank implied.

"You may call me Walter when we are alone … Victoria."

Victoria smiled: she knew she had me. I smiled: I knew I was going to have her.

There was a long silence between us, which I finally broke.

"How did you get here?"

Victoria sat on an old, battered sofa and motioned for me to join her. She told me how news of my location had been brought back to Fort Drum by the fuel-truck drivers. Supplies of fuel were being stocked in depots in Syracuse and across Threecor from the cache that Colonel Omar had discovered onboard the tanker in Montreal. Victoria hitched a ride in one of the trucks. She said she did the driver a favor. How casually she said that. She remained a whore.

I asked her about her life in the brothel and how she ended up there. I was surprised how candid she was. She confided without reserve or hesitation all the sordid details of her life. In a soft but serious voice, she told me how she had been raised in the underworld gangs of Toronto. Her mother was the reluctant girlfriend of a senior leader in a powerful gang. Victoria claimed her mother was more beautiful than her, although I could scarcely believe that. Her mother never told her who Victoria's father was, and Victoria was convinced her mother didn't actually know. Her mother was promiscuous and was frequently caught in the act by the gang leader. She was beaten for her betrayals, but that did little to stop her. She hated the gang leader, but was powerless to escape. She fought back in the only way available to her.

Once when the leader caught her mother in bed with a man from his own gang, the leader didn't beat her but instead found a better punishment. He grabbed Victoria and threw her into the arms of the mother's lover and threatened him with a gun. The man shrugged and led Victoria into his bedroom. Fortunately, in a rare act of kindness within the world of the gangs, the man didn't rape her. He told her to bounce on the bed for five minutes. Victoria thought this great fun—after all she was only eleven. When she had finished the man left without a word. Nevertheless, her mother learned her lesson and stopped her affairs. Thereafter, her mother became sullen and depressed, and she hardly ever spoke to her daughter. Victoria believed her mother blamed her for being trapped.

Three years later, government control failed in Toronto and anarchy erupted. Open gang warfare began and her mother saw her opportunity to escape. In the confusion, she fled with

Victoria to the western edge of the city. One of Cottick's patrols captured them. Her mother was raped by the soldiers then and there. Victoria was to be next, but before anything happened a captain appeared. He ordered that the two of them be taken back to Kitchener for General Cottick. Her mother suddenly pushed Victoria at the captain and ran away. She disappeared into a nearby building and that was the last Victoria saw of her.

At fourteen, Victoria was already a well-developed beauty, fresh in face and firm in body. The captain saw her as an opportunity to curry favor with his commanding general. He forbade any of his soldiers to touch her and personally took her all the way back to General Cottick's headquarters. Victoria was ushered by the captain into Cottick's office. The general eyed her body hungrily. He thanked the captain and ordered him to take Victoria to his sleeping quarters. The captain had correctly judged his general.

Victoria was left alone in the room for some time until Cottick arrived. She was frightened but knew what to expect. She had lived in the violent world of the gangs and at fourteen she wasn't innocent or inexperienced. Cottick undressed in silence and Victoria did the same. He pushed her on to his bed and handled her roughly with his huge hands. Victoria submitted and the deed was quickly over. Cottick was an aggressive, thoughtless and impatient lover, but Victoria knew no better.

After three months Cottick became bored with her and found a new interest. She was sent to the Third's infamous officers' brothel. Victoria claimed that life in the brothel was better than her life with the gangs. Some of the officers were kind and gentle. She had plenty to eat and the other women were friendly. Cottick's brief attentions gave Victoria status, of a sort, with the other prostitutes.

With her story finished, we lapsed into silence. I was very aware of her presence on the sofa beside me.

Finally, to dispel the somber mood, Victoria asked me if I had eaten breakfast for it wasn't yet nine-thirty, and she offered to cook something for me. I replied honestly that I had and then instantly regretted it.

"Never mind, Walter. That gives me more time to create something really special for lunch. Let's see what we have in the kitchen. Have you got any wild fowl? Pigeon, grouse, duck, anything? I could make something tasty—a specialty of mine. Would you like to help me?"

I replied that I would like that very much.

The kitchen had been well stocked by Colonel Hunt, but there was no wild fowl. I ordered a few of my men to shoot some ducks which I spied congregating in a nearby marsh. It was a terrible waste of precious ammunition but I threw away such considerations for a day.

Victoria commandeered the kitchen and I took orders from her like a private. The modest idea of a small private lunch was abandoned in favor of a celebratory feast for everyone— me, Victoria, my bodyguards, and the soldier from the 132nd. Nobody bothered to ask what we were celebrating. Perhaps it was just the joy of being alive.

We worked all morning and finally created a feast for all. The guards from the 132nd and my own security detail sat down to the best meal they had eaten in years. For a few brief hours, rank was ignored and we chatted and laughed as comrades, pleasantly oblivious to the rigors of the world outside.

Someone produced a battered set of playing cards and a game of poker quickly got underway. Money was useless, so we bet food rations. I wasn't very good at card games and was soon bankrupt. It didn't help that I had a string of bad hands. In contrast to my poor performance, Victoria had an excellent game. Superb hands such as a full house and four twos helped, but I think it was the way she bent over to collect the ration slips that encouraged the men to lose to her. She was just doing what came naturally to her.

After she had cleaned out the last survivor at the table, she magnanimously offered to use her horde of rations to prepare another feast for all of us tomorrow. On that happy note and long after the sun had set, Victoria led me upstairs with the eyes of my men following me. Victoria's status was now assured. Behind me I heard hoots and whistles, but I didn't care. I was truly happy for the first time in years.

* * *

I awoke slowly, with a feeling of profound relaxation. My exertions of the night before had left me content and lazy. I was in no hurry to get out of bed. Victoria's arm lay casually over my chest; her naked body pressed close to mine. From her breathing, I could tell she was still asleep. I didn't want to disturb her and I was content to remain where I was.

The previous night had been wonderful. She made it easy for me and I was pleased with my performance. I hadn't been with a woman for a long, long time and to be honest I was not that experienced in bed. As my career got underway I had little time or interest in romance. My duty came first.

There was no doubt that Victoria was excellent in bed and I was attracted to her beautiful body, but there was something missing when I was with her. A closeness, a tenderness, something intangible. It was something I had once, but that was a long time ago when I was a brash, youthful second lieutenant straight from West Point. I was on my first combat mission when I saved a young woman's life—an act which almost ruined my career. Her name was Svetlana Tunguska and I loved her.

Svetlana was a Siberian and I met her when war came to her young country. The newly-independent Siberia had enemies on all sides. Many wanted access to its wealth of natural resources, including the United States. The rump of Russia, now called the Moscova Republic, was in disarray and couldn't reclaim its Siberian territories, but the same was not true for China.

The Chinese government was in trouble. In the north, the Gobi Desert was advancing relentlessly on Beijing and prolonged droughts were decimating crops; in the south, Shanghai was under water and vast refugee camps covered the dry land around the drowned city. With its population becoming rebellious, the government did what governments throughout history have done to deflect responsibility: it found an external enemy to blame. To assert its newfound independence, Siberia decided to reduce natural gas shipments to China. This act was used by China as justification for its invasion of Siberia and Mongolia. However, the United States coveted the minerals of Siberia and quickly built international support for intervening in the Siberian War.

The Tenth Mountain Division was the first major American combat unit deployed in Siberia. The division was airlifted to Komsomolsk on the Amur River in the southeastern Siberia. I graduated from West Point on a Saturday and the following Tuesday was in the air en route to Siberia. After arrival, the division immediately moved south to meet the Chinese, but I was ordered to remain behind as part of a detachment which was guarding the airport. It was in Komsomolsk where I met Svetlana, the eldest daughter of the town magistrate.

While the war raged to the south, I had little to do. The Siberians were thankful for our presence and friendly toward us. Officers, including junior ones such as me, were frequently invited to dine with the locals. I remember seeing Svetlana for the first time. She was helping her mother and younger sister bring out food to where her father and the officers were dining. She placed a plate of goat meat and soybeans in front of me. As she did so, she laughed. She chatted to her sister, who then also laughed. Her father half-heartedly scolded her and then translated for my benefit.

"I must apologize for my daughter," he said. "She finds it amusing that you manage to keep your uniform so clean in this dusty town."

I noticed smiles on the faces of the other officers at the table. My uniform was indeed crisp, pressed and spotless. The creases were razor-sharp and the buttons were shiny. I have always taken particular pride in my uniform. I felt a little disgruntled at this young woman making fun of me in front of my captain and my fellow officers.

I glared at her, but she just looked back at me and smiled. I was mesmerized by her beguiling smile. The next day I made a point of visiting the magistrate's house. Svetlana answered the door. She looked at me intently, but as soon as she realized she was staring she quickly lowered her gaze and studied my feet.

"Sorry," she said with a thick accent. Her father must have schooled her in what to say because that was the only English word she knew at the time.

I held my hand out to shake hers, as a gesture of forgiveness. She misunderstood the gesture, and instead of shaking my hand she bent and kissed it. I became flustered and left hastily. Throughout the day I kept looking at my hand where Svetlana had placed her lips.

After that, we met every day. I told her my name, which she always pronounced as Valtar. We held hands while I taught her some English words, but otherwise we said very little to each other. Little needed to be said, and in our silence a profound bond between us grew.

With the war raging only miles to the south and life uncertain, perhaps it was inevitable that two young people such as us would become lovers. One sunny day, I led her to an abandoned barn and laid her on a bed of straw. We lay beside each other and kissed. We remained clothed for the longest time, but ever so slowly our clothes came off. Every touch was full of meaning; every gesture was momentous. It wasn't like that with Victoria. Not at all. With her it was fun and light. Pleasure unaffected by deep emotions.

I loved Svetlana without reservation and she returned my love with the same intensity, but our happiness couldn't last. War was coming to Komsomolsk. The Chinese were driving the Tenth before them and our losses were high. Wounded soldiers streamed into the town. The locals began to realize who was winning and our relations with them cooled. Svetlana's father forbade her to leave the house and especially to see me.

I was ordered south to reinforce our depleted lines. I led my squad along the western bank of the Amur River, and beside that river I saw my first combat and killed my first man. When I arrived, over on the far bank a Chinese squad was attacking another American unit. I ordered my men to lie flat in the mud and fire into the flank of the Chinese. My men killed all the enemy, save one. A solitary survivor fled. I carefully aimed my rifle and pulled the trigger. The soldier fell forward and disappeared into the long grass. I felt exhilarated. I had led my men to victory and I had blooded myself in battle. My father would be proud.

My successful skirmish had no effect on the outcome. The entire division retreated into Komsomolsk, and it was then that events started to get ugly. Major General Batrid, commander of the Tenth, was searching for a scapegoat for the debacle. A spy was found among the Siberian locals and Batrid had him shot. Fair enough, but then the general made the outrageous claim that many other locals were involved. He had no evidence but he nevertheless ordered more executions. The soldiers of the Tenth had seen a lot of death by then and thought little of more killing. They obeyed without question. The civilians rioted and two soldiers were killed. This triggered an orgy of killing and raping by our soldiers in retaliation.

My only thoughts were of Svetlana and I rushed to her house. Her father, after seeing what other American soldiers were doing, lunged at me with an ancient sword. I wrestled him off and explained I was there to help. He was doubtful, but Svetlana helped me to convince him. I wanted to lead Svetlana and her family into the hills to the west, but as we left the house we were caught by General Batrid. He took out his pistol and shot Svetlana's father in the head.

"Lieutenant," he ordered me, "take these spies to the center of town. Burn their house down."

I was stunned. Svetlana and her sister cringed behind me, while her mother knelt beside her fallen husband.

"Now, Lieutenant!" Without warning, Batrid shot Svetlana's mother, who fell across the body of her dead husband.

I aimed my rifle at the general's chest. "No sir, I won't! These people are not spies. Drop your gun!"

The general's face flushed with rage. "Lieutenant, I gave you an order."

I pressed my rifle's muzzle into his chest. His hand opened and his gun fell to the ground.

"You're finished, Lieutenant. I'll break you for this."

Ignoring the general's threats, I turned to Svetlana and pushed her away. I gestured with my free hand that she and her sister should run away. After a moment of hesitation, they fled. I remained with my rifle pointing at the general. I glanced around just in time to see Svetlana disappear over the crest of a hill. I never saw her again.

Other soldiers arrived, and now that Svetlana was safe I lowered my rifle. Batrid had me arrested and threatened me with a court martial. I was led away under heavy guard, while behind me Svetlana's house was set alight.

I was flown back to the States, but the court martial never happened. General Batrid's actions at Komsomolsk were hushed up by the Army and he was quietly retired. I was transferred to another division and the matter was dropped. Nevertheless, I had disobeyed a direct order from a general, regardless of the nature of that order, and that was something the Army did not forget. I wallowed in obscurity without a promotion for years. My father wasn't pleased with my actions that day, but I never regretted them. I had saved Svetlana's life, and that was worth far more than the Army's displeasure—or my father's.

I keep the memory of Svetlana deep within me, and I have never mentioned her to anyone. I can still feel our love deep within my chest, but I won't permit it to come to the surface. That emotion has no part to play in the world in which I now live.

– Chapter 15 –

Fort Drum

From my oasis of happiness on the shores of Oneida Lake, I returned to the concerns and worries of my life at Fort Drum. The debris from Cottick's brief occupation of the base had been tidied away and it was once again looking smart and orderly. Victoria installed herself in my quarters. Each night when I came off duty, she greeted me at the door. She kissed me passionately and led me to our bed. We made love nightly. I don't know how I managed it at my age. Victoria was amazing. I hadn't felt so young and virile in years. She made all my worries seem small and manageable. Even General Cottick faded into the background when I was with Victoria.

My troops picked up on my mood and everyone seemed buoyant. We had much to be cheerful about. The fuel trucks kept arriving at the base loaded with diesel from the tanker in Montreal, and the disassembled parts of the satellite control system were arriving from Saint-Hubert. I had ordered that the system be reassembled in the command building. I wanted that equipment close by. It would take some weeks to get the system operating again, but once it was I would have an unparalleled strategic advantage over Cottick. Some of the reassembly work required my personal attention because I had considerable expertise with satellite systems, and only Lieutenant Colonel Woo and I had the access codes. I enjoyed the technical work. Between my work and Victoria, I was extremely busy. The days flew by.

Two weeks after I returned to Fort Drum, Colonel Hunt sent me a strange report from Syracuse. Under his guidance, the 3rd Syracuse Militia Regiment was being organized and training of its officers was underway. It was these militia officers who had told Hunt about strangers appearing in the city. It began with just a few starving people staggering out of the hills to the south of Syracuse. The first group of refugees came from nearby Tully and Cortland, at the southern border of Threecor. As the number of strangers grew, so did the distances they had traveled. People had walked, staggered or been carried from Binghamton, Elmira and Corning, even from the mountains of northern Pennsylvania. These people, who had eked out a life of sorts outside my protected domain, had finally decided to flee chaos and seek order. According to the refugees, small bands of marauders were riding into the villages and pillaging everything the refugees had struggled to protect.

As a precaution, Colonel Hunt increased the number of patrols south of Syracuse. He was being prudent but I doubted anything would come of it. My forces were more than a match for any bands of marauders. A more pressing issue was: what was I going to do with all these refugees? There were now many thousands of them on the streets of Syracuse. The residents were complaining bitterly to Colonel Hunt about these starving and desperate people who were begging for food and causing disturbances. These refugees would be nothing but trouble unless I did something about them.

That night in bed I mentioned the problem to Victoria. As I was discussing it with her, an idea came to me. Why not just put them to work? I told Victoria my idea and the more I talked about it, the more I liked it. Victoria said little but acted as a sounding board to my idea. She occasionally nodded in agreement or offered some positive feedback. I worked out all the details right there in bed.

It was a brilliant idea. Farmers throughout Threecor were short handed, particularly during harvest. I would send these non-citizens to the farmers to be employed as needed. The non-citizens would work for their food. This would also free up the citizens of Threecor to devote more time to militia duties. Not only that, but I could replace machines on the farms with people and consequently reduce the farmers' fuel allocation. My army would have more fuel reserves and would therefore become even more maneuverable. I immediately stopped thinking of these refugees as a problem and started to view them as a resource to be used.

The next morning, I ordered Colonel Hunt to round up the refugees and send them to Fort Drum. I didn't want to waste precious fuel transporting them, so I ordered Hunt to march them up Interstate 81 to Fort Drum. It took days longer than I estimated for the pathetic collection of people to make the seventy-mile journey. I was sorry to hear that dozens died on the march north. It was too much for them in their state of starvation.

I watched as the long column of refugees shuffled into the base. The emaciated creatures were poorly clothed and had vacant expressions, their eyes devoid of life. They were fed, washed and deloused. I ordered that the refugees be temporarily housed in the base's prison and that the distribution of these non-citizens was to start the next day.

The citizens of Syracuse were pleased to get rid of these unwanted strangers, the farmers of Threecor were eager to get the free help, and I was thankful for the reduced draw on my fuel reserves. Everyone was happy—everyone except perhaps the refugees, but no one thought much about that. They were being fed and that should be good enough for them.

* * *

Kellerman had returned from his scouting mission. He stood in front of my desk and gave me his report. "Sir, General Cottick's forces are in disarray."

With that assessment, a wave of relief washed over me.

Kellerman continued: "I discovered that upon his return to Kitchener, General Cottick purged his officer corps of anyone suspected of having any residual loyalties to you. Even Cottick's fanatics thought it was brutal and largely unnecessary."

This was excellent. Cottick's troops would be leaderless, uncertain and dispirited.

Kellerman continued with his good news. "While the slaughter was underway, the Fifth Guard Division was attacked by unknown forces southwest of Buffalo. The Fifth managed to repulse the attack but with heavy losses. Morale is rock-bottom throughout General Cottick's forces but particularly with the guardsmen of the Fifth."

Splendid! Until Cottick had reorganized his forces and repaired the morale of his troops, he would be vulnerable. There was no way his forces could mount a sustained attack on my base. I was secure for the moment. The strategic initiative was mine. I could move on Cottick whenever I was ready and meet him in battle on terms of my choosing.

"And what about Cottick himself?" I asked. "What's his state of mind?"

"I couldn't say, sir. He remains in his headquarters and never comes out. The building is heavily guarded, and in keeping with your orders I didn't attempt entry."

I noted a hint of annoyance in Kellerman's voice. He believed that he could have entered Cottick's headquarters and killed the traitorous general, but I had ordered him not to take any risks.

"If Cottick stays hidden," I mused, "it means he'll lose touch with the mood of his men."

"I don't think so, sir. General Cottick has enforcers and informers throughout his army. I think he knows everything that's going on."

"Maybe, but only what his informers choose to tell him. How much bad news will his informers dare to share with him? Even if he is accurately informed, men fight better for a leader they see and who they know is taking the same risks as they are."

Kellerman absorbed this assertion without comment.

"Thank you, Sergeant. Dismissed. Go get yourself some food and a good night's sleep. I'll be going after Cottick soon enough, and then I'll have some work for you."

Kellerman saluted and left my office.

I leaned back in my chair and smiled. Everything was going so well. My army was recovering and the militia was being trained. I had procured fuel and free labor, and the threat from General Cottick was diminished. And I had Victoria. My circumstances couldn't get any better.

Part III

Hell Received

Abandon all hope, ye who enter here!
– Dante Alighieri
The inscription over the entrance to Hell

– Chapter 16 –

Syracuse

My senior officers were arguing again. Colonel Rourke was for the second time complaining about the lack of fuel for his armored battalion and Colonel Omar's improper distribution of supplies (as Rourke saw it). He added many colorful swear words to his complaints. I try to discourage foul language in my presence, but Rourke was oblivious to my preference in this regard. I don't think he even noticed what he was saying. I had given up cautioning him on this occasion.

This meeting of my senior commanders stationed at Fort Drum, Omar, Rourke, and Holcomb, was supposed to be productive. Instead it had degenerated into an attack on Colonel Omar and his Quartermaster Regiment. Both Colonel Rourke and Colonel Holcomb were united in their assault on the regiment's poor foraging results, but they differed on where Omar should be putting his priorities. Rourke wanted more fuel to make the tanks in his armored battalion mobile; Holcomb wanted ammunition for training exercises, and everyday items like paper and pencils to enable his officer cadets to take notes in their classes.

Colonel Omar finally lost his temper—a rare event for this usually jovial man. "My men are doing everything they can do," Omar shouted. "While your men laze about polishing their tanks or strutting around the parade ground, my men are out there working eighteen-hour days searching crumbling buildings and decaying factories. It's dangerous work."

"Surely, finding paper—," Holcomb started to say.

"Enough with the paper! If it wasn't for my men discovering that paper-mill north of Trenton with its undamaged stocks, you wouldn't have—."

"Gentlemen. Please," I interrupted.

"General, my men are stretched too thin," Omar stated. "Look at what I have to put up with." He waved a scrap of paper at Holcomb and Rourke. "This morning, I get this. Colonel King sends me a message saying that the fighting spirit of her soldiers is plummeting and she blames me. She demands—demands!—as a top priority that I find her battalion a supply of shampoo. I mean, General, this is too much. No one makes the stuff anymore, so I would have to assign men to forage for an overlooked stock hidden in an abandoned warehouse. What a waste! As if my men didn't have enough to do."

"This is stupid," Rourke shouted. "I need more fuel."

I put my hand to my forehead. I was getting a headache. Shampoo? Why couldn't King's women be content with rock-hard soap like the rest of us?

"This is getting us nowhere," I said. "It's clear to me that the Quartermaster Regiment has too many demands on it and not enough men. Colonel Omar, I will assign more men to your command. I want you to liaise with the militia. They know their regions better than us. Colonel Holcomb, design a course on foraging and send your cadets to Colonel Omar for training."

Holcomb was about to say something, but I cut him off with a curt dismissal.

The three officers rose and left my office. I remained behind with my headache. I longed for an aspirin, but such medication was irreplaceable and was used only on the truly sick. My head pounded and I felt truly sick. Surely I deserved just one aspirin.

Feeling very sorry for myself, I dragged a file across my

desk and opened it. It was a lengthy and verbose operational status report by the militia colonel in command of the 2nd Adirondack Militia Regiment stationed in Lake Placid. What a waste of precious paper! I would censure this commander, and then I would send Colonel Holcomb to him to procure additional supplies of paper for his cadets from this wasteful officer's stocks.

I read the boring report without absorbing any of it, and I was about to attempt to read it again when Victoria entered my office. It was getting late, so I welcomed her with relief and pleasure.

"I've missed you today," she said with a playful pout.

"And I, you."

Victoria winked and then playfully shimmied her chest in front of me. Her breasts jiggled beneath her loose clothing. Needing no further encouragement, I pushed myself out of my chair and hurried over to her. She felt good in my arms.

"Let's go to our quarters," I said at last.

"What about doing it here?"

"Here? In my office?" I laughed.

No sooner were the words out of my mouth than there was a knock at my door.

"My quarters, I think—where we won't be disturbed."

I opened the door and led Victoria out. My aide stood to one side and saluted.

"Sorry to disturb you, sir."

"Yes, Captain, what is it?" I asked with a sigh.

"Sir, Colonel Hunt is calling from Syracuse. He wants to speak with you. It sounded urgent."

It was always urgent. Why couldn't my senior commanders solve problems for themselves? Why did they always have to run to me for everything? I had created independent battalions to be independent. I knew I should hear what Hunt had to say but Victoria looked especially desirable this evening. She gently tugged on my arm. I decided Hunt could manage on his own.

"Captain, tell Colonel Hunt that I will talk to him in the morning. He can handle whatever it is in the meantime. I don't want to be disturbed tonight by anyone—not unless General Cottick himself is driving through the main gate. Understood, Captain?"

"Yes, sir," the captain said smartly. He gave me a crisp salute and I made a halfhearted gesture in return.

I was a bit too gruff with the captain (it wasn't his fault that Hunt had called), but I was fed up with babysitting my senior commanders.

Victoria led me away from my office and all my worries.

* * *

I awoke late after a restful night. I stretched and rolled over to view Victoria's beautiful naked body next to me. Arousing to be sure, but after last night I had no more energy left for such things. It was time for work. I struggled out of bed, yawned and began to get dressed. I must have disturbed Victoria for she mumbled something unintelligible and then closed her eyes and went back to sleep. I watched her exposed breasts slowly rise and fall with her breathing.

I sighed. Duty called.

I put on my uniform and walked out the door. I turned around to close it and looked longingly at Victoria's nakedness in my bed. Life was pleasant with her—simple and uncomplicated. With another sigh, I closed the door and left for my office. I prayed I wouldn't have another day with my senior officers arguing about irritating supply issues.

No sooner had I entered my office than my aide appeared. He informed me that Colonel Hunt had called several more times that night. Each time, as I had ordered, Hunt was told that I wasn't to be disturbed. I told my aide that I would talk to Colonel Hunt now. I yawned heavily.

My aide and I walked to the adjoining communications room, where I ordered the radio operator to contact Colonel Hunt. The operator made a number of attempts, but to no avail. Given the poverty of our functioning communications equipment and the inexperience of many of the radio operators, this wasn't all that unusual.

After a while, I asked if any messages had been left the previous night. The operator checked the log and informed me that there were two messages from Colonel Hunt. He pointed out the two and I read them for myself. The first, logged just before ten o'clock, said: "Raid underway. Forces unknown. Investigating." The second, logged just after midnight, said: "Battalion pursuing south. Militia ordered to follow."

Neither of these messages was very clear. Obviously, Hunt had a situation on his hands, but what was it? The first message indicated a raid by unknown forces. I doubted these could be Cottick's soldiers. According to Kellerman, Cottick's command was in a mess. Furthermore, the second message said the battalion was pursuing southward, not westward, as it would if it had been a raid by Cottick's Fifth Guard Division. I suspected it was probably an attack by refugees coming out of the hills south of Syracuse. It was unlikely the refugees would number more than one or two hundred at most, and they wouldn't be well armed. Nothing to worry about. But then why did the second message imply that the entire battalion had been mobilized and the militia was following? Probably the message meant only small parts of the battalion and militia were involved. The messages were tantalizing but obscure. It was imperative that I talk to Colonel Hunt to clarify the situation.

The radio operator tried repeatedly to raise Colonel Hunt or anyone in the 132nd Battalion, but there was only static. I ordered the operator to contact the 3rd Militia Regiment and later anyone at all in Syracuse. I was growing increasingly concerned. This could no longer be blamed on the usual communication breakdowns. Something bad had occurred in Syracuse last night, and I didn't know what that something was. It wasn't a comfortable feeling—not one bit.

By noon, we still hadn't raised anyone in Syracuse, so I decided I had to travel there to see what was going on. I felt that speed was necessary so I authorized the use of a car for me and a truck for my bodyguard detail.

Less than an hour later, as I approached Syracuse along Interstate 81, I was greeted by the ominous sight of several tall plumes of billowing black smoke. I ordered my driver to go faster. We flew through empty streets and soon arrived at the headquarters of the 132nd on the west side of the city. It was deserted and evidently abandoned in a hurry. I traveled into the center of the city and headed towards the headquarters of the 3rd Syracuse Militia Regiment.

At last, people!

It was a scene of chaos. Soldiers and civilians were running in every direction. A car sat in front of the militia's headquarters, driverless but with its engine idling and wasting precious fuel.

I climbed out of my car and strode into the militia headquarters. I grabbed the first officer I saw and demanded to know what had happened. The young, fresh-faced militia lieutenant was clearly in a state of high agitation. He was overjoyed that help had come at last. The lieutenant launched into details of what had happened during the night and my heart sank further with every word he uttered.

According to the lieutenant, at dusk a force of hundreds of horsemen, possibly numbering as high as one thousand, had attacked areas across the southern districts of the city. They pillaged food, raided weapons depots and kidnapped women. Colonel Hunt's young wife was among the women taken (a very recent marriage of which I was unaware). They murdered anyone who got in their way. Hundreds had died. When the horsemen withdrew, they set fire to buildings and fuel depots.

The raid happened so quickly and so unexpectedly that no organized resistance had been mounted. After the horsemen had retired into the hills to the south, Colonel Hunt had ordered the entire 132nd to pursue and the militia to follow as soon as it was ready. The militia colonel was leaving within the hour, and I demanded to know where I could find him. The lieutenant promptly led me outside and around the corner to a parking lot where many militiamen were assembled. The colonel was talking with other militia officers but stopped as soon as he saw me striding towards him.

The colonel repeated the same story the lieutenant had told me, but added some additional information to which the lieutenant wasn't privy. A corporal, who Hunt sent back to Syracuse, had reported that early in the morning Colonel Hunt had led the 132nd along Interstate 81 to a village called Tully, some thirty miles south of Syracuse. They had been ambushed and had suffered very heavy casualties. Colonel Hunt had been severely wounded. The surviving men of the battalion had retreated into Tully and had taken defensive positions inside the buildings of the village.

A disaster! How did this happen? Hunt was an experienced and cautious soldier. To walk into a trap like this indicated gross negligence on his part. What was he thinking?

I had to act quickly. The militia colonel was even now moving the 3rd Militia to rescue the trapped men. If these unknown horsemen had routed the veteran 132nd, they would make quick work of the 3rd Militia. I couldn't send the barely-trained militiamen into battle unsupported, but I couldn't find any support before darkness fell. The survivors of the 132nd would have to hold out until tomorrow. I ordered the militia colonel to advance on Tully cautiously but not to attack until first light tomorrow. I promised him I would be there with reinforcements. I ordered scouting parties out to gather intelligence on the forces that I faced. I had to know who I was dealing with. How strong were they? Who was their leader?

Why had they attacked?

I had to get back to Fort Drum to mobilize my forces, but I also needed to revive the sagging morale of my men. I made a hurried tour of the damaged parts of the city. Bodies lay in the streets, homes were on fire, and storehouses and arsenals had been plundered. Burial details were moving through the streets searching for the dead. In the distance, I could see a vast column of thick black smoke rising into the air. Syracuse's fuel depot, newly refilled with diesel from the tanker in Montreal, was burning. Irreplaceable fuel had been lost. A catastrophe!

At the site of one attack, several civilians were helping the militiamen drag a body from beneath a fallen wall. The mangled body was that of a boy about three years old. A young woman, probably his mother, was grasping his limp hand. Her face was pale and tears ran freely down both cheeks.

"They killed my boy," she wailed.

A flash of recognition swept across her face when she realized it was me watching her. Her eyes narrowed and her expression changed from all-consuming sadness to burning hate.

She said with an anger which startled me: "Kill them, General. Kill them all!"

She looked into my eyes and saw something there that satisfied her. She nodded to me and then returned to attending her dead son. I watched her for a moment and then hurried away.

I made my way over to the hospital. Dozens of my soldiers and a hundred or more civilians were lying on beds, sofa, mats, or directly on the bare floor. Others, less hurt, were standing or sitting on the floor, patiently waiting for the hard-pressed medical staff to attend to their needs. There was an air of hopelessness about the place. I hadn't visited such a place since I was a young lieutenant serving with the Tenth Mountain Division in Siberia. It was depressing. A key part of my army had been defeated. I made a short speech about revenge and retribution. I tried to be inspirational and reassuring, but my soldiers didn't seem to react. They were silent but their eyes stared at me. I knew what they were thinking: how did I allow this to happen? I had no answer for them. My experienced, battle-hardened soldiers had been routed by common raiders twice: once here in Syracuse and again near Tully. Their confidence had been shattered. Unless I did something decisive, these soldiers would be useless to me in the war against General Cottick. Worse, such defeatism could spread. No words on my part would do; action was required. I had to prove to these men that we were still the best.

I fled back to Fort Drum to make my plans.

Why didn't someone inform me of this situation last night when I could have done something to prevent it? Although I said I didn't want to be disturbed, couldn't anyone see this was important? Damn my staff's lack of initiative—and damn Victoria. Anger flooded through me.

– Chapter 17 –

Tully

I stormed out of a meeting with Lieutenant Colonel Woo. I was furious. My satellite system was still not operational. His complex technical explanations, valid or not, were irrelevant. Now, when I needed it the most, I couldn't use my best intelligence tool. I was blind to what was happening south of Syracuse.

I regained my composure and began to search for other solutions. There was another source of information which I had yet to fully tap: the refugees from the south. They might know more about these mysterious horsemen, but no one had bothered to ask them. Many of the refugees remained in Fort Drum's prison, awaiting allocation to local farmers. I ordered their immediate interrogation—a thorough one this time.

Most of the refugees were quite talkative, and several expressed surprise about never being asked who had attacked them and driven them from their homes. The stories were all the same. Weeks ago, they had been attacked by bands of marauding horsemen, usually no more than twenty or thirty at one time. No one mentioned any number close to the thousand or more that raided Syracuse. These raiders swept into a community, usually at dusk, stealing food, raping and kidnapping women, murdering whole families, and burning whatever was left. Several survivors claimed to have heard them speak Spanish, while others said they spoke English with a southern drawl. According to the tales of survivors, these raiders had traveled up from the southern states, leaving destruction and misery in their wake.

One attractive woman claimed to have been brought before their leader, an evil-looking, bestial man who called himself El Acero, which is, so I was informed, Spanish for The Steel. The leader gave this woman to one of his men, a tall man with a jagged scar across his face and one eye white and unseeing. After he raped her, another man wanted a turn and there was a fight. The woman made her escape during the confusion.

A corporal came towards me and saluted. He reported that radio communications with Syracuse had been reestablished. Finally! I went over to the communications room and the officer-on-duty informed me that he had received a message from the 3rd Militia Regiment. The 3rd reported that a messenger from the 132nd had made his way back from Tully. The 132nd was surrounded in the village and was barely holding its own against repeated attacks. Ammunition was dangerously low, and food and water were non-existent. The force attacking them was now estimated to be more than two thousand irregular cavalry with a plentiful supply of heavy weapons (some of which had probably been looted from my arsenals in Syracuse). The effective strength of the 132nd was down to less than two hundred soldiers. The condition of Colonel Hunt was deteriorating and he required immediate medical attention.

I had to act fast to save both the men of 132nd and the confidence of my army. I strode purposely towards my main briefing room.

On the way, Victoria came up to me. "I heard what has happened. Can you save them?"

"Not now!" I snapped. Couldn't she see I was busy?

I left Victoria behind in the hallway and entered the briefing room. Two officers had assembled as ordered, Colonel Rourke, commander of the 88th Armored Battalion, and Major Bokuk, in her role as the commander of the Aviation Support Group.

"We need to hit these marauders fast and hard," I said without preamble.

"The 88th is ready to go," Rourke said proudly. "I can have my tanks underway within two hours."

"That's excellent, Colonel. But we aren't taking them all. The heavy tanks are too slow. On this operation, we need speed—above all speed. We are dealing with a highly mobile cavalry force. I don't want it escaping and disappearing into the hills. I want the enemy completely destroyed and my southern flank secure. Is that understood?"

"Yes, sir, but if I go in with only the faster urban tanks, we will be light for taking on an enemy a thousand strong. I think we will need the heavies."

"We can't take them, Colonel. They're too slow. And it gets worse. The soldiers of the 132nd estimate they are facing a force of more than two thousand. But the 88th isn't doing this alone. I don't just want the 132nd rescued—I want this El Acero and his marauders annihilated."

"What other forces? The militiamen? They're useless."

"The militia will play its part, but I have another force in mind. I intend to send a fleet of trucks and cars over to the 200th in Utica. I want Colonel King's soldiers mobile and driving down to Tully as soon as the transport arrives. The objective of this mission is to trap the enemy and annihilate them. The ground around Tully is perfect for that. There are lakes and marshes to the west, steep hills to the east and open farmland in between. The 200th will hit the marauders from the northeast, and in the northwest the 3rd Militia will pin them while the 88th drives through from the north and destroys them."

"What about in the south?" asked Rourke. "They'll scatter as soon as they see our tanks. If they can get into those hills, we'll never catch them."

I turned to Major Bokuk. "What air assets do we have ready to go immediately?"

"A helicopter gunship and two transport helicopters. I might be able to get a third helicopter operational if I had another day."

"You don't."

"Yes, sir. We also have four light fixed-wing aircraft, but stocks of the high-octane aviation gasoline are getting very low."

"We'll use one of the planes as a scout and observer. As for the helicopters, I want you to send the two transport helicopters over to Colonel King. Load them to the limit with her soldiers. The soldiers in the two transports will land and hold the southern exit. The gunship will support them. The 88th, the 200th and the 3rd Militia will crush the enemy, and your task force's mission is to stop them escaping. Questions?"

"No, sir," Major Bokuk replied. "I'll fly the gunship myself. With its powerful support, my men will hold." It was Bokuk's first important battle command, but I had confidence in her. Under normal circumstances, I would have preferred her to be on the ground with her men, but her superb flying skills might make the difference. Colonel King would assign the appropriate ground commander for this force from within her battalion.

"Thank you all. You have your orders. Dismissed."

"We are going to burn a lot of fuel on this," Rourke pointed out as we all stood up from the briefing table.

"So be it. I must have my southern flank secure."

Rourke broke into a broad grin. After the constant fuel restrictions I had been forced to impose on his command, he was now free of them.

"Let's roll!" he said with unabashed enthusiasm.

* * *

I sat in the turret of one of the 88th's ten-wheeled urban tanks. The battered machine had seen a lot of hard service, and it was dented in many places from bullets and shrapnel. Its coat of olive-green paint had for the most part flaked off revealing a flat-white color beneath. It was a camouflage scheme from some long-forgotten winter campaign in, perhaps, Arctic Canada or the Rocky Mountain states.

I had chosen this fighting vehicle purposely because of its out-of-place white camouflage scheme. The tank would stand out on the battlefield and my soldiers would know where I was. They would know that I was personally going into battle. To be honest, there was no way I was going to miss this. I wasn't going to wait around in headquarters again as I had during the Battle of Saranac Lake and before that the Battle of Kemptville. This time I wanted to be a part of the fight and I wanted my men to know that their general shared their risks and dangers. It would be good for morale.

Colonel Rourke was very concerned about me going into battle. He had cautioned me that anything could happen and that I should not be taking such an unnecessary risk. A single bullet through my heart, he had warned, would bring chaos to Threecor. No victory was worth that.

I dismissed Rourke's concerns. I had been in battle before and knew the risks. There were risks all around and this was no different. For this battle, coordination was less important than speed, so I convinced myself that I had to be at the front to ensure nothing slowed us down. To emphasize that point, before we left Fort Drum I gave my troops an order I had never given before: take no prisoners! I was going into this battle outnumbered and I hadn't the manpower, time or inclination to guard prisoners. And what would I do with prisoners anyway? These marauders couldn't be integrated into my disciplined army. It was best to be rid of them straightaway.

Last night had been hot and humid, and today would be scorching. It was mid June and the first real heat of summer had arrived. By noon it would reach at least 115°F. I had to conclude this battle in the relative cool of the morning before the interior of the tanks became unbearable.

I had pushed my officers and they had responded. Some minor delays had occurred, but my forces were now driving hard in the darkness towards Tully to rescue the beleaguered men of the 132nd and to destroy El Acero's horsemen. There was one disappointment so far: Major Bokuk reported that our supply of specialized high-octane aviation gasoline for the fixed-wing planes was contaminated with water and therefore useless. The planes couldn't fly and so I would have to attack without any preliminary reconnaissance. However, on the plus side, the absence of an airplane overhead meant that El Acero wouldn't have any advance warning of our approach.

Just as the sun rose, a column of seventeen urban tanks from the 88th drove through Syracuse along Interstate 81. Far to the east, a truck convoy with Colonel King and many of her soldiers onboard was speeding along rural roads. Farther to the east Major Bokuk's airborne force was flying in a wide arc so that it could approach the battlefield undetected over the eastern hills. We were each running about thirty to forty minutes behind schedule. I had wanted to hit the enemy at first light when they would be the least prepared, but now it would be a little later than that. I prayed the delay wouldn't matter.

My tank was at the head of the column and would lead a force of nine tanks down Route 11 to the east. Colonel Rourke, who was in the middle of the column, would continue with the remaining eight tanks down Interstate 81 to the west. There was about a half-mile or so of flat, open farmland between these two parallel roads. Between us, I hoped to trap and destroy the horsemen.

The column hit the first of the enemy, a small covering cavalry force to the north of Tully. We brushed them aside. Another small force, which was blocking the area around the Tully exit off the interstate, was similarly pushed away. I wasn't interested in these tiny forces; I wanted to eliminate the main force to the south.

The column split and I led my half off the interstate and

towards Tully. From my open turret I watched in horror as a mile to the south the militiamen were retreating in disarray across open ground. Contrary to my orders the militia colonel had prematurely attacked a large, disused factory. An intelligence report had suggested that the women who had been taken from Syracuse were being held in that building. The marauders had quickly counterattacked, which stopped cold the attack by the militia. My inexperienced troops had been routed. The militia colonel was supposed to have waited for my arrival before he attacked. Damn him!

My nine tanks flew through the streets of Tully to the waves and cheers of the beleaguered men of the 132nd. The siege had been broken, but many dead were visible. Without slowing, I turned my tanks on to Route 11 and drove south. A large force of cavalry, emboldened by the retreat of the militia, was preparing to charge on the fleeing militiamen. My tanks emerged from Tully and hit the horsemen just as they started their attack. I had arrived just in time. My tanks poured shell after shell into the enemy. Men and horses were cut down by the powerful cannons and machine guns mounted on the tanks. In less than two minutes we had wiped out half the force and sent the other half reeling over to the east, right into the deadly embrace of King's women, who had just arrived and were now deploying. Through my binoculars, I watched as the soldiers of the 200th dismounted from their transport trucks and set up a defensive line. The marauders were no longer dealing with inexperienced militiamen or defenseless farmers. A few survivors fled south. The helicopter gunship piloted by Major Bokuk skimmed low over the trees and let loose with its 20-millimetre cannon. The remaining horsemen were all killed.

My tanks continued southward. We soon hit El Acero's main force, which was already retreating. Major Bokuk's gunship swung south and fired its only remaining air-to-surface missile. It was the last such missile in our ammunition stores. At the same time the troops disembarked from the two helicopter transports and blocked the southern exit. The marauders turned away. The gunship came around from another attack and then disaster occurred. The enemy let loose at point-blank range a portable surface-to-air missile, probably one stolen from my arsenals in Syracuse. The missile hit the gunship's engine and the gunship exploded and crashed in a fiery heap. Major Bokuk was killed instantly.

I threw down my binoculars and grabbed the turret's co-axial machine gun. It vibrated in my hands as I poured murderous fire into the retreating horsemen. Dozens fell. Bullets sprayed from my machine gun. Dozens more fell. Adrenalin surged through my body. I was in full battle-fury and it felt good—a release of stresses and frustrations built up over the previous day. A stray bullet ricocheted off my helmet. Startled, I stopped firing for a moment. As soon as I realized I was unhurt, I squeezed the machine gun's trigger and renewed my attack.

The enemy fled eastward only to come under fire from Colonel Rourke's tanks. They turned south again and attempted to escape the trap, but we had them. Bullets and shells blanketed the killing-ground between Interstate 81 and Route 11. Within ten minutes, nothing moved; all the marauders and their horses were dead.

I ordered a ceasefire and turned my tanks around and headed back north. The slaughter was over. Now, I had to assess the cost of my victory.

* * *

The scorching hot sun and the swarms of flies feeding off the dead made outside unbearable. I trudged over brown, dead grass which crunched underfoot. There was no moisture in the soil—not enough even for a cactus.

Passing dozens of dead marauders, I felt nothing but satisfaction and pride in the performance of my soldiers, even that of the militiamen. Although they had retreated, they had killed many of the enemy before doing so. Now the swarms of flies were dining on an unexpected bounty which my men had provided. The flies attacked everything and everyone—dead or alive. The corpses couldn't be left to attract the flies so I ordered mass graves to be dug as soon as the heat of the day was over.

Along with Colonel Rourke, the militia colonel, and several junior officers, I retreated to the relative cool and shade of the factory to the south of Tully. Inside the factory, the captured women of Syracuse were waiting for us. They had been abandoned when the enemy fled. The marauders holding the factory had escaped and were the only enemy force of significance to do so. Some of the women had been killed by El Acero and his men but most had not. The survivors were grateful beyond words to me and my soldiers.

The militia colonel felt the need to show me a tragic little scene, as he called it. He led me to two bodies and informed me that the woman was Colonel Hunt's young bride. She had bled to death from several stab wounds to her chest. However, she hadn't died alone. Lying beside her was a tall man with an old scar across his jaw and a damaged eye. Now both his eyes were lifeless. He too had bled to death. The woman still gripped the knife she had plunged into the man's throat. The private struggle had taken both their lives.

Perhaps it was best that Colonel Hunt hadn't lived to see this scene. Hunt had succumbed from his wounds just before the 88th arrived. He was a cautious man who, in a moment of incaution driven by his desire to save his bride, had lost his own life and almost destroyed his battalion. Maybe he would have judged it a noble cause to die for, but I had lost a valuable and experienced commander and one of the few men I trusted. Such a loss, such a waste. I needed him.

I ordered the bodies of Colonel Hunt and his wife to be buried in a private grave just outside the factory. The militia colonel was right: it was a tragic little scene.

Colonel Hunt had found love, but such an emotion couldn't survive in this hellish world. I reflected for a moment on my relationship with Victoria and a profound realization came to me: I didn't love her. I was using Victoria to sedate my needs, but then she was using me to obtain security, food and shelter. No love, just lust. No commitment, just use. How cheerless and bleak was that? I sighed and turned away.

I continued my inspection of the ruined factory, but I didn't really notice my surroundings as I was lost in thought. El Acero and his marauders had cost me a lot. I had lost Colonel Hunt and Major Bokuk—two irreplaceable officers. The 132nd had been effectively wiped out. I would have to reassign the surviving soldiers to other battalions. The 3rd Syracuse Militia Regiment had been severely mauled and its confidence shattered, possibly irreparably. The 200th had suffered some casualties and I had lost my only helicopter gunship. Inevitably, I had expended a lot of valuable supplies. Small caliber ammunition was still in plentiful supply, but the stock of shells for the urban tanks' main guns was now alarmingly low.

And the fuel!

How much of my precious fuel supplies had been used up in this operation? How much had gone up in smoke in the fires in Syracuse? I needed it all to fight Cottick. His engineers would be pumping as much oil as they could out of the old reservoirs under southwestern Ontario. How much fuel did I have left? Would it be enough? I would have to make a thorough inventory of fuel supplies when I returned to Fort Drum. My plans would have to be adjusted accordingly.

I'm glad that I ordered no prisoners to be taken. It was the right thing to do. With less than six hundred soldiers and eight hundred militiamen, I had crushed a force now estimated at over three thousand. Over twenty-seven hundred of El Acero's men lay dead on the field of battle and less than three hundred had escaped. It was a massacre—as I had planned. Nevertheless, it concerned me that their leader might have slipped out of my net.

Interrogations of the women abandoned in the factory led me to believe that the leader of the marauders was in the factory at the time of our attack. I ordered all women who could recognize El Acero to search among the dead for him, but by evening his body still had not been identified. That was very disappointing. El Acero wasn't dead. I had to face the regrettable fact that he had indeed escaped. I consoled myself that he would have at most three hundred men with him and he would flee southward. It was unlikely that he would come north to trouble me again—but he might and I couldn't afford to take that risk. My southern flank had to be secure.

– Chapter 18 –

Binghamton

"Reporting for duty, sir." Captain Nuoi saluted crisply. Nuoi was Colonel Rourke's intelligence officer and except for Colonel Rourke he was the senior officer in the 88th with me at Tully.

The small man tried to look his best for me but his uniform, torn, frayed and stained with sweat, marred his efforts. All our uniforms were becoming shabby and threadbare, including my own. I sensed that this bothered the captain as much as it did me, which was a mark in his favor as far as I was concerned. There was a time when I would never have been seen dead in such a tattered uniform, and I would have severely disciplined anyone in my command who dishonored the uniform like this. I would have to do something about our uniforms, but that was for a later, more peaceful time. Right now, I had a job to finish.

"Very good, Captain. I have a mission for you. Walk with me."

Together we left the column of urban tanks parked on Route 11, some three miles south of Tully, and walked across a field. On the horizon a deep-orange sun was setting in a cloudless sky. Only half of it remained above the hills to the west. Behind us, the first few stars were visible in the dark eastern sky.

A fierce wind was building from the south. I removed my cap lest it be blown away and tucked it under my arm. There would be a violent windstorm tonight. My troops called them 'blasts'. All the conditions were present and we all could read the signs. We knew what to expect. No clouds would form, no rain would fall, but the wind would howl. In this valley with hills to the east and west, the windstorm would be funneled and its strength amplified. Such powerful windstorms were increasingly frequent as the atmosphere vented the energy it accumulated from the scorching heat of the day. I would have to order precautions. My men would have to find shelter from blowing debris. The tanks and trucks would have to be protected from dust being blasted into their machinery. My helicopters would be the most vulnerable of my vehicles. They would have to be lashed down tight and covered with tarps. I lost one helicopter today. I couldn't afford to lose any more.

With Captain Nuoi in tow, I headed towards the smoking pyre that marked the grave of Major Bokuk. I was going to pay my last respects to a fine officer. The helicopter gunship still smoldered where it had crashed twelve hours before. I made a mental note that I would have to detail some men to ensure that there were no fires left burning in the wreck. The windstorm would fan any residual flames and blow cinders all over the valley. I couldn't risk waking up tomorrow to find a raging fire sweeping through my camp.

As Captain Nuoi and I walked across the field towards the site of the crash, I gave him his mission. I ordered him to find and capture or kill El Acero. It was a straightforward search and destroy mission with just one target. Once the leader of the marauders was out of the way, his leaderless horde—at least what was left of it after the slaughter on the fields of Tully— would disperse and trouble me no more. I assigned to Nuoi two urban tanks from our column, two trucks with as many of Colonel King's soldiers as they could carry, and for scouting purposes one of the two surviving helicopters.

"I want the helicopter back in one piece," I warned him. "Is that clearly understood, Captain?"

"Yes, sir."

"I want El Acero captured or killed. Either way, I want to see his body. Take someone who speaks Spanish, as well as one of the women who was held captive by El Acero. She'll be able to identify him."

"Yes, sir." Nuoi was eager to please me.

I dismissed the captain, leaving him to make his plans and assemble his men, and continued towards the crash site by myself.

Somewhere in the mangled, smoldering wreck lay the charred body of Major Belinda Bokuk. The gathering dusk obscured the gruesome details—which was a blessing for I had seen enough death today. I saluted and privately gave my thanks to the major.

* * *

I decided to remain in the Tully area with the soldiers who had fought the battle until the results of Captain Nuoi's mission were known. My forces protected gravediggers from the 3rd Syracuse Militia Regiment from any surprise attacks by overlooked bands of surviving horsemen. The work of burying so many dead was time-consuming, but I didn't want to risk an epidemic springing from the corpses of the marauders if I left them to rot in the fields. Everyone who lived through the Adepi plague years ago took the risk of epidemics very seriously indeed. Although it was grueling work in the heat, made worse by the thick swarms of engorged flies, everyone knew it was necessary.

As expected, the windstorm blasted through the valley during the night. We had taken all the precautions that we could think of, but still we experienced some damage. One of the trucks toppled over, and dust and grit fouled the engine of an urban tank. Fortunately, none of my men were hurt. For two hours during the night the wind howled, but finally it weakened and then disappeared altogether. With no breeze, the flies returned. The pests were relentless enemies that couldn't be defeated. Frankly, I preferred living through the windstorm to the constant aggravation of flies. They got everywhere. I sought refuge in my tent.

Tossing my cap on to a small folding desk which functioned as my portable office, I lay down on my cot for a nap. I hadn't slept more than three hours in the past two days. Exhausted, I pulled the mosquito netting over my face. Such netting was exceedingly rare and most of my men didn't have such a luxury. Usually I chose to share my men's hardships but these flies were an exception. I loathed their incessant attacks, so I commandeered one of the last mosquito nets.

I fell asleep right away, but in what seemed only an instant later I was awoken by my orderly. He informed me that Colonel Rourke was asking if I could come over to the communications tent. I struggled to my feet and stretched my weary muscles. A huge yawn escaped from me and I belatedly put my hand over my mouth. Thirsty, I grabbed my canteen, which lay near my desk, and took a deep gulp of water. I put on my cap and left for the communications tent, which was set up not far away in the ruins of Tully.

Rourke had some news for me. I was informed that Captain Nuoi was in a 'meeting engagement' with the horsemen. A meeting engagement was a battle in which the two opposing forces arrived at a place at the same time but didn't expect the other side to be there. Such an unexpected battle could test the mettle of any commander. I hoped Nuoi was up to the challenge. Anxiously I awaited his report via the radio.

A corporal powered up the radio with the hand-crank. After the preliminary coded identification of both parties, Nuoi's voice came on. The static hissed loudly, but it didn't mask Nuoi's voice and he could be heard clearly enough.

Nuoi reported that his tankmen had discovered an automobile scrap-yard and had taken the opportunity to see if they could recover any air-conditioning gases from the wrecks.

Chances of this were very slim indeed, but no one who lived in this heat (and particularly those who inhabited the interior of a metal tank) would overlook the possibility of obtaining these much-sought-after gases.

Nuoi's tankmen had only just started their work when the horsemen arrived. A large column of mounted men suddenly appeared in the center of the scrap-yard. Neither side expected to see the other. The scrap-yard was a terrible place to deploy cavalry, because sharp shards of rusting metal which lay all about the place could easily pierce the unprotected hoof of a horse. The marauders, thinking they faced only a few scroungers, dismounted and attacked the tankmen on foot. Fortunately, as per my standing orders, the tankmen had left a guard with each urban tank. While one tank raked the enemy with machine-gun fire, the other drove over to where the tankmen were taking cover. A fierce firefight developed. One of the urban tanks was immobilized when its tires were torn by jagged metal scraps. Not willing to abandon the disabled tank, the outnumbered tankmen fought tenaciously. The marauders, seeing a rare prize for the taking, were also reluctant to retreat. The two truck-loads of King's soldiers arrived just in time. Captain Nuoi deployed one group immediately and sent the other on a flanking maneuver.

The dead and wounded mounted up on both sides, but the tide turned in our favor when the second truck-load of soldiers arrived at the rear of the marauders. The enemy panicked and fled. The helicopter arrived in time to follow the fleeing horsemen to the town of Binghamton, located some fifty miles south of Tully on Interstate 81. Nuoi left a small detachment to secure the disabled tank and protect the wounded. The rest of Nuoi's force pursued the marauders into the town.

The capture of El Acero was anti-climactic. A woman volunteer onboard the helicopter recognized the leader riding below. The pilot remained overhead and directed Nuoi's ground forces to wherever El Acero fled. The marauders realized it was their leader who was our target, so one by one they abandoned him to his fate. He took refuge in the ruins of a hotel. Guided by the helicopter overhead, my soldiers arrived and undertook a systematic room by room search. El Acero, the terrifying brute who was the bane of all that was decent, was found cowering in a filthy bathtub.

El Acero had been captured alive and Captain Nuoi was asking for my orders. I was curious about this man who had caused me so much unanticipated trouble, so I ordered Nuoi to hold him until I arrived.

* * *

My helicopter flew over the ruins of Binghamton, a town that had never been under my command. It wasn't like Watertown or Syracuse or Kingston, where people could go about their business under the protection of my army. It wasn't even like Plattsburgh, where Mayor Keese had once maintained order. It wasn't just that the buildings of Binghamton were ruined; the social structure of the town had also collapsed.

The pilot landed the helicopter on the front parking lot of the ruined hotel. A large crowd had gathered, held back by Nuoi's soldiers and the threat of the urban tank's machine gun.

I climbed out of the helicopter, followed by my bodyguards, and walked over to where Nuoi was waiting. I felt buoyed up and hardly needed my cane. I had in my power the man who had attacked Syracuse, stolen my supplies, destroyed the 132nd Regiment, and threatened my southern flank. He was mine to do with what I wished.

I gestured at the shouting crowd. "What's going on here?"

"They gathered as soon as we arrived," Captain Nuoi responded. "They are howling for blood. They demand we give them El Acero. He's been terrorizing them for months."

"Hmm. I see."

I walked over towards the crowd and scanned the faces. I

saw rage in them. It took me a moment to realize there were no women.

"Where are the women?" I asked.

Nuoi shrugged.

Either taken by El Acero's men long ago, I surmised, or, if they were lucky, in hiding.

I turned my back on the crowd and walked into the wrecked lobby of the abandoned hotel. Nuoi guided me to a room on the second floor. He opened a door and I came face to face with a medium height, very broad and muscular man in his early forties with a face that could only be described as ravaged and evil. Three women of the 200th stood guard over El Acero and had their rifles leveled at him. They looked like they would take pleasure in shooting him if he so much as breathed too hard.

I studied him for a time and then said: "You've caused me a lot of trouble."

"What are you going to do with me?" he whimpered in English but with a thick Spanish accent. "Don't kill me, por favor. Permítame vivir! Let me live!" He was terrified—you could see it in his eyes.

I don't know what I expected him to say, but it wasn't that. Maybe I expected defiance or anger or threats, but not craven begging—not from a man who had hurt my army like this man had. He wasn't a worthy opponent.

"What did you do with the women you took from Syracuse? Did you spare them when they begged for mercy?"

He fell to his knees and pleaded for his life. This was degrading to watch.

"Captain, bring him," I ordered.

El Acero looked relieved. Perhaps he thought I was going to take him back to Fort Drum.

We left the hotel and walked towards the waiting crowd. The mob went wild when they saw El Acero led out under arrest. Their shouts of anger turned to screams of madness. I stopped some ten yards from the cordon of soldiers that held the crowd back, and put up my hand for silence. Slowly the shouting died down.

"Captain, withdraw your lines thirty paces," I said loudly. With that, the crowd fell absolutely silent. My actions weren't what they expected.

After a moment of hesitation, Nuoi shouted the order to his soldiers. Slowly they backed away from the crowd, but with their rifles still aimed at the motionless mass of people.

There was now only me and Captain Nuoi between El Acero and the mob. Slowly it dawned on him what was about to happen. Again he fell to his knees and started to wail for me to save him. I wasn't inclined to do so—in fact, I had a quite different fate in mind for him.

"Captain," I said. "Our work here is done."

We backed away from El Acero.

The mob surged forward and consumed the man who had terrorized them. Consumed—yes, that was the right word to describe what occurred. If El Acero screamed, I didn't hear it over the joyful cries of the mob.

My soldiers and I stood passively by as the mob beat and pummeled El Acero with their fists and feet. Someone produced a rope and tied it around El Acero's lifeless legs. The battered body was dragged through the street and away from the hotel, surrounded by the mob howling with insane joy.

Even though I had let this happen, I found the sight of this madness disturbing. It was as though the veneer of humanity had been stripped away from these people, and I didn't like what was revealed beneath.

I ordered my forces to depart and headed for the waiting helicopter. Binghamton left me with an unpleasant memory and I wanted to leave immediately, but I was momentarily detained. I stopped when I heard a voice call my name, and I turned to see a man waving at me from the other side of a line of my bodyguards.

"Walter Eastland," this man shouted. "You knew my father."

I ordered the man searched and then brought before me. He was in his mid forties, prematurely gray and balding. He had sunken cheeks, a bony face and his eyes appeared larger than they should. This man was starving.

"General Eastland," he gasped. "My father was Senator Nicholas Jonack. He sat on the Defense Armed Services Committee many years ago. You testified before him regarding your escape from Libya."

I cast my mind back to those events many, many years ago and remembered Senator Jonack. An honorable man. He viewed my actions during the escape of my regiment from Libya as the actions of a brave and imaginative officer. Most of the others on the committee had chosen to believe—for political purposes, I might add—that my miraculous escape was in fact an ignominious rout caused by an inexperienced commander who had abandoned his post. The senator was a friend when I needed one.

"I remember him."

"Don't leave. Please don't send your soldiers away. This is an awful place to live. We need your help."

I looked about at the crazed mob dragging the mangled body of El Acero through the streets. I wanted no part of this place. These people were beyond help.

"No, I'm leaving," I stated with finality.

"But General, we could become part of your command. You could set up a militia here as you have elsewhere."

I wasn't at all tempted to extend my domain. General Cottick, before his betrayal, had once argued that I should extend my control over Michigan and northern Indiana, but I had rejected his arguments. I wasn't going to overextend my meager resources—not then and certainly not now. My takeover of Plattsburgh was an exception, and only warranted because of the natural defense offered by Lake Champlain. In this case, the natural defensive line was the hills between Syracuse and Binghamton. The town of Binghamton itself was of no use to me. I had also to consider that much of my free labor in Threecor came from the refugees from this area. If I extended my domain into Binghamton, their secondary status within Threecor would become less clear and I might lose their valuable services.

"No," I repeated.

The poor man looked crestfallen.

In a moment of charity, I offered him a seat on my helicopter in repayment of an old debt which I owed his father.

His face lit up. "Thank you, General. But my son?" He pointed to someone in the distance.

"Very well, bring him. But we're leaving now."

He waved and his teenage son, a skinny, dull-looking lad, ran towards us.

I climbed onboard the helicopter, with the two newly liberated citizens of Binghamton right behind me, and ordered the pilot to take off. It was time to leave this unsettling place. The behavior of the mob bothered me and on hindsight maybe I was wrong to pander to its savagery. El Acero deserved to die, but perhaps a bullet in the head or a noose around the neck would have been more civilized. Too late for second thoughts. My conscience was placated sufficiently by my small act of charity towards Senator Jonack's son and grandson.

I decided I would waste no more time dwelling on the gruesome fate of El Acero. He deserved what he received. It was time to get back to my real fight: the battle against General Cottick. It had been on hold for far too long.

– Chapter 19 –

Port Hope

Lieutenant Colonel Woo and the engineers had finally got my satellite system working. The system should have been operating when I had to deal with El Acero and his marauders, but it wasn't. However, it was now. I had at my disposal God-like powers to observe anything, anywhere, at any time (within some irritating orbital parameters and equipment constraints). I had five satellites at my disposal: three communications satellites, which were all but useless as there was no one to communicate with, a weather satellite, which was useful, and one other. This last satellite was the jewel in my orbital crown. The last military surveillance satellite ever launched was mine to use as required. Built long ago by a country which I had honorably served but which now no longer existed, this superbly equipped spy satellite contained thousands of technological marvels which we once took for granted.

My first order for the spy satellite was the observation of Cottick's headquarters at Kitchener. What a marvelous strategic advantage I had—and even better, Cottick wasn't aware I had it.

Cottick's army was stirring. Surveillance images showed a convoy of one hundred and fifty trucks and twenty heavy tanks was moving eastward. The convoy was north of Toronto, skirting the edge of that necropolis. It was the evening of an incredibly hot day in July. The thermometer had peaked at a searing 125°F during mid-afternoon and was still hovering around100°F. Cottick wasn't crazy enough to move his men in the heat of the day, but even travel during the relative cool of the evening was difficult. Cottick must be making the effort in the hope that his forces could catch me by surprise.

My interpretation of Cottick's movement was that he was aiming for an early morning engagement with my forces north of the Saint Lawrence River. I was, however, puzzled as to Cottick's final objective. With all the bridges across the wide river long since destroyed, how was Cottick planning to get his tanks and trucks across to drive on Fort Drum? At first, I suspected this was just a feint. It would make much more sense for Cottick to go south through Buffalo and attack my forces to the west of Syracuse. The marauders' attack on Syracuse and the Battle of Tully had left me very weak in that region. I had been forced to leave Colonel Rourke and all his urban tanks in Syracuse, as well as the survivors of the 132nd and a third of Colonel King's soldiers. The rebuilding and retraining of the 3rd Syracuse Militia Regiment was going to take a long time. My southwest flank was weak, and a determined thrust from Cottick in that direction could have caused me severe difficulties.

But no. Satellite images of the roads to the east of Buffalo showed no movement, and the bases of the Fifth Guard Division weren't making any preparations. Cottick's forces around Buffalo were strangely inactive. His northern convoy was going it alone. Was it a probe? A reconnaissance-in-force? No, it was too big for that. Was it an effort to destroy all my forces north of the Saint Lawrence River? No, it was too small for that. Was there bridging equipment in some of those trucks? Or rafts? What was Cottick up to? I stood staring at the satellite images of the convoy. All these unknowns were disturbing.

The convoy had to be intercepted and delayed while I marshaled my forces—that much was obvious. I called to my senior communications officer, who was on the far side of the room. The lieutenant colonel came over and saluted. His dark complexion and darker beard glistened with sweat. It was stifling in the enclosed room. Between the heat outside and the crowd inside, the air-conditioning unit wasn't coping.

"Get a message to the 317th," I said. "Make sure it's coded. I don't want Cottick getting one whiff of this." I dictated an order for Colonel Sheflin to attack the convoy during the night with whatever she could mobilize. She was to attack and then withdraw—hit-and-run tactics only. The engagement was to be limited to a short-but-sharp delaying action. I emphasized that the 317th wasn't to get bogged down in a large scale battle. The lieutenant colonel saluted and left to prepare the message to Colonel Sheflin.

I then composed mobilization orders to my other forces north of the Saint Lawrence River, as well as my forces in and around Fort Drum. After Cottick's soldiers brushed aside Sheflin's cavalrymen, which they inevitably would, Cottick could either attempt a river crossing or move east toward Montreal. I couldn't see how he could do both with the limited forces in the convoy. If Cottick attempted a river crossing I would hit his flank; if he went for Montreal I would ferry my forces at Fort Drum across the river and hit his rear. Either way, Cottick would come off badly.

What was Cottick doing? What was he thinking? Was he being clever and devious or overconfident and careless?

At this moment, Victoria came into the room. She had free access to anywhere on the base because no officer dared interfere with her movements. She came and went as she pleased.

"Walter," she said smiling, "are you free to come to dinner? I made something special. Something you'll really like."

She knew I didn't like to be called by my first name in front of my men, but ever since I had returned from Tully, she had made a point of doing so. I had asked her not to and she had promised she wouldn't, but she soon broke her word. I think it had less to do with me and more to do with reinforcing her position with my officers. It may have been partially my own fault. I had blamed her for distracting me on the night Syracuse was attacked—unreasonably, I suppose. I had deliberately ignored her for over a week after my return and that had shaken her. Eventually I conceded that I had behaved badly and I apologized. Nevertheless, I realized that I had a power over her which I hadn't previously understood. I liked that feeling.

"No, I'm not free," I replied curtly. "Cottick is on the move."

"Oh, is he?"

I could tell from Victoria's tone of voice that she considered this news to be unimportant. She held an annoying view that my war with General Cottick was nothing more than a stupid game. More than once she had accused me of being obsessed with taking my revenge on the traitorous general. What nonsense! Cottick was a dangerous threat and had to be utterly destroyed. There would be no peace until he was dead.

"Yes, he is!" I shouted.

Her face blanched at my anger. She turned and fled, crying.

I closed my eyes and cursed to myself. All she wanted to do was feed me. I sighed. My orders were given and my men were well-trained to carry them out. Perhaps I did have time for a meal, and I was hungry. Without a word to my men, I left the room and walked over to my quarters. I opened the door and stood in the doorway. Before me, the table was laid with a meal of mashed turnips, wild rhubarb, tiny carrots and Victoria's special pork meatloaf (a particular favorite of mine). A glass of wine, presumably from the vineyards on the Isle of Quinte, was beside my plate.

I could hear sobbing coming from our bedroom. With all I had to worry about, now I had to comfort this young woman. I had been a bachelor far too long for this aggravation.

"I'm here. The meal looks lovely." I attempted to put as much conviction into the words as I could muster.

The sobbing stopped. "I'll be out in a minute."

I knew she was wiping her eyes and composing herself before she came out of the bedroom.

Victoria emerged smiling as though nothing had happened. She ushered me to my chair and chatted away happily. I gave brief compliments at the appropriate times, but said very little else. The meal was delicious and Victoria was beautiful, but both were wasted on me. My mind was on another woman. What was Colonel Sheflin doing now? How long would it be before the 317th engaged the enemy? This was the first large scale battle against Cottick's forces since the Battle of Saranac Lake. Sheflin's small-but-mobile cavalry battalion was outnumbered by at least five to one and it had no heavy support. If Sheflin wasn't very prudent, Cottick's heavy tanks would make mincemeat of her light forces.

Would she be prudent? A grain of doubt remained in my mind. Since my return from Oneida Lake with Victoria, Sheflin had been distant and formal. I hoped she could overcome any emotional issues regarding me and be the superb commander I knew her to be. I was ninety-nine percent certain she would focus on the task at hand and wouldn't let me or her men down. That one percent, however, gave me considerable angst.

After the meal, Victoria came over and held my hand. I stood and she led me towards the bedroom. I wasn't in the mood, but for the sake of peace I reluctantly followed.

There was a knock at the door. I wasn't going to ignore my duties, as I had on the night Syracuse was attacked. I dropped Victoria's hand and bid the person enter. The door opened and a young lieutenant informed me that Colonel Sheflin was preparing to attack. I left my quarters with the lieutenant and didn't look back.

* * *

The satellite imaging software was adjusted to compensate for the darkness of the night, and with the exception of a slight greenish glow, it looked just like daytime. I could follow Cottick's convoy as it traveled east along Highway 401. Sheflin had prepared a series of roadblocks around the town of Port Hope. She had sent two smaller forces on a flanking movement to the north along Route 74. I realized what Sheflin was doing: she was attempting to recreate the conditions which had brought me victory at the Battle of Saranac Lake. While the roadblocks held the lead tanks in check, the two flanking forces would hit the column of trucks from the side. However, she had little time to prepare and the terrain was all wrong. The open farmland couldn't be as effective as the dense forests of the Adirondacks in hiding her forces, and Cottick's men wouldn't be taken unaware a second time. He would have reconnaissance units guarding both flanks. But it was dark—so anything was possible. Sheflin had only to delay the column, not destroy it as I had at Saranac Lake.

The first roadblock stopped Cottick's tanks momentarily, but they soon fanned out in an attempt to outflank it. Sheflin's cavalrymen retreated to a second roadblock. Both forces were becoming scattered and the action was becoming localized and confused. There was no way Sheflin could be maintaining any sort of control over her battalion.

The firefight at the second roadblock raged for fifteen minutes before Sheflin's two flanking forces were in position. Their attacks were poorly coordinated, but nevertheless effective in distracting the enemy. Cottick's soldiers poured out of the trucks and searched for cover. Several trucks were set ablaze, but Sheflin's small flanking force was soon spent. The cavalrymen turned their horses about and rapidly withdrew. The second roadblock fell and all her forces were now in headlong retreat. In the confusing battle, Cottick had lost only three trucks, no tanks, and maybe a dozen men. Sheflin's losses were probably just as light.

Cottick's forces were now free to continue eastward, but they remained motionless for over an hour and then simply turned around and headed back towards Toronto. Incredible! It had never occurred to me that Cottick's forces would retreat after such a small firefight. The commander of the column (which I now assumed wasn't General Cottick himself) had simply lost his nerve. Maybe the fear of repeating the Battle of Saranac Lake had worked on his mind, or perhaps his heart wasn't in the enterprise in the first place. Either way, the enemy slinked back to Kitchener and the crisis evaporated.

I didn't return to my quarters and Victoria that night, but instead left the base in the company of my bodyguards and headed north to congratulate Colonel Sheflin and her cavalrymen. Although the 317th had lost its battle, it had won a great victory of another sort. I realized that I had achieved a psychological dominance over Cottick's men. They feared me—and that was my victory. General Cottick's forces wouldn't again stray out of their zone of control to attack me, and I expected no further interference from them. I had time to develop my plans to the full.

I arrived at Sheflin's headquarters the next day after some hard riding. The colonel greeted me at the entrance to her headquarters, which was located in an old hotel in the small town of Picton. I could see why Sheflin had chosen this site, for the hotel lay at the junction of three roads. These roads provided Sheflin with excellent communications with the rest of her command, which was spread out across the Isle of Quinte. Very sensible.

I sat down on a comfortable leather chair opposite Sheflin's desk. The desk was bare except for a small pile of neatly stacked papers, and the rest of the office was spartan and without any personal touches. On the wall there was an old blackboard on which a crude map of the Port Hope area was sketched. Circles and arrows covered the board. It was Sheflin's plan of attack, done in haste before the battle. I studied it and could visualize

Sheflin's tactics. I was impressed.

"I'm sorry we let you down, sir," Sheflin said.

She didn't understand the true outcome of the battle.

"Nonsense, Colonel. You and your men fought splendidly." I explained what had happened after the 317th retreated and how Cottick's forces had withdrawn. Sheflin lapped up my praise.

We sat alone in her small office in comfortable chairs. Feeling relaxed, I leaned back and stated: "I wish I was with you during the fight."

"So do I, sir."

"It must have been exhilarating to charge into a night time battle on horseback."

Sheflin laughed. "I was scared to death."

I smiled. "I'm envious, Colonel. Back at Fort Drum, I felt remote and detached from the action."

There was a pause. "How are things back at Fort Drum?" she asked. "How is …? … How are you …?" Her voice trailed off.

Alarm bells went off in my head. Sheflin wasn't asking about the efficiency of my command staff or the morale of the men; she was asking about my relationship with Victoria.

"Everything in Fort Drum is going well," I said defensively.

There was an awkward silence for a second or two and then the strangest thing happened: the alarm bells in my head fell silent and I opened up to Jan Sheflin. "I find that I'm being distracted from what needs to be done. There are too many complications. Too many demands on my time."

"Can you do anything about these … demands?"

"It would be awkward. And I'm not sure what I want to do."

Neither of us mentioned Victoria by name, but we both knew who the subject of our conversion was.

"Can I help, sir? I once told you that I would do anything for you."

"I haven't forgotten and I value that promise—value it highly."

Over the next two hours, I poured out my concerns and anxieties. I discussed Cottick and the war, my assessment of why the war had started, and how I had failed to read Cottick's intentions. Eventually, however, my barriers fell and I discussed my relationship with Victoria. Perhaps Sheflin prompted me to open up but I can't recall anything she said to nudge the conversation in that direction. I complained about Victoria's neediness, her occasional embarrassing behavior, and her informality with me in front of my staff. Sheflin listened without comment, with only the occasional nod of sympathy. Words kept pouring out of my mouth. At the end of my monologue, I felt emotionally exhausted.

I had neither possessed nor sought a confidant such as this for many years, but it appeared I now had one.

Jan reached across the desk and placed her hands on mine. They were scratched and callused—unlike Victoria's soft and graceful hands—but they were also warm and gentle.

"I'm always here for you ... Walter."

"Thank you, Jan."

– Chapter 20 –

Olcott

As if the heat wasn't enough, I had to contend with a plague of insects of biblical proportions. Billions of the tiny creatures were making our lives utterly miserable. The only relief was when the strong, hot wind blew and scattered the pests away.

Grasshoppers ate our wilting crops, flies got into our diminishing food stores, and mosquitoes fed liberally on the blood of my exhausted troops. Insect swarms like this had occurred over the past few summers, but never as bad as this. A war with the insects wasn't one I could win. My only strategy was to wait them out. For myself, I decided to retreat into the satellite operations room. Because the room's air-conditioning unit still functioned, it was one of the few rooms on the base which could be sealed off from the outside.

Buildings could only be cooled with open windows and fans which circulated the air (and the insects), or they could be closed off from the outside and cooled by air-conditioning. With the electricity from the two wind-turbine power stations at Sackets Harbor and Picton, I had more than enough power to run my base, but the special gases used in air-conditioning units were exceedingly rare. I could cool only the satellite operations room (which had to be done to keep the computers functional), the hospital, and one-tenth of the sleeping quarters. I had established a strict rotation for my men in the air-conditioned quarters. The threat of removal of that privilege kept my hard-pressed troops obedient.

I confess I spent much more time in the satellite operations room than I needed to, but I wasn't alone. Anyone with clearance and the slightest excuse found their way into the room as often as possible. Today was no exception. The room was full of officers and technicians. However, this time I was in the room on legitimate business. Colonel Woo had called to inform me of strange developments in the city of Buffalo, which was the headquarters of the Fifth Guard Division. This was the smaller of Cottick's two combat divisions.

I hurried over to Colonel Woo, who was examining a large table screen. The colonel saluted and informed me the image on the screen was a live feed from the spy satellite. He drew my attention to a large number of burning buildings. There could be many explanations for this, including accidental fires caused by frequent lightning strikes. One explanation, however, came to my mind immediately: a revolt against Cottick. Had the officers and soldiers of Cottick's smaller division risen up against him?

I ordered the colonel to zoom in on the bridges over the Niagara River. A great deal could be inferred from the identity of whoever controlled those bridges. If soldiers of the Third guarded them, Cottick could rush forces to suppress a rebellion (if there was one). If, on the other hand, soldiers of the Fifth held them, the rebellion might succeed.

"How interesting," Woo mumbled, as he pointed to a particular spot on the image.

I, too, noticed the destroyed bridge at Buffalo. Someone had blown it up.

Woo scrolled the image northward to the town of Niagara Falls. The great horseshoe-shaped waterfall was still there. The mist formed by the plunging waters of the Niagara River lingered in the air, partially obscuring the vast waterfall. The falls had been there for eons and would still be there long after we faded into history. The vegetation on the cliffs surrounding the falls was kept lush by the mist and was a marked contrast to the dried and withered plant life outside the radius of the life-giving mist. I noted all this in passing because my attention was on the central object on the screen. The bridge was gone. Its remnants had been swallowed by the raging rapids below.

Woo scrolled further north and we could see that the bridge at Lewiston was also destroyed. There was no way Cottick could get across the river to crush the soldiers of the Fifth. The division was isolated, and so it was now mine to destroy or, better, convert.

Woo pointed to a burning structure by the river: the hydroelectric power station at Lewiston was in flames. Scanning further north, we could see the tall tower of the Olcott wind-turbine power station fallen on its side. The massive blades lay bent and twisted on the ground. Buffalo had lost its last remaining sources of electricity.

Woo typed instructions to the imaging table and the picture changed back to a view of Buffalo. Zooming in on what was the headquarters of the Fifth, we could see nothing but smoke. Woo adjusted the image to the infra-red spectra. The flames of the burning buildings stood out, as did the tiny pinpoints of light indicating human beings. At random, Woo zoomed in on one group. We could see the flashes from the muzzles of rifles (my spy satellite was that good). A battle was raging in Buffalo, but with the bridges down, who was fighting who? Presumably the forces of the Fifth still loyal to Cottick were attempting to stop the rebellion. But who was winning? There was only so much satellite reconnaissance could tell. I needed some intelligence assets on the ground in Buffalo. Someone had to get there as quickly as possible.

I had to act fast to ensure that if the rebellion succeeded, the surviving soldiers would swear loyalty to me and not some other leader, who I would then have to take the time to deal with one way or another. There was only one way to ensure that the rebels swore loyalty to me: I had to be there in person. I had to get to Buffalo.

But how? And if events didn't turn out as I hoped, how would I withdraw safely?

Since the marauders' attack on Syracuse, my fuel situation was precarious so using land transportation was problematic (and it was too hot to be trapped inside the metal box of a vehicle). A helicopter was possible, but my two surviving helicopters were being prepared for my final attack on Cottick's main forces at Kitchener. Furthermore, my stocks of the helicopters' jet-fuel were even more precarious than my stocks of diesel fuel. I decided the time had arrived for me to make use of my fledgling navy, an asset I hadn't used before.

Being an Army man through and through, I had an instinctive distrust of large bodies of water. Rivers and lakes limited the maneuvers of an army. They simply got in the way of the proper development of land-based strategy. However, I had studied enough military history to know that army commanders who weren't afraid of the possibilities offered by large bodies of water were almost always successful in war. I had Lake Ontario before me and I had created a navy to control it. The time had come to take advantage of that.

* * *

Major Bors Barovscu was an irreverent officer with a flare for getting things done. He had a rogue's face, with piercing, pale blue eyes and a charismatic smile. His short black hair and his well-groomed beard rounded off a flamboyant look which he carefully fostered, but more to the point he had proven to be a resourceful officer. He had persuaded me to create a navy to control the eastern end of Lake Ontario and the headwaters of the Saint Lawrence River, and I had let his boundless energy loose on the problem. He hadn't disappointed me. He had created for me a navy—but I use that word very loosely. The fleet was stationed at Sackets Harbor at the eastern end of Lake Ontario and close to Fort Drum. At the core of the fleet were four old but well-armed Coast Guard patrol boats. There was little in the way of fuel to drive these diesel-powered boats, so Barovscu had also gathered together a motley fleet of large yachts and smaller sailing craft. These sailboats had been rescued from abandoned marinas and made seaworthy once again with whatever materials could be scrounged in these lean times. They were once the toys of rich sailing enthusiasts, but only people of my generation could remember such a time of luxury and pleasure.

For this mission, Major Barovscu had selected a small flotilla of six yachts, ranging in length from thirty-three to forty-five feet. These boats were the most seaworthy vessels of the fleet. We packed the boats full with Barovscu's sailors, my bodyguard detail, including Sergeant Kellerman, and a few militiamen from the nearby 1st Jefferson Militia Regiment. A strong wind was howling, as it often did, but from the south, not the usual west. Barovscu assured me this was a welcome development and would speed our voyage. We set sail with Barovscu putting the boats on a broad reach, as he called it.

The journey would take two days or so, but it was the safest and most covert method for me to get to Buffalo. My arrival wouldn't be announced by the distinctive sound of helicopter blades cutting the air or by scouts observing the roads. Barovscu assured me we could approach the coast near Olcott, just north of Buffalo, without being observed. We would land in secret and make a reconnaissance before I decided on my next action. Just to be safe, I was in constant communication with Fort Drum, and one of the helicopters had been placed on standby in case there was an emergency.

The journey was surprisingly pleasant. After a few hours of queasiness, I got my sea legs and settled in to enjoy the trip. It was cool and refreshing on the lake and a welcome relief from the sweltering heat of the land. I listened with amusement to the arcane language of the sailors. Sails were trimmed (meaning tightened), and sheets were hauled (meaning ropes were pulled, not carried). One moment we were bearing away and the next luffing up, and all the while we were making headway (which I was assured was a good thing to be making). Tacking was a time of activity, while running was (oddly) a time of relaxation.

Leaving the sailors to their business, I relaxed in the shade of the sails with a pleasant breeze blowing on my face. I had time to think. This small reconnaissance was the first action on Cottick's forces since my recapture of Fort Drum back in the winter. Eventually the path I was on would lead to my killing Cottick—or his killing me. Either way, our destructive conflict would end. It didn't have to turn out that way. Our relationship began well enough.

As a newly promoted lieutenant general, I was given command of III Corps and the task of assisting rebel Canadian generals seize power in their country. In return, they promised to increase Canadian water shipments to drought-ridden America. Among the forces assigned to III Corps was the Third Infantry Division. It was the largest and most powerful of my divisions, but the only one not based in the northeast. The home of the Third was Fort Stewart in Georgia, and I decided to fly there to meet its commander, Major General Hollis Cottick III.

I had never met General Cottick, but I had heard he was extremely popular with his men and very ambitious. He was the son of a general and the grandson of a general. An Army man through and through.

Cottick was there to meet my airplane when I arrived. He was a big, broad, brawny man, a year or two younger than me. He had not yet shaved off his thinning hair. There was the usual welcoming ceremony and the customary exchange of pleasantries. It wasn't until that evening, at a reception held in my honor, that I had a chance to talk with Cottick in private. I was standing quietly with some type of southern drink in my hand. In the center of the room, I observed Cottick chatting and laughing with his senior officers. He seemed completely at ease with them, and they with him. It was an ease which

I never quite had with officers under my command. Cottick noticed me watching him. He lightheartedly waved his men away and made his way over to me.

"General Eastland, come and take a look at the view. You can see most of the base from here."

Cottick led me out on to a veranda. The chill of the January night was not unpleasant and indeed a welcome relief from the stuffy reception room.

"You've a fine command," I said.

"Thank you, sir. I'm very proud of my boys. It was tough going in Atlanta last summer, but they did well."

Too well, I thought. The thirst-crazed citizens of Atlanta had rioted the previous summer, as they did most summers. Cottick's brutal tactics had killed the ringleaders and crushed the riots. The state government was both thankful and angry. Control had been re-established, but many of its citizens had been killed and the hospitals had been overwhelmed with casualties. The Third Division couldn't remain in Georgia, which is why it was transferred to my northern command. Another division would patrol the streets of Atlanta the following summer.

We began to discuss the specifics of the upcoming Canadian operation. Cottick was keen to understand the political agreement we had with the Canadian generals with regard to the water shipments. Cottick, living in the Deep South, was particularly attuned to the issue of water shortages, which were far worse there than in the North.

I told him the Canadian generals had promised to increase water shipments three-fold after they seized power.

"Hmm. It will be welcomed to be sure," Cottick mused. "But will it be enough? The cities of the North will get most. And what about agricultural needs? The South will get nothing, and there hasn't been a decent crop in these parts in years. Famine is not far away."

"I agree. It's not enough water, but it's the only supply around."

"Is anyone thinking of persuading the Canadians to increase the shipments even more?"

"They have their own needs. A three-fold increase is, I think, the best that we can get."

"But we will be there in force, surely——."

I cut Cottick off immediately. I knew what he was thinking, for I too had thought the same thing. I was required to state, forcefully, the official line. "No, General. We're going into Canada as allies. Is that clearly understood?"

"Yes, sir. I'm sure everybody understands that."

Obviously Cottick didn't believe that we could resist the temptation to take more water by force—but then neither did I.

We then began to discuss the distribution of forces of III Corps and the role of the Third Division.

The next day I departed Fort Stewart and returned north. I left with the impression of General Cottick as a tough, resourceful commander who saw the larger picture clearly and without bias. He was dedicated to the Army and popular with his men. I could trust him to do whatever was necessary to fulfill our mission. General Cottick and the Third Division would be a welcome addition to my corps.

How could I know then what would befall us all?

* * *

After an uneventful journey we arrived off the coast east of Olcott at just after midnight. While the rest of us waited on the boats far from shore, I ordered Sergeant Kellerman to take a dinghy and land on the dark shore. He was to make a reconnaissance of the destroyed Olcott wind-turbine power station. The Fifth once had an engineering company stationed there and I hoped a few stragglers would still be in the area. They would be captured and interrogated.

Major Barovscu and I waited in silence for nearly an hour until we saw a signal lamp flashing from the shore. The message began with Kellerman's recognition code and then went on to say that I should land with minimal contingent. I immediately became suspicious. Why would Kellerman of all people suggest that I come ashore with only a few bodyguards? I suspected a trap, but the message had begun with Kellerman's recognition code and he wouldn't have told that to anyone. Even if he had been captured and tortured, he could easily have given his interrogators a false code. Something was wrong and I didn't know what. I resolved to land, but contrary to Kellerman's recommendation, I would arrive with a full complement of bodyguards.

The small flotilla of sailboats approached the shore in silence. Major Barovscu ordered the anchors dropped about fifty yards out, where he, and most of the men, climbed into dinghies to row the final distance. Once they reached land, they quickly fanned out to secure the area. After a few minutes, Barovscu assured me it was safe. I climbed into the last dinghy and rowed to the rocky beach.

Once ashore, I approached Barovscu in the darkness while he was talking to another soldier. It was Kellerman, alive and well.

"Report, Sergeant," I commanded. "Explain your message."

Kellerman replied in barely a whisper: "Sir, I don't think you want too many people to know what's going on here."

"Why not? What's happened?"

"It's best that I show you—just you."

In the faint glow of moonlight, I studied Kellerman's face. It was clear he was in earnest.

"Major, set a perimeter and hold here."

Barovscu immediately protested, but I assured him I would be safe with Sergeant Kellerman for protection. I ordered the major to guard the boats and set a picket line.

Leaving the security of my soldiers, I headed out into the darkness with Kellerman. I had no idea where I was going as he led me through the dark countryside. Although I had sent Kellerman on many missions before, this was the first occasion I had actually accompanied him. It was exhilarating.

Stealthily we approached a squat, rectangular building which had once been a portable office for the Olcott power station. It sat on concrete blocks and there was a gap of a foot or so between the ground and the floor. The gap was covered with decaying plywood, but Kellerman had found a break in the plywood and he indicated that we were going to crawl through it. I followed him under the floor, and for once my bad leg didn't give me any trouble. Once underneath the building, Kellerman cupped his ear to indicate that I should listen to the proceedings above.

I positioned one ear close to the floorboards and strained to hear the faint voices.

"These two prisoners are the last officers of our division," one voice said.

"So, let's kill them now," another stated.

"What's your rush? They aren't going anywhere."

A third voice stated with authority, "The Committee has ordered that all prisoners must be read the list of their crimes before being executed."

"What's the point? Just kill them so we can get back to having some fun."

"Enough! The Committee's rules must be obeyed."

"I've obeyed idiots long enough. No one asked me if the Committee could take charge. I've had enough of them. No more rules. I'm going to kill these officers now."

"Put that gun back or I will shoot you where you stand."

There was a chilling pause for what seemed a very long time.

"Fine. Obey the Committee's rules, but I'm telling you that I'm getting sick of them. The Committee men are no better than officers were."

"Can we get on with this?" asked another.

"All right, all right. … You two prisoners are officers of the Fifth. Your crimes include hoarding food and medicine, not sharing the air-conditioned quarters, keeping the women to yourselves—"

"Sounds like the Committee men."

"Shut up! That mouth of yours will get us all into trouble."

There was silence for a moment.

"So we're finished?"

"Yes. You can execute them now."

Two shots rang out immediately.

A shiver ran through my body. This was a mutiny. Soldiers were rising up against their officers.

I understood why Kellerman had insisted that only I hear this. The soldiers of the Fifth had just finished murdering all their officers. They were seen as the enemy by their men and the chain of command had disintegrated. First it was the officers who were killed, next it would be the leaders of the Committee, and then anarchy would follow. I couldn't let this contagion spread to my army. If the soldiers of Threecor ever believed their officers were the enemy, everyone would be doomed. The idea of a mutiny brought back bad memories for me because I had seen it happen before.

I was a first lieutenant in the Fourth Mechanized Division when it was assigned to a United Nations peacekeeping mission in Kenya. That country, which for decades had been the symbol of stability in Africa, had succumbed to anarchy. Droughts and famines plagued the country, but the event that tipped Kenya over the edge was a massive surge in malaria. Warmer temperatures had extended the range of the disease carrying mosquitoes. Medicine was already in short supply, but that year there were many malaria cases in Italy and Spain. The Europeans had panicked and horded supplies of quinine and other anti-malaria drugs as well as mosquito-netting; the Africans got none. The disease ran rampant throughout Africa, and the hardest hit country was Kenya. Nairobi, the capital, with a population of millions, was decimated. The city was once high enough and cool enough to be outside of the malaria-carrying mosquitoes' habitat, but not any more. As the numbers of the dead and sick climbed, food production fell and anarchy came to the streets of Nairobi. On the brink of collapse, the Kenyan government appealed to the United Nations. As its contribution to the UN peacekeeping force, the United States sent the Fourth Division.

Well dosed up with anti-malaria drugs, I arrived in Nairobi and assumed my duties. Initially my platoon aided in keeping the roads open for the UN trucks to carry medicine to the worst affected areas of the city, but as the situation deteriorated we were ordered to protect the main hospital. It was there where I befriended a young Kenyan officer who was also stationed at the hospital. Lieutenant Kibwezi was responsible for guarding high government officials who were patients.

As the weeks of ever worsening crisis dragged by, the false notion that hospitals and medicine were making the situation worse by creating breeding grounds for malaria gained credence with the terrified citizens of Nairobi. Frequent demonstrations and riots began to occur in front of the hospital, but with the assistance of the Kenyan army we managed to protect the patients and medical staff.

Under mounting pressure the government collapsed and fanatics seized control. Their first act was to demand the withdrawal of UN forces from the country, irrationally blaming them for the rising death toll. The UN was only too pleased to comply and leave this troubled and ungrateful country behind. There were too many other problems in the world with which the UN had to contend.

My platoon was on guard at the hospital perimeter, along with Lieutenant Kibwezi and his platoon, when the news of our withdrawal arrived. The mob surrounding the hospital was unusually quiet. It was as though the people were waiting for something to happen. My company commander had only just finished explaining our new orders when a bad situation got worse. Kibwezi ordered his men to take our place guarding the hospital. He was determined to protect the patients, but his men refused. Many of them now believed the false notion that hospitals were evil places. Kibwezi held his ground and demanded his orders be obeyed. A sergeant punched him. The lieutenant struggled back to his feet and attempted to draw his pistol, but before he could he was knocked down again.

I moved to help my friend, but my commander ordered me to remain where I was. We were leaving this country and we were not to get involved any more. I could have disobeyed, but then how would I be different from the Kenyan soldiers? This was not Siberia, and Kibwezi was not Svetlana. I stayed where I was, as ordered, and watched my friend being kicked, beaten and finally shot.

With their officer dead, the Kenyan soldiers ran into the hospital firing their rifles wildly. The mob surged past us and followed the soldiers into the building. My commander ordered us to depart the area with haste and go to the airport. We fled the hospital with the sound of screams in our ears.

Kibwezi's soldiers had mutinied, and horror had followed. I was determined that a mutiny would never happen to my command, and my soldiers would always obey their officers. The actions of the soldiers of the Fifth Guard Division would be kept a secret.

Kellerman tapped me on my shoulder. It was time to leave. We crawled out from under the building and made our way back to the landing party. Dawn was breaking as we arrived. I informed Major Barovscu that there was nothing for us here and that we should set sail immediately for Sackets Harbor. I gave him no explanation.

I resolved, upon my return to Fort Drum, to order Colonel Rourke to seal our border with the Fifth Guard Division. Anyone who attempted entry, civilian, soldier or even escaping officer, would be killed. There would be no exceptions; the quarantine would be total. No one would be permitted to spread the news of what had occurred in Buffalo. The disease of mutiny had to be contained.

– Chapter 21 –

Sackets Harbor

To escape the fierce sun, Major Barovscu and I sought refuge in the shadow of a genoa, a huge front sail which the sailors had raised. The temperature was unbearable. The wind, which cooled us on the outward journey, was blowing just as strongly, but now directly from the west, and we were running before it (another of Barovscu's odd sailing terms, but at least this one made some sense because the boat was moving fast). Unfortunately for us, the sailboat and the wind were traveling in the same direction and more or less at the same speed, so we couldn't feel anything of the refreshing breeze that we felt on the outward journey.

As far as I could see, sailing with the wind directly behind us was effortless. There was little activity on any of the boats in our little fleet. Fifty yards away, I aimlessly watched one energetic sailor on a nearby boat, struggling to put up a large, brightly colored sail at the front of the boat—the bow, I corrected myself. I marveled at the man's energy in this heat.

"Sorry, sir," Barovscu said as he flopped down beside me. "I should have made sure this boat was equipped with one of those."

"One of what, Major?"

"A spinnaker." Barovscu pointed to the colorful sail the sailor was struggling with on the nearby boat. "We could get this boat really flying." After a pause, the major added, with apparent deep regret, "I had to issue spinnakers only to

198

the slowest boats. The sails are very fragile and there aren't many left. But, if we had one, General, it would be a fast and exciting sail. A couple of months ago, we had this wind from the southeast—unusual, but what a ride! We were racing off Stony Point and I had just set my spinnaker—."

I interrupted the major before he launched into a long sailing story, full of arcane and incomprehensible sailing terms.

"Major, I'm impressed with your command."

"Thank you, sir."

"I think we should make more use of it."

"Yes, sir." Barovscu was clearly pleased with this assessment.

"Yes indeed. With the Fifth Guard Division no longer a factor, I think we should start probing General Cottick's defenses."

"Have you something in mind, sir?"

"Let's see a map of the western end of the lake."

Barovscu ordered a private below to retrieve the map. The private struggled to his feet and descended into the oven that was the cabin. Moments later, he returned and handed a battered map to the major. That small amount of effort had left the private drenched with sweat. Fortunately, we were sailing on one of the largest bodies of freshwater in the world. The private threw a bucket into the lake and pulled it back by the rope attached to its handle. He drank heavily from the bucket and then poured the remainder over his head. It was ironic that the fall of our technological society had done wonders for cleaning up the waters of the once heavily polluted Lake Ontario.

The private's example was tempting to follow, but I was busy making my plans. Barovscu opened the deeply creased map, and we studied the western end of Lake Ontario.

"I would like a reconnaissance in force to penetrate behind Cottick's front lines. Intelligence suggests his forces are deployed along the western edge of Toronto, but I would like a patrol to make sure."

I didn't mention that the intelligence was from images provided by my spy satellite. Barovscu knew of my special asset, but the others on the yacht didn't. I couldn't take the chance that one of these soldiers could be captured one day and be made to tell Cottick of my supreme strategic advantage.

"I see, sir. If we landed a shore party near ..." Barovscu studied the map. "... near Burlington or Hamilton, then we might be able to capture a stray soldier for interrogation."

"Exactly, Major. Cottick has a fuel depot in Hamilton, and there would be supply officers nearby. I would dearly like to know how much fuel Cottick has." That was something my spy satellite couldn't tell me.

Barovscu examined the map again. "If, under cover of darkness, we landed on the docks of the old steel factories in Hamilton Bay, we could sneak in and snatch one of Cottick's officers. If we landed with enough force, we could even destroy the fuel depot afterwards."

I liked how the major was thinking. "Very tempting, Major. The fuel depot should be destroyed, but it's to be a secondary objective. The priority must remain the covert intelligence gathering operation."

"Yes, sir."

I liked this young major.

* * *

We arrived back in Sackets Harbor after a hot but uneventful voyage. I was pleasantly surprised to find Victoria waiting on the dock. She was standing in a patchwork swimsuit she had made. I knew her well enough to know she was reveling in the attention from the nearby soldiers. Curvaceous and buxom—what a beauty! She had a body to die for—and it was all mine.

Victoria waved at me. I would have waved back but

preserving my dignity in front of the men forbade it. The yacht inched closer to the dock and I climbed off. Victoria rushed over and hugged me. My body longed for hers, but I felt awkward about such a public display. If only she'd waited until we were in my quarters.

She lifted her head in an effort to kiss me, but I pulled away. "Later," I whispered. Her arms dropped away and she stepped back and frowned at me. I had upset her, but I would make it up to her later.

Major Barovscu and I, with Victoria in tow, walked towards the major's command post. I wanted to develop the plans for his raid on Cottick's Hamilton fuel depot before I returned to Fort Drum with Victoria.

No sooner had I entered the command post than a lieutenant approached. He saluted and I automatically returned the gesture.

"Report, Lieutenant."

"Sir, Lieutenant Colonel Woo requests your immediate return to Fort Drum."

"Did he say what it was about?"

"He just said 'God is looking down'. I don't know what he meant by it."

But I did. It was our code for intelligence provided by my spy satellite. For Woo to send a messenger meant he had important news he thought I should hear straightaway.

"Thank you, lieutenant." I turned to Major Barovscu. "Major, I must return to Fort Drum immediately. Develop your plans. I'll return tomorrow to discuss them."

"Yes, sir."

"Can I stay here? Victoria interrupted. "The water is wonderfully cool."

My mind was focused on what news Woo could have for me. "Yes, certainly," I said. "I will be back tomorrow. Enjoy yourself."

I left immediately with the lieutenant and my bodyguard detail. We rode on horseback the fifteen miles back to Fort Drum. It felt good to have Judge once again under me. I much preferred her rhythmic trot to the unpredictable waves on the lake. I could control one but not the other.

The journey was hot and I was greatly relieved when I entered the air-conditioned satellite control room. Lieutenant Colonel Woo looked remarkably fresh wearing his dry uniform. Mine was drenched in sweat.

Woo saluted and then reported that the satellite had observed activity by Cottick's forces in a town called Grimsby, on the southwest shore of Lake Ontario halfway between Niagara Falls and Hamilton.

"It's all over now," Woo reported, "but there was quite a battle raging in Grimsby for a time. I can replay the video if you like."

"Yes, I'll look at it, but first give me your assessment."

"It appears to have been a battle between Cottick's force on the west side of the town and another smaller force on the east side. We haven't been able to identify the force, but I am thinking it's either soldiers of the Fifth trapped on the west side of the Niagara River after the bridges were destroyed, or elements of the Third staging a revolt in support of the men of the Fifth. It's clear that the battle was between regular forces. This was no civilian uprising or a raid by marauders."

Woo pressed buttons on the console and brought up a replay of the last part of the battle on the main screen. I watched as Cottick's larger force wiped out the smaller force, but not before sustaining heavy casualties. I suspected it was Cottick crushing an isolated pocket of mutinous soldiers from the Fifth. However, it was possible they were men from the Third who had rebelled. If so, it meant the mutiny had spread like a cancer throughout Cottick's army. I had to find out which.

The raid that Barovscu was planning took on more

importance, and it would have to be larger than I had originally foreseen. I needed to provide Barovscu more soldiers for his raid, and the only ones readily available were the militiamen from the nearby 1st Jefferson Militia Regiment. I left the delightful cool of the air-conditioned room and returned to the heat outside. I rode to nearby Watertown, the headquarters of the regiment, and discussed with the militia colonel the situation and the readiness of his troops.

I spent the night in Watertown as a guest of the regiment and the next morning I did the colonel the honor of inspecting one of his companies. The militiamen were green but eager to undertake a mission. I ordered the colonel and two of his officers to return to Fort Drum to make plans. I also sent a message to Major Barovscu to travel from Sackets Harbor to join us. I had decided that we would need to make a secondary raid on Grimsby, in addition to the primary raid on Hamilton.

I hadn't forgotten about Victoria but I had work to do and plans to make. In any case, she would be happier swimming in the cool water of the lake. I would call for her later once I had finalized my plans and set the operation in motion.

– Chapter 22 –

Fort Drum

It was a week after my return from Sackets Harbor and the plans for the raid were progressing nicely. Barovscu and his navy would transport troops from the 1st Jefferson Militia Regiment to Hamilton and Grimsby. I would accompany them part of the way. I was going to take advantage of this troop movement to be dropped off at Picton on the Isle of Quinte so I could visit Colonel Sheflin and inspect her soldiers. Hers was a distant command and I felt it important to reconnect with these soldiers. The cavalrymen of the 317th would be at the forefront of the battle when the final push on Cottick's army began. Furthermore, I wished to thank her troops once again for their splendid fight which had turned back Cottick's abortive attack. I had some medals to award the cavalrymen of the 317th. I also wanted to see Jan again. I missed talking to her.

Major Barovscu was ordered to come to Fort Drum to finalize the plans for his raid, and Victoria returned with him. I had been too busy to spend any time with her—and I felt bad about that. It was nearly midnight and I was getting tired. I hadn't seen my bed before two in the morning for several days. Maybe I should be with her tonight. She would be pleased.

I pushed away the satellite photographs of Hamilton harbor and leaned back in my well-worn chair. A huge yawn overwhelmed me. I was tired and should be going to bed, but I wasn't satisfied that Barovscu had selected the best location to land his men. He had tried to convince me with arguments about currents and wind direction, but I was becoming increasingly worried about the distance the men would have to travel in the dark. I wished our night-vision goggles still functioned. They would have made everything much easier, but my wishes wouldn't fix their worn-out components or corroded batteries. I forced my eyes to open wide and with a sigh picked up my old, cracked magnifying glass and returned to my study of the photographs.

There was a quiet knock on my door and I beckoned the person in. I expected it to be Victoria asking me to come to bed. Tonight I would go with her, I decided.

It wasn't Victoria at my door, but Sergeant Kellerman.

"Yes, Sergeant?"

"Sir, could you accompany me, please?" he said in a whisper.

"What is it?" I became alert.

Kellerman turned and peered into the hallway outside my office. "Please, sir, follow me."

I was concerned. If my trusted assassin was acting in this cautious manner, something bad was happening.

Kellerman led me to the hallway in which my own quarters were located. He motioned to me to move into the shadows and indicated that I should remain absolutely quiet. Bewildered by this, I nevertheless complied. I trusted Kellerman like no other person. He and I shared too many unpleasant secrets for it to be otherwise.

There was a barely audible click as the door handle to my quarters moved. From the shadows I saw the door open and to my complete amazement Major Barovscu stepped out. He looked furtively up and down the hall. He turned to face the open door. A hand appeared and gently stroked his beard. He kissed the hand and then turned and quietly fled.

What an old fool I was!

I felt the hallway close in on me. My knees weakened and I started to slump to the floor. Kellerman put his arm around my waist and propped me up.

I don't remember anything more until I found myself back at the desk in my office. Kellerman sat in silence in the chair opposite. He must have led me back there, but for the life of me I couldn't remember the journey. All I could remember was the vision of the hand stroking Barovscu's beard. Victoria had betrayed me. They both had.

Traitors!

"How long?" I stammered.

"Since Sackets Harbor," Kellerman replied without a hint of emotion. "I thought you should know."

"How many others know?"

"No one. They've been very careful."

My body shuddered and I placed my head in my hands. I was too numb to think.

After a long silence, Kellerman spoke. "General, do you know why I was court-martialed, stripped of my rank and sent to prison?"

My mind was in too much of a fog to remember or to work out why Kellerman was asking this question.

"I remember the defending officer's summation perfectly," he went on. "I had returned home to find my wife raped. When I opened the door, I saw her battered and beaten body lying on the floor. Standing over her was the rapist, a knife in his hand. I instinctively attacked and killed the man with his own knife. The prosecuting officer stated that if I had stopped there I would haven't have been charged with murder. What husband wouldn't have done what I did? But I didn't stop there, did I? I stabbed the rapist over forty times. There wasn't much left of him. Even then, I would have been let off lightly, but I finally went too far for military justice to bear. My wife had been raped and I thought she was dying. I put her out of her misery with a quick slash across her throat."

My head was reeling from the image of Victoria's hand. I heard Kellerman's words but wasn't concentrating on them.

"General!" he said sharply. "Do you remember my story?"

His sharp tone jolted me back. "Yes, I remember." I had reviewed the files from Kellerman's court-martial when he first came to my attention.

"Then you remember nothing but lies. My wife wasn't the tragic victim of a deranged rapist. She was cheating on me and I killed her. I killed them both."

I began to see where Kellerman's story was going—and I didn't like it.

"I found them together on the carpet. For the only time in my life, I couldn't control my emotions. A few quick slashes with my knife and it was all over. When I regained control of myself, I realized that there I was with my wife and her lover dead on the floor of my house and their blood on my uniform. I was facing the death penalty."

Kellerman explained that he saw his only chance of avoiding execution was to have the court believe he had gone temporarily insane in defense of his wife. He wanted everyone to think he had found his wife being raped by the man and that had been too much for him to cope with. He carefully rearranged the scene to make it more consistent with his story. To achieve the illusion of madness, Kellerman stabbed an already dead man forty times in cold blood. I reeled in horror at the truly cold nature of this man before me. He was capable of anything.

"My wife's affair had been too secret," he continued. "No one suspected they even knew each other. As far as everyone was concerned, he was a stranger I found in my house. The investigators accepted my tragic story of a husband protecting his wife and then mercifully putting her out of her misery.

Unfortunately, the prosecuting officer was a woman and she didn't look too favorably on, in her words, a husband putting his wife down like a dog. I didn't get off, but I escaped the death penalty and my sentence was only half the maximum."

I could never look at Kellerman in the same way. He was even colder than I suspected.

"Why are you telling me all this, Sergeant?"

"No one knows, General. No one knows but me and you what went on here tonight. If the news gets out, you'll lose the respect of your officers and then lose control of your army. I've seen enough anarchy out there—I don't want it to happen here. Sometimes I need a quiet home to come back to."

I understood all too clearly what Kellerman was suggesting.

"Dismissed, Sergeant," I said abruptly.

Without another word, Kellerman rose from his chair, saluted and left.

I was alone with the vision of Victoria's hand stroking Barovscu's beard. In my head, Kellerman's words echoed: no one knows.

I had been betrayed by someone I trusted. I don't think I really loved Victoria, but I trusted her. She had been disloyal to me—and I couldn't accept that.

How could she?

Traitor.

– Chapter 23 –

Lake Ontario

I didn't sleep that night. I remained in my chair in my office deep in thought. My familiar office was soothing. A gloomy light gradually appeared in the window; dawn was breaking. I stirred from my self-pity. The night had been endless and full of bewilderment and pain, but now that dawn was here I tried to distract myself with activity. I ordered that the raid be brought forward twenty-four hours, so we would leave that afternoon. I gave my officers some excuse about arriving at Grimsby before the evidence of the battle disappeared, but it was really because I wanted to get away and, more important, to get Major Barovscu as far away from Victoria as possible.

During the black night, I had finally decided to reject Kellerman's solution in favor of a much less brutal one. Immediately after the current operation, I would transfer the base of operations for Barovscu's navy from Sackets Harbor to the more distant harbor at Picton on the Isle of Quinte. No one would question such a relocation, because Picton was much closer to Cottick's army and it made eminent strategic sense to shorten the navy's patrol routes. Neither Victoria nor Barovscu would suspect my true motives, but they would be as far apart as I could manage. I resolved to be more attentive to Victoria and she would soon forget him. I would forgive her one act of disloyalty. She had once saved my life by warning me of Cottick's treachery, and now I had repaid that debt by sparing her life.

I avoided Victoria all day, but it was impossible not to see her when I departed. She hugged me and wished me luck. There was no indication she had been with another man the night before. I responded as normally as possible, but I had an uneasy feeling that everyone could see through my charade.

To reassure myself, I repeated over and over again the words Kellerman had used: no one knows, no one knows, no one knows. It didn't help very much.

I mounted Judge and prepared to get underway. Major Barovscu rode up beside me and waited for the signal from me to ride to Sackets Harbor. I observed Victoria and Barovscu as closely as I dared. Neither betrayed the slightest interest in the other. Kellerman appeared beside me, inscrutable as ever. Here were the four of us—all with our secrets.

No one knows, no one knows, no one knows, I repeated.

Without another word, I turned Judge around and rode out of the base. Barovscu and his officers rode beside me and my bodyguards surrounded us. The militiamen from the 1st Jefferson were already marching from their base in Watertown to the boats in Sackets Harbor, where we would rendezvous with them.

The journey to Sackets Harbor seemed endless. I remained silent and morose throughout the ride, and none of my officers dared disturb me from my black thoughts.

No one knows, no one knows, no one knows.

It wasn't working. Kellerman was wrong. Someone did know: I knew.

* * *

At Sackets Harbor, I stood on the dock watching the bustling activity. Over four hundred men were busy cramming themselves into fifty-seven yachts and sailboats, which were already packed full of supplies and sailing equipment. When one boat was filled it maneuvered out into the harbor to allow room at the dock for the next. The militiamen were in fine form and high spirits as they climbed on the various boats. They were excited to be on their first real mission.

I spoke briefly to the militia colonel who was commanding the raid on the fuel depot in Hamilton. He was caught up in the same excitement as his troops. I praised him for the fine job he had done training his men. This wasn't just morale boosting—the 1st Jefferson was the best of my new militia regiments. The colonel deserved the compliments that I bestowed on him and his men.

When all was ready, Major Barovscu ordered the last of the boats, the largest of the big yachts, to approach the dock. This fifty-two-foot beauty had been hidden from view in a forgotten marina building in Clayton, in the Thousand Islands. Barovscu's men had recently discovered the yacht and had worked hard preparing it for service. Barovscu wanted to use it for our mission to Olcott, and it had arrived in Sackets Harbor only this morning, just in time to be loaded for the mission.

Barovscu jumped aboard and relieved the sailor behind the wheel. He beckoned me aboard, smiling and acting like a friend. I steeled myself and tried to act normally. I stepped on to the hull and Kellerman and my bodyguards followed. I wasn't going to accompany Barovscu and the militiamen on the raids on Hamilton and Grimsby; instead, my bodyguards and I were to be dropped off at Picton. I would spend some time there with Colonel Sheflin discussing the possibility of a probing attack on some of Cottick's forces north of Toronto.

It was gray and overcast when we left, but Barovscu assured me the wind was perfect. It was blowing from the southeast and we would make excellent time on the first leg of the voyage.

I made no reply. Barovscu's presence was unavoidable but that didn't make it any easier for me to tolerate. I had made up my mind to spare Victoria, but what should I do about Barovscu?

* * *

After many hours of sailing with a favorable breeze, the wind grew in strength and blew fiercely from the northwest. The gentle rolling waves were replaced by irregular breaking waves. Spray often drenched the men. Although overcast, it remained hot and humid and the cool spray provided a modicum of relief for my tightly packed soldiers.

Barovscu wasn't concerned, even when the boats of his fleet drew apart as they dealt with the deteriorating weather conditions. I couldn't see many of the boats, but Barovscu assured me his men had sailed in worse than this. He pointed to a low gray line on the horizon and informed me that was the coast of the Isle of Quinte.

To travel into the wind, the sailboats had to move in a zigzag pattern. Each time we changed direction there was a flurry of activity, during which sailors cranked on winches to move the front sail from one side of the boat to the other. Barovscu shouted strange expressions like 'helms alee', 'watch the trim', 'luff', 'start reefing' and 'raise the storm jib'. With each command his shouts became more urgent, and this concerned me.

We were heading towards the coast but also towards a black and ominous sky. Static electricity permeated the air. Barovscu noticed it too.

"We will have to veer westward and take shelter in Prince Edward Bay," he informed me. He called to a private, "Signal the fleet to follow me westward."

The private raised some colorful flags and waved them at nearest boat, which in turn relayed the message to the next boat. Most of the boats had no radios and those few that did had no power with which to operate them.

Our yacht plowed through the growing waves and gradually we approached the distant coastline. I kept my eyes focused on the safety of land, but then to my dismay the coastline disappeared from view. A wall of gray clouds shrouded the land.

Minutes ticked by.

Suddenly, the sails hung limp as the wind temporarily died away.

"Get the sails down!" Barovscu screamed at his men. From his experience, he sensed what was about to happen, but I had no clue—other than whatever it was would be bad.

Too late! A powerful blast of bitterly cold wind from the north hit the sails, and the yacht tipped over. Most of the men on the crowded boat fell into the lake. I grabbed a nearby metal pole and held on for dear life. One of the wires that held up the mast snapped and hit a militiaman across the face. He fell into the water and disappeared beneath the waves. The blast of wind subsided and the boat slowly came upright.

Something hit my head and then my hand. It was hailing—but this wasn't like any hail I had ever seen. Hailstones the size of baseballs pounded the yacht and the men remaining on it. I covered my head with my free hand, but I kept the other glued to the metal pole. I wouldn't let go.

A second blast of wind hit the sails, more powerful than the first. The boat tipped all the way over and the sails touched the water and lay floating on the churning surface of the lake. The giant hailstones continued to plummet from the heavens. One hit the back of my leg. Moments later, another hit my head. I almost blacked out. Barely conscious, I was lucid enough to realize I had to cling to the pole. Without warning, the boat flipped back so quickly I was almost flung over the other side.

The hail stopped as abruptly as it had begun. I quickly surveyed the scene of carnage. I was alone on the boat. The mainsail was holed in many places by hailstones, and the front sail was gone, blown away by the wind. The boat floated low in the water, because of the large quantity of water that had poured into the cabin when the boat was on its side.

The wind hit the remnants of the torn and holed mainsail and drove the boat before it. I spied a few men in the water struggling to catch up to the boat, but the large waves were making swimming nearly impossible.

I leaned over the edge of the boat to pull the nearest man onboard. He held his hand out for me to grab. It was Major Barovscu.

I hesitated for a moment.

No one knows, no one knows, no one knows. The phrase drummed through my head. It wouldn't go away.

Slowly, I pulled back my hand. Barovscu got caught in the waves and was driven away from the boat. I could see in his eyes he knew why I hadn't saved him. I turned away.

Another man was struggling in the water. He clung to a rope hanging from the side of the boat. I leaned over and pulled the rope and the man came closer. It was Kellerman. I pulled him towards me and somehow managed to drag him onboard. He had wrenched his shoulder but he was alive. Together we managed to rescue two more men but Major Bors Barovscu wasn't one of them.

The wind pushed the boat southward, away from the safety of land. I needed to get the yacht under control—and quickly. One of the men I had rescued was a sailor. Although his leg was broken and his head bleeding, he was conscious. Kellerman and the other survivor, a militiaman, dragged him to a bench near the yacht's large steering wheel, where Kellerman propped him up. Although in great pain, the sailor explained what we had to do. Kellerman and the militiaman pulled down the ripped and holed mainsail and worked to replace it with a smaller sail which was stored in the front of the cabin. The cabin itself was under two feet of water, but we could bail it out later. With the new mainsail hoisted, the sailor explained how to trim it. Kellerman found a spare crank handle and cranked with his good arm to the correct trim of the sail. I stood behind the wheel and steered the boat to the nearest shore. The waves subsided when we entered a sheltered bay.

After a half hour of anxious sailing through the relatively calm waters of the bay, I pulled the boat alongside a decrepit dock at a deserted marina. The militiaman jumped ashore on to the ancient dock and tied the boat to a rotting wooden pole. Kellerman and I lifted the wounded sailor and helped him over the side into the arms of the militiaman. Kellerman climbed off the boat and, with the militiaman, carried the wounded sailor to an abandoned building. I stepped off the boat and hurried along the dock. My feet welcomed the feel of dry land beneath them. What a relief! I was safe.

Leaving the militiaman to care for the sailor, Kellerman and I hiked off to find soldiers of Sheflin's battalion. My bad leg had been bruised in the disaster and I had lost my old cane, but I limped along beside Kellerman as quickly as I could.

During that walk with Kellerman, I began to grasp what I had done out there on the lake. I could have saved Major Barovscu but I chose not to. What did that make me? How was I different from Kellerman?

* * *

Kellerman and I hobbled into Colonel Sheflin's command post in Picton. I had been here before, just after the skirmish with Cottick's forces at Port Hope. Sheflin greeted me as I arrived and ushered me into her office. I informed her of the location of the wounded sailor and the militiaman and she gave orders to her cavalrymen to retrieve them. Kellerman left to get his damaged shoulder treated at the battalion's field hospital, and others departed to carry out their orders. Sheflin and I found ourselves alone.

She insisted I tell her what happened on the boat, and I gave her a slightly edited version, never mentioning that Major Barovscu was on the same boat as me. How could I tell her I had deliberately failed to rescue him? That would only lead to the question why.

Sheflin watched me intently during my account of the storm and the sinking of the fleet. My mind swirled around in a mad race going nowhere. Part of me wanted to tell her and ask for her understanding, even for her forgiveness. My guilt needed sedating, but another part of me could never allow such a display. Losing control and confessing weakness to an officer I commanded was unthinkable. But Jan was so near.

When I finished, she rose from her chair and came around her desk. She squatted in front of me and reached out and held my hand. I was aware of her closeness, her presence. I didn't hear anything except my breathing, which had become heavy and laborious. As I closed my eyes, Jan began gently to stroke my hand. I don't know what instinct this woman had but she knew there was more to my story than I had told. Having her touch me weakened my resolve. I was losing control. I could feel myself slipping into darkness—to a place I feared.

I opened my mouth to tell her she needn't worry about me, but other words flooded out. I couldn't stop. I told her everything: Victoria's betrayal, Kellerman's advice, and my failure to save Barovscu. By the end, I was drained and I felt ashamed.

Jan said nothing. She just continued to stroke my hand.

– Chapter 24 –

Watertown

Jan Sheflin never said a word about my admission of guilt for my failure to save Major Barovscu. Not reproach, not condemnation, not sympathy—nothing. It was as though I never told her. What was she thinking? I couldn't read her. Was she disappointed in me? Her approval—or at least understanding—of my actions was important to me. I found that realization surprising.

After a good night's sleep, my emotional walls were restored. It was a strain but I managed to distance myself from my feelings, and returned to being a professional soldier. I was distant with Sheflin and she was the same with me. Obviously neither of us wanted to deal with the secret we now shared. We were far too busy to be distracted by personal complications.

Any discussion with Sheflin regarding an attack on Cottick was abandoned, because managing the fallout from this disaster required my complete and immediate attention. I remained with her to take stock of the disaster. She detailed men from her battalion to collect the dead that washed up on the shore and give them a proper burial. Her cavalrymen would also continue to search for survivors. Over four hundred men sailed with me, but only one hundred and fifty-three made it to shore—and of those who did, two died of their wounds, and one, the brave sailor who guided me to a safe harbor, lost his leg. Watertown, the headquarters of the 1st Jefferson Militia Regiment, was a tightly connected community which had gone through much and survived. The loss of so many would touch the lives of everyone, and morale among the surviving militiamen would plummet.

After a day of visiting the wounded in the field hospital, it was time for me to return to Watertown to personally offer my condolences to the families of the dead militiamen. Sheflin provided me with an escort, because all the soldiers of my bodyguard detail, except Sergeant Kellerman, were dead. The ride back was quiet and somber.

Although I should have been preparing to deal with the grief I knew I would find in Watertown, I was distracted by my memories of what had happened on the lake and afterwards in Sheflin's office. I could see clearly that moment when I had deliberately pulled my hand away from a drowning man. Did Barovscu's betrayal warrant such a punishment? I had sentenced others to death less guilty of disloyalty than Barovscu, but he threatened my control of my army, and without my army Threecor would descend into anarchy just like the rest of the world. There had to be control. No, Barovscu had to die—but why did I confide to Colonel Sheflin?

I entered Watertown. It was silent and still. Although a messenger I had sent before me had given the loyal citizens of Watertown news of disaster, none of them knew who had died and who had lived. I carried with me a list of those who had survived and were recovering on the Isle of Quinte.

People silently congregated around me as I rode slowly forward. I stopped in front of the militia's headquarters and climbed a few steps so I could be seen by all. I made a short speech thanking the citizens of Watertown for their bravery and loyalty. After a brief description of the freakish storm that had killed so many of their loved ones, I read the names of the living. The silence of the crowd was total while I read the list. It wasn't until I stopped reading and hung my head that the weeping started.

I left the citizens of Watertown to deal with their grief and returned to Fort Drum. The base was equally subdued. I avoided everyone and headed directly for my quarters. I was physically exhausted and emotionally drained. When I opened the door, I saw Victoria waiting for me. She ran to me and hugged me. For a second, I wanted to return the hug, but my arms wouldn't move. Something was holding them back, and I knew what that something was: it was the image of Major Barovscu's outstretched hand. Rage and guilt swirled around in my mind.

"I'm so relieved to have you back alive," Victoria said as she pulled away from me.

I said nothing and showed no emotion.

"So many dead. It's terrible. The list … Is …?"

I knew what she was going to ask: is Major Barovscu on the list? Is he alive? Fury rose up in me—unbidden and uncontrollable.

Victoria saw it in my eyes. She knew. She backed away, but not quickly enough.

A madness consumed me. How could she be so disloyal after all I had given her? All the rage and frustration I had chained up within me over these many months exploded. Cottick's treason, El Acero's raid, Hunt's folly, Barovscu's betrayal, and now Victoria's infidelity. My hand swung through the air and struck the side of Victoria's beautiful face. The blow knocked her to the floor. I fell upon her. My hands encircled her throat and squeezed. Her hands clutched at my arms but she was no match for my fury. There would be no more betrayal!

Her eyes looked pleadingly at me and pierced my heart.

I froze. What was I doing?

I fought to control my anger. The battle was intense. I closed my eyes in order to concentrate. Slowly I opened my eyes and relaxed my grip. I removed my hands from her throat and struggled to my knees. The madness was dissipating and I felt myself returning from the abyss.

Victoria gasped for breath. She rolled over and crawled away to the far side of the room. She grabbed a pillow from the bed and held it against her chest as a shield. She began to sob.

For a minute—or was it an hour?—I sat on the floor in the middle of the room. I was shocked that I could feel that much anger. My mind whirled around and around. I had almost killed Victoria. I had lost control.

Eventually I struggled to my feet and slowly, as if drugged, I staggered out of the room.

* * *

I awoke on the cold floor of my office. I stood and looked out the window. It was mid morning on an overcast day. I had sought refuge in my office. It was a place where I was in control. Under no circumstances could I have returned to my quarters—rooms that I shared with Victoria.

After fleeing from her the previous night, I had ordered her to be placed under arrest and taken to a house in a remote suburb of Watertown. It was more for her protection from me than anything else.

I stood in front of the window staring out at the cloudy sky. I thought about Victoria; I thought about nothing else. I enjoyed feeling youthful when I was with her. She was a whore—I knew that. She never hid what she was. She had been one most of her life. I tried to convince myself that Barovscu was nothing to her. I was busy and I ignored her. She craved security and it might have seemed to her that I was abandoning her. She found shelter in someone else's arms—it was nothing more than that. She knew no different. Why should I blame her for that? Did she betray me, or did the time with Barovscu mean nothing to her? If it meant nothing to her, why should it mean anything to me?

I wanted her back. I shook my head in disbelief at what I was going to do. I was going to forgive her, and more surprising yet, I was going to tell her how sorry I was for my attack on her. Yes, I, commander of an army and leader of Threecor, would ask the forgiveness of an unfaithful whore. Damn my dignity and my pride.

I left my office and walked to the stables. I saddled Judge and rode off. I refused all help and company. I rode alone out of the main gate and headed towards Watertown.

After a journey with only my impatience and regret for company, I neared the house in which I had ordered Victoria imprisoned. Excitement rose in my chest, because I would soon see her. She would forgive me as I had forgiven her and all would be as it once was. We would be together and we would be happy again.

I dismounted Judge and strode purposefully over to the house. The guard at the door saluted and I automatically returned the salute. I climbed the stairs to the second floor. My leg ached and I regretted not bringing my new cane. Another guard, another salute. He opened the door and I entered.

The captain of the guards, a lieutenant and Sergeant Kellerman were in the room gathered around something on the floor. They swung around to face me. Their faces betrayed deep concern. I approached and they parted so I could see what was hidden behind them. Lying on the floor was Victoria, her head resting in a pool of blood. An army pistol lay on the floor beside her.

I rushed over and knelt beside her. I reached out and held her hand. It was cold.

I stood and glared at Kellerman.

"Did you do this?"

It was the first time I saw fear in Kellerman's eyes. He backed away from me.

"No, sir. She shot herself."

"Where did she get the gun? How did it get into her room?

I glared at the lieutenant who was on duty. The blood

drained from his face.

"Sorry, sir," he stammered. "I did search the room. She seemed happy. I didn't think—."

"We found a note," the captain said to deflect my attention from the terrified lieutenant. "Sergeant."

Kellerman came forward and held out a torn scrap of paper. "I found this under her pillow. No one has read it but me."

"That's correct, General," the captain said. "The sergeant refused my direct order to hand it over. He claims you will support his actions."

Ignoring the peeved captain, I snatched the scrap of paper from Kellerman. I opened it and read the first line, written in Victoria's handwriting: 'My Dearest Walter, I love you.'

I immediately refolded the paper and placed it in my pocket. I wouldn't read any more of the letter in front of these men. She loved me—did I need to read any more?

"Thank you, gentlemen. Captain, please attend to the burial detail at once. Inform me when you are ready."

Victoria's body was taken away, while I remained in the room. I turned away from the pool of blood on the floor and walked to the bed on which Victoria had slept last night. I sat on the edge of the bed and gently ran my hand over the sheets.

About an hour later, the captain entered the room to inform me they were ready to bury Victoria's body. I followed him to where a grave had been dug. I stood mute while soldiers carefully lowered Victoria's wrapped body into the grave.

It started to drizzle gently as the soldiers shoveled dirt into the grave. When they finished, everyone left and only I remained standing over Victoria's grave. No one disturbed me—no one dared.

I whispered goodbye to Victoria Hewitt, and then reached into my pocket and extracted the scrap of paper on which she had written her goodbye to me. It read:

My Dearest Walter,

I love you.

Please forgive me because I cannot forgive myself. I have let you down terribly. How could I have been so selfish? You have so much to worry about and so much to achieve. This is for the best. I know it is. You will be better off without me. You have important things to do and I am in your way. Please remember me as I was when we were together at the house by the lake. I was happier then than I had ever been.

I love you with all my heart. I am so very sorry.

Victoria

My legs buckled and I fell to my knees. I clutched her note in my fist. Why had she done this?

Part IV

Hell Reconciled

If you are going through Hell, keep going.
                    – Winston Churchill

– Chapter 25 –

Hospital

Noises swirled through the darkness as consciousness returned slowly. Where was I?

I struggled with the haziness in my mind to remember. I was falling—falling from a horse. I was riding Judge back to Fort Drum when I became dizzy and everything went dark. Where had I been?

The fog in my mind thinned and fragments returned. It was raining and I remembered feeling upset. I wondered why that was. The fog lifted and memories flooded back. An overwhelming emptiness consumed me. Victoria was dead.

I must have let out a moan because voices started way off in the darkness. Disconnected phrases floated into my consciousness.

Moments later, someone grabbed my finger and pinched it hard. I forced my hand to move. Someone shouted something—I couldn't grasp the meaning of the words. My eyes were prized open and a bright light blasted into them. I tried closing my eyes and raising my hand as a shield against the painful light.

"He's coming to," a voice said.

I fought to open my eyes; everything was blurry. I blinked rapidly and a face came into focus. It was Major Runciman, commander of Fort Drum's hospital and its chief surgeon.

"Welcome back, General," he said.

I struggled to form words. "Where? … What?"

"Relax, General. You're in hospital recovering from a mild stroke."

A stroke? What was he talking about? I was riding back to the base and then …?

Suddenly, my mind cleared. I was riding back from Victoria's burial. Judge was walking slowly, in a steady, soothing rhythm. It was raining. I was remembering Victoria smiling at me when she served me dinner at the house by the lake. A bitter happiness had welled up in my chest and then a sudden dizziness had overwhelmed me. The image of Victoria's beautiful face had faded and everything had gone black. I fell from Judge's saddle but I didn't remember hitting the ground.

I brought myself back to the present and scanned the hospital room. Runciman was beside me and a medical orderly stood motionless at the foot of my bed. Over by the open door, I could see the backs of two soldiers guarding the entranceway, and beyond them I spied Colonel Holcomb and Colonel Omar peering in at me. They looked worried.

I found my voice at last. "Major, report. What happened? Why am I here?"

"As I said, General, you suffered a mild stroke. But don't worry, you aren't in any danger. You should make a complete recovery. It was very mild."

"Why did this happen?" What a strange question for me to ask. It was as though I was angry at my body for interfering with me in this way.

Runciman took the question in his stride. He smiled and said in a tone of understanding: "It happened, General, because a small blood vessel in your brain burst. But you're in good hands and you'll recover. You'll be on your feet in a few days or a week at most."

A week!

"Major, I will not be in this bed for a week. I've things to do. I've an army to run."

"Hmm. We'll see. We can discuss this later when I think you are ready to return to duty, but for now you must remain in bed."

Runciman was acting differently towards me than in the past. Gone was his crisp 'Yes sir, no sir.' Why had he changed? I then realized it was I who had changed. I was no longer his commander but his patient. I hated my new role.

An irrational anger surged through me. I wasn't going to be a helpless patient for a week—or even a day.

"Major, I want Colonel Holcomb and Colonel Omar in here immediately."

"Sorry, sir, you need rest. I'll let you know when you're well enough to see them."

"Major, I gave you an order."

Runciman frowned at me and gave me his best I-am-the-doctor look. "Sir, your body needs time to recover. I cannot permit you to jeopardize that recovery by prematurely going back to duty. You must stay in bed and rest. The soldiers of Threecor need you, and I don't intend to let them down by allowing you to kill yourself by stupidly going back to duty before your body is ready. Is that understood, sir?"

Without waiting for me to dismiss him, Runciman turned and left with the medial orderly. He put his hand on the doorknob and was about to close the door when I called out to him.

"You didn't answer my question, Major. Why did this happen?"

"I told you, General. A blood vessel in your brain burst."

"But why now?"

"Stress, sir. You suffered a great loss. Please accept my condolences. She was a lovely woman."

Yes, she was, I thought.

Runciman continued: "Sir, I can treat your symptoms but I cannot treat the underlying cause—at least not alone. You must work with me. You must somehow reduce the stress that you are living with or else your next stroke may not be a mild one."

With that, Runciman shut the door and I was left alone—alone with my thoughts. Some instinct told me the major had said something important but I couldn't quite grasp what it was.

* * *

I stood beside the hospital bed and examined my threadbare uniform, which I had taken from my closet and laid neatly on the bed. Someone had washed it and repaired several small holes. My medals and service board had been carefully shined and the silver general's stars on the shoulders were gleaming: three on the right shoulder but only two on the left. Many months ago, after I recaptured Fort Drum from Cottick's forces, I had promised myself I would replace the missing star from Cottick's uniform. This war had gone on too long and I was fed up. No more delays; it was time to kill Cottick.

Over the four long and tedious days of my enforced rest in the hospital, I had come to realize where I had gone wrong all this time. In Runciman's words, I had been treating the symptoms but not the underlying cause. Shortages, rebellions, marauders, mutinies, suicides—they were all just symptoms. The cause was Cottick; he was at the root of everything bad. He had to die. Nothing would distract me from that task; nothing else mattered.

I disrobed and picked up my uniform. The familiar, reassuring feel of the worn and faded material felt good in my hands. I dressed quickly and went over to the mirror to make the final adjustments. The old mirror was cracked and chipped but it served its purpose adequately. I placed my cap on my head and studied my image. I was back. I was back in command once again.

I hated hospitals. My father had died in a hospital. He was a strong, hard man, who had fought in secret battles all over the world. He shunned praise and awards for he only needed to know that he had done his duty. The only battle he ever lost was in a hospital. He was a strong man with a weak heart. I had rushed back from a mission abroad only to arrive less than an hour after his death. There were no final words of reconciliation between us; no acceptance of what I did to save Svetlana. He just lay there—dead and diminished. And I was alone for the first time in my life, with only my duty for companionship.

I walked to the door and, after a moment of hesitation, opened it. Runciman, Omar, Holcomb and Woo were waiting in the hall. They all snapped to attention. I returned their salute.

"Thank you, Major Runciman, for your care," I said dismissively. I was no longer his helpless patient. "Gentlemen, it's time to finish this war with General Cottick. Please join me in the conference room."

I strode off, and Omar, Holcomb and Woo trailed behind. For some reason, I felt empowered and energized. The world had simplified for me and its future had crystallized in my mind.

I sat at the head of the table in the conference room. Colonel Holcomb, who had been acting commander of my army in my enforced absence, made his report.

"Sir, in your absence, there have been two serious developments—."

"Three," interrupted Lieutenant Colonel Woo.

"Yes, three."

Holcomb seemed very disturbed. Commanding Threecor wasn't an easy task, even if only for four days.

"First, sir, the town of Plattsburgh is in open revolt. Rumors of your death precipitated it. There is fighting in the streets and the surrounding countryside. The 15th is being pressed very hard. There is a report, unconfirmed at present, that Colonel Flores is dead. Should we withdraw and regroup?

I remained silent.

Holcomb took the hint and continued with his report. "There is also unrest in Syracuse. The soldiers are complaining about the harshness of your orders in regards to refugees from Buffalo. Colonel Rourke reports a number of incidences— nothing major but together they indicate an underlying discontent. The troops don't understand why everyone coming from Buffalo must turn back or be killed. Some of the men once had friends in the Fifth Guard Division."

I said nothing.

Woo spoke up next. "Sir, our weather satellite has shown a very powerful hurricane forming up in the Atlantic Ocean. The meteorological staff forecast that its track will come just west of the base."

This was an interesting development and an idea came immediately to me.

"Strength?" I asked.

"A big one. Category seven when it hits North Carolina, but still a category three or four when it gets here."

"Does that conclude your report, gentlemen?"

Omar shifted in his chair. "Sir, I have been reviewing the fuel situation. Colonel Rourke's continuous patrols to stop the refugees from Buffalo entering Syracuse are consuming more fuel than I realized. He must reduce the patrols or we will be running short soon."

I sat in silent thought for quite some time. The others sensed my mood and didn't interrupt.

Finally, I broke the silence. "Gentlemen, the time has come to end this. Our primary objective is the destruction of Third Division and the capture or elimination of General Cottick. The heat of the summer has faded and it's now cool enough for combat operations. This hurricane couldn't have come at a better time. Thanks to our satellite system we will be prepared for it, but Cottick's forces won't. It will batter them, and after it has, we'll sweep in and smash whatever is left."

"But Plattsburgh—," Holcomb started to say.

"You will inform whoever is commanding the 15th to hold their ground. Contact Colonel King and inform her I want the entire 200th in Plattsburgh by tomorrow night. She may use whatever transportation assets and fuel supplies she deems necessary. I'm ordering her to crush this rebellion with whatever means necessary—and I mean crush. I've given the citizens of Plattsburgh every opportunity to contribute to the welfare and security of Threecor. They have shown themselves unworthy. King is to consider them all enemies of the state. Is that clear?"

"Yes, sir, I will see that your orders are transmitted to Colonel King immediately."

"Next, I will write a note to Colonel Rourke explaining my reasons for the total blockade of Buffalo. He'll then understand my reasons and will act accordingly. A courier will hand-deliver the note to Colonel Rourke. Colonel Omar, you will issue the courier with an automobile and enough gasoline to make the return journey. No one is to read the note except Colonel Rourke. Sergeant Kellerman of my security detail will be the courier."

I wanted someone completely trustworthy and unquestioningly loyal to be the courier of the dangerous news of the mutiny in Buffalo.

Colonel Omar nodded.

"Gentlemen, we have been distracted from our real mission for far too long. Colonel Holcomb, you will contact Colonel Sheflin and Colonel Petras and inform them that I want the 317th and the 41st ready to move west in two days. I want the 7th and 8th militia regiments to support them."

"What about our foraging operations in Montreal?" Omar

protested. "With the 41st gone, there will be no security for my troops."

"Colonel Omar, your men in Montreal are soldiers first. They won't remain in Montreal scavenging while others fight. They'll attach themselves to the 41st for this operation and prepared for battle. Understood?"

"Yes, sir."

Omar wasn't happy, but I didn't care. I needed every man I could get for my move on Cottick.

"Colonel Holcomb, how many cadet officers do you have in the Kingston Military College?"

"Just under a hundred."

"They will form themselves into a company and attach themselves to the militia. They will complete their training in battle. The soldiers in the training school here in Fort Drum will join them."

Holcomb acknowledged the order.

I stood and walked to the door. "You have your orders. Carry them out."

Holcomb, Omar and Woo stood and saluted.

I left the conference room feeling more alive than I had in days. I had set events in motion and nothing would stop them. Cottick would be hit by a hurricane—no, two hurricanes. I would be the second. The first one would weaken him, but I would be the one to kill him.

– Chapter 26 –

Toronto

Operation SWORD was underway. Colonel Holcomb suggested the codename. Sword of justice, sword of vengeance, sword of deliverance—the codename had many meanings to the men, and to me.

All was progressing as well as could be expected. Of course there were problems here and there, but nothing of real importance. I had provided Colonel Petras most of my available transport trucks, over one hundred vehicles in all, to move the one thousand men of the 41st Battalion. Unfortunately they were delayed. In order to get the vehicles on the main highway from Montreal to Toronto, Petras's engineers had to build several pontoon bridges over the rivers to the west of Montreal.

A twenty-four-hour delay for the men of the 41st couldn't be helped, but it wasn't going to stop me. I left Fort Drum right on schedule on my way to join Colonel Sheflin and her cavalrymen, who were already riding westward to Toronto.

On the first leg of my journey, I rode north to Alexandria Bay in the company of Sergeant Kellerman and a small contingent of mounted militiamen from the 1st Jefferson and 6th Seaway regiments (about one hundred strong). Three heavy tanks from the 88th Armor Battalion followed us. My engineers at Alexandria Bay had constructed a ferry to transport us across the Saint Lawrence River to Rockport on the north shore. I traveled over on the first trip so I could discuss Operation SWORD with the colonel of the 7th Frontenac Militia Regiment. His militiamen would have to walk to Toronto because I had no transport available for them. They wouldn't make it to Toronto in time for the rendezvous, but would follow behind the main force and act as my reserves.

The colonel and I stood by the dock at Rockport on the north side of the Saint Lawrence River watching the ferrying operation. After four hours, my small mounted contingent was across. As the ferry departed from the south side with the first of the heavy tanks, we all looked on with a mix of fascination and dread. Would the makeshift ferry carry the load? The commander of the engineering detail was confident that it would. Nevertheless, we all watched the slow progress of the ferry across the river with considerable apprehension. When the ferry arrived in Rockport with the first tank onboard, I noted that it was riding very low in the water. When the tank drove off, the ferry tipped alarmingly but then bounced back.

The second tank also made it across, but not the third. I watched through my binoculars as the ferry broke in two in the middle of the river and the tank plunged into the water. The two halves of the ferry floated away. Fortunately the commander of the engineers had a small boat following and all aboard the ferry were rescued.

It was a pity about the tank. It was built long ago with technology that couldn't be replaced. However, it wasn't pivotal to my strategy. The most important aspect of the operation was that my army be in position and ready to pounce immediately after the hurricane had roared through and thrown Cottick's forces into disarray.

The two remaining heavy tanks drove away, with the crew of the sunken tank and the ferry engineers riding on their hulls. They would make their way independently to Toronto along the main highway. My force of mounted militiamen would ride along a road south of the main highway and closer to Lake Ontario, so we would have better access to water for ourselves and our horses. I left the militia colonel to get his men organized for their long march.

My small contingent of mounted militiamen rode west at a steady pace. Just to the west of Belleville, we passed the militiamen of the 8th Quinte Militia Regiment, who were already marching along the road to Toronto. They cheered as I passed. All of us, including myself, were in good spirits and morale was high. Everyone was confident in the outcome.

I rode on through the night until at last I joined up with Colonel Sheflin and her battalion on the outskirts of the greater Toronto urban area. Toronto had for a short time served as my headquarters for III Corps, but that was long ago and in a different world. So much had changed since then, including me. I was answerable to no one now but my conscience and my duty to my people.

Sheflin greeted me warmly. I didn't know what to say and averted my eyes. I hadn't seen her since confessing my guilt to her about the death of Major Barovscu.

"Don't worry, sir, we'll win though. General Cottick doesn't stand a chance."

Sheflin's cheerful message told me what I needed to hear: she would pretend that nothing had happened. And so would I.

At dawn, after five hours sleep, I mounted Judge and rode to the top of a high hill. I sat there for some time looking over a deserted wasteland which had once been a massive metropolitan area with a population of millions. The bones of the city's citizens had long since decayed and derelict buildings lined rubble-filled streets. There was nothing alive but weeds, scrubby vegetation, insects and rodents. They were now the masters of the city.

Judge fidgeted to indicate her impatience with me. She was right: it was time to move on. I had a schedule to keep for the hurricane wouldn't wait for me. Already there was a thin line of dark clouds on the southern horizon, marring an otherwise cloudless day.

* * *

Colonel Sheflin had selected as our haven from the approaching hurricane the subterranean parking lot of a tall tower in what was once the financial district of Toronto. The tower had been subjected to many windstorms in the past, each one seemingly fiercer than the last, but the building had endured. The glass in its windows had long since been blown out and now lay shattered among the rubble on the streets surrounding the tower. The tower's skeleton frame would simply let the wind pass through its pillars and, I hoped, wouldn't seriously be affected by the approaching hurricane.

Sheflin had selected this refuge because of its extensive and intact underground parking area, which could offer safe accommodation for our force of over six hundred cavalrymen and their horses. I approved of her choice.

I was much more concerned about my other forces. My tanks had found an underground parking lot further to the north, but the 41st had still not arrived. Colonel Petras had only just left Montreal and he had a seven hour drive before him. All being well, he would arrive in Toronto just before the hurricane. The militiamen of the 8th Quinte would shelter in buildings in an eastern suburb of Toronto, but the men of the 7th Frontenac would be dreadfully exposed. They would have to find what shelter they could. Fortunately for them, they wouldn't get the full fury of the hurricane as the eye of the storm was forecasted to pass west of Toronto, approximately halfway between my location and Cottick's headquarters in Kitchener.

I turned on the hand-cranked radio at a prearranged time in order to listen to Lieutenant Colonel Woo, who was back at Fort Drum, give a coded update of the weather. Reception was awful but I managed to understand that the hurricane had hit the North Carolina coast as a category seven and that there was massive flooding in its wake. The eye of the hurricane was now northeast of Pittsburgh. Woo forecasted that it would weaken to a category four by the time it reached the southern shore of Lake Erie, but it would increase in strength to a category five when it crossed the very warm waters of that shallow lake and fed on the heat from the water. If it lingered over the lake it might even strengthen to a category six. I didn't reply to Woo, because I didn't know if Cottick's forces would be listening and could use the radio signal to triangulate on my position. I was doubtful that they could do this with all the static in the air, but why take the risk?

I left the safety of the underground parking area and climbed up the ramp to the outside. Once on the rubble-filled street, I looked up between the ruined towers. The sky was dark and forbidding. The storm was coming. Would it aid me in my quest or be my undoing? I had risked much in timing my attack on Cottick to coincide with the hurricane. Had I risked too much? I had deliberately put my men in the path of a powerful hurricane, but it was too late for second thoughts now. The die was cast.

I found Kellerman standing beside me. I hadn't heard him approach. He stood there silently waiting for me to acknowledge him.

"Yes, Sergeant," I said without looking at him. "What is it?"

"Sir, there is something I think you should know."

"Go on." I thought Kellerman was going to tell me something about the men's morale or suggest a dangerous mission for himself in the upcoming battle with Cottick's forces, but I was wrong.

"Sir, it's something about Colonel Sheflin."

The way Kellerman said that brief sentence told me that he had some distasteful news to tell. I briefly thought that Sheflin had told others the truth about Barovscu's drowning, but that idea died quickly. Jan Sheflin would never betray me.

"Get on with it," I snapped.

"Sir, I have reason to believe that Colonel Sheflin might have been in Victoria Hewitt's room an hour or so before she killed herself."

"What?" I was astonished by Kellerman's statement.

"Colonel Woo has asked me to inform you that Colonel Sheflin was missing from her command for a period of thirty-two hours around the time of the suicide. Her staff didn't know where she was and her horse was missing. When Colonel Sheflin returned, she told her staff she was scouting out defensive positions, but her horse had been ridden very hard and was close to death. Colonel Woo, when he inspected the area around the house in Watertown, noticed hoof prints of a horse galloping northward."

"Is that all?" There had to be more.

"No, sir. Colonel Woo has traced the pistol that Hewitt used to one issued to a captain in Colonel Sheflin's command. The captain died a few weeks ago of a fever. Furthermore, I noticed blood on the windowsill of Hewitt's room. It appears that someone climbed in or out of that window and cut themselves on a nail. I pointed this out to Colonel Woo, but he said that he has no equipment to test this blood."

"Anything more?"

"Just that the lieutenant on duty that night remembered a noise coming from Hewitt's room an hour before she killed herself. He entered the room and found Hewitt sitting on her bed. She yelled at him to leave. The lieutenant looked around the room and seeing nothing amiss he left."

Kellerman fell silent.

As the clouds darkened above, I stood motionless and deep in thought. It was all circumstantial evidence. Someone else could have entered the room by the window and that could have been weeks ago. Sheflin could have been scouting as she claimed. Victoria could have found and hidden the gun herself. As for the suicide note, it was genuine enough for I recognized Victoria's distinctive scrawl. There was no doubt in my mind that she had written it. Furthermore, the guards had rushed into the room only moments after the shot, so there was no time for anyone to escape.

And yet, in my mind I could see Sheflin standing over Victoria, intimidating and tormenting her. She would have told Victoria how she had let me down and was wrecking all that I had built. She was being selfish and she was in my way. Victoria's letter had said that. Victoria would have been fragile and suggestible that night. I remembered my own overwhelming feeling of remorse. How much guilt and shame had Victoria felt? Sheflin may not have pulled the trigger but did she coerce Victoria into committing suicide?

Did Sheflin do this to clear the way for me to carry on with my crusade against Cottick, undistracted by Victoria and her betrayal, or did Sheflin do it to clear the way for herself?

Did she do it at all?

Did it matter?

Jan was loyal to me and I needed her. It was that simple. I ordered Kellerman to drop the investigation.

I returned to the underground parking lot. The hurricane was almost upon us.

* * *

The noise was deafening. A constant roar of wind drowned out all other sound. The hurricane had arrived.

I stood looking up at the ramp to the outside. A river of water flowed down it and over my feet. The ground dipped slightly in front of the tower. I had thought nothing of this when we arrived, but now I realized that the torrents of rain were being funneled to this site.

I felt a tap on my shoulder and turned to see Colonel Sheflin. Her mouth was moving but I couldn't hear anything.

I cupped my hand to my ear and she screamed into it. I could barely make out a few key words: flooding, rising, underwater. She beckoned me to follow her. An image of Sheflin standing over Victoria flashed into my mind but I dismissed it. It was unwelcome and distracting.

We descended to the second sublevel of the underground parking lot. I was greeted by the sight of a mass of men and horses standing packed together. The men were attempting, with only limited success, to calm their terrified mounts. Sheflin and I pushed our way through the crowd towards the ramp down to the third sublevel. When we arrived, Sheflin pointed to the rising water. I instantly understood her concern. The lowest sublevel of the parking structure was already underwater and the water was rising quickly. If the sublevel that we were on flooded we would all have to squeeze on to the uppermost sublevel, and if that were also to flood we would have to go outside—something that we couldn't do while the hurricane was pounding the city.

I waited there by the ramp with Sheflin and watched the rising water. There was nothing else to do. Once the level reached my knees, I indicated to Sheflin that we should evacuate this level and get the men and horses to the uppermost sublevel.

The men were wet and scared and the animals were terrified, but somehow we managed to squeeze over six hundred men and six hundred horses on the last unflooded sublevel.

We waited.

A young lieutenant had taken it upon himself to take precise measurements of the water level and the rate at which it was rising. I was enormously relieved when he showed me a chart of the water level in the parking area which he had scratched into a concrete wall. The chart indicated the rate of rise was slowing. At last, the storm was moving away to the north. I ordered the lieutenant to pass his good news along to the men and assure them that the worst was over.

Twenty minutes later, with the water nearly up to my waist, and shivering badly, I left the flooded parking area and walked up the exit ramp to the surface. Rain still poured down, but the wind had weakened. The remnants of the hurricane were little more than a bad rainstorm. We could now survive outside. I ordered the cavalrymen of the 317th to leave their underground haven and make their way to the surface.

Besides some bumps and bruises, the 317th had made it through the hurricane with no casualties. I was anxious to discover the fate of my other forces. Sheflin's communications officer contacted the 41st, the 7th and the 8th, as well as the two independent heavy tanks. I had to know what was going on, regardless of the risk of Cottick's forces overhearing. I hoped that they would be too busy with their own difficulties.

The news was bad. The 8th Quinte reported two dead and six wounded, and the 7th Frontenac reported thirteen dead, thirty-five wounded and twelve missing. The two tanks, their crews and the accompanying engineers were unharmed, but there was no word from the 41st.

The 41st had sought refuge from the hurricane in two buildings to the north of my location and not far from the site of the two tanks. I ordered the tanks to drive over to the last known location of the 41st.

I waited and waited. I was almost ready to rush over there myself to investigate when the commander of the lead tank radioed in. There had been a disaster. One of the two buildings in which the men of the 41st had sought shelter had collapsed during the hurricane. There were ninety-two dead, hundreds wounded, many mortally, and hundreds missing, including Colonel Petras. Half of the 41st was out of action, including most of its command staff. I immediately ordered all my forces to rendezvous at the site of the disaster to lend assistance.

I mounted Judge and, with Colonel Sheflin and Sergeant Kellerman on either side of me, I rode northward with the cavalrymen of the 317th to rescue the men of the 41st.

– Chapter 27 –

Guelph

Over three hundred dead, including an experienced and popular battalion commander—a very high price indeed. The body of Colonel Petras was never found under the rubble of the collapsed building, neither were the bodies of hundreds of his men.

Wounded men had been pulled from the rubble by their surviving comrades and had been laid in rows. They awaited attention from the overwhelmed medical staff from the 317th and the few surviving medics from the 41st. Some of the men screamed in pain, while many lay there quietly and slipped into death with little more than an inaudible moan. I watched one medic, with his face covered in dried blood, reset a broken collarbone on a very young lieutenant. The brave lieutenant refused to cry out despite what must have been excruciating pain. The medic finished his work and moved on to his next patient without looking back. The lieutenant, unnoticed by everyone but me, slipped into blissful unconsciousness.

I assigned half the surviving trucks to transport the wounded back to Fort Drum to receive proper medical attention in the base's hospital. After the wounded had departed, I conducted a solemn ceremony over the rubble for the benefit of the remaining survivors. The dead soldiers of the 41st and their commander were left in the tomb that the hurricane had made for them. Afterwards, my soldiers were very quiet and there was little conversation about the hurricane or our upcoming battle with Cottick.

My gamble with the hurricane had cost me a lot, but now it was time to see if it was worth it. I began to organize the next part of Operation SWORD. I wouldn't stop to mourn the dead; I wouldn't stop for anything.

The remaining trucks were loaded with the unhurt survivors of the 41st. These trucks, combined with the two heavy tanks, formed a mobile mechanized column. The column would stay on the main highway and approach Kitchener from the south, while I would lead the slower main force by a more northerly route along Highway 7 and attack Kitchener from the northeast. The militiamen of the 7th Frontenac were a day's march behind us and would form my reserve. That was the plan. An attack on two fronts would, I hoped, sow panic in Cottick's headquarters, but dividing my forces in front of a numerically superior enemy ran against my training and caused me some anxiety.

The progress of my main force along Highway 7 was slow. Many of the low-lying areas were flooded and a number of bridges had been washed away. Nevertheless, my foot-bound force was, under the circumstances, more mobile than the mechanized column that I had created. I was informed that the mechanized column was stuck. An important bridge over a large and swollen river had collapsed and the column had to seek an alternative route. One of the tanks had tried to navigate across open ground and had become mired in the mud, and the other tank had thrown a track, which would take hours to repair. My reserve, the 7th Frontenac, was still trapped in Toronto attempting to find a route that wasn't flooded. My northern force was on its own. I had originally planned to attack Cottick with nearly seven thousand men, but now I was approaching him and his army with barely two-and-a-half thousand. It would have to be enough.

After many detours and delays, the northern force finally reached Guelph, a town only twelve miles from Kitchener.

Guelph, with rolling hills surrounding the area and a river running through the center of the town, made for an obvious defensive position. My troops approached cautiously. I ordered cavalry units to fan out to the north and south of the town, while the militiamen approached from the east.

The air was completely still, which was remarkable given that a powerful hurricane had blasted through here only four days before, and a dense and eerie morning fog enveloped the town. The pale gray mist made every shape indistinct and I felt as though I was floating through nothingness as I approached the town.

Everything was deathly quiet. No enemies, no civilians, no animals, no birds, no insects—nothing.

I left Judge behind and, surrounded by the militiamen, I made my way into the town on foot. Because of the damp, my bad leg throbbed, making walking difficult even with my new cane; however, going by foot was infinitely safer than riding boldly on top of Judge exposed to any sniper in the area.

There was a terrible stench about the place. At first I thought the foul odor was of rotting carcasses from animals drowned in the floods, but a militiaman drew my attention to the real cause. He pointed upwards. Above my head, a dead soldier hung from an old streetlight. He had been dead at least a day. There were others—many others. From every streetlight and overhead sign which could be seen through the fog, there hung the corpse of a soldier.

I ordered one cut down so I could examine his uniform. It was despoiled with grotesque graffiti. I ignored the graphic pictures and instead examined the uniform's shoulder patches. This soldier was from the 22nd Infantry Regiment, which was part of Cottick's army.

The search of Guelph continued. In all, some five hundred of Cottick's soldiers had been hung. Officers and men from various regiments and battalions in the 3rd Brigade were among the dead. Apart from the corpses, we saw no evidence of Cottick's army. Someone had executed Cottick's men, but who, and more important, why?

I ordered my men to set up a defensive perimeter in Guelph, while I organized a reconnaissance of the surrounding area and along Highway 7 towards Kitchener. The thick fog remained all day and it hampered our reconnaissance. I was eager for it to lift so my advance on Kitchener could continue.

Just as the light began to fade at the end of a gloomy evening, there was a development. Colonel Sheflin approached and informed me that her soldiers were bringing in two prisoners.

Sheflin and I watched as these prisoners were marched down the main street, surrounded on their flanks and rear by cavalrymen. Rifles were pointed at their backs. One of the prisoners clutched a torn and dirty rag next to his chest—the instrument of his surrender, I surmised.

The commander of the guarding cavalrymen made a brief report. "Sir, we captured these two a few miles to the east. They were just standing there in the middle of the road waving a rag at us."

One started to speak but a jab in the back from a rifle shut him up.

I examined the two prisoners carefully. There was before me a major from the 3rd Brigade and a captain from the 4th. Both of their uniforms were resplendent with graffiti, and through a sizable tear in the captain's uniform I notice an elaborate tattoo on his chest —of what I couldn't discern.

"Speak," I said flatly, trying to mask my eagerness to hear first hand news of Cottick's army.

The major started to raise a hand in a salute, but a jab in the back with a rifle froze him in mid gesture. He slowly placed his hand by his side.

"General Eastland, I'm hear to negotiate the surrender of the 3rd and 4th brigades," the major said formally. I noted the nervousness his voice betrayed.

I said nothing. My minded whirled at the possibilities that the major's statement implied. Was he offering the surrender of two entire brigades or just some splinter group? Did he speak for the brigade commanders or just junior officers? How many of Cottick's soldiers would meekly surrender to me?

As though Colonel Sheflin was reading my mind, she demanded: "Who do you speak for? What units? How many men?"

The major glanced nervously from me to Colonel Sheflin and then back again.

"Sir, I'm authorized to speak on behalf of all surviving officers at the rank of major and below and all the troops who remain under our command."

"How many is that?" Sheflin prompted.

"Two thousand. The rest are dead, have deserted or have fled with General Cottick."

Only two thousand? The Third had once numbered fifteen thousand officers and men. I had captured six thousand after the Battle of Saranac Lake and the fall of Fort Drum, but what of the rest? What had Cottick done to his division?

"Where's General Cottick?" I demanded in an icy voice.

"General Cottick, his surviving senior commanders and a handful of soldiers are holed up in an old office building on the west side of Kitchener. Our soldiers have him surrounded and we are offering him to you as part of our surrender.

So the betrayer had been betrayed. How gratifying.

"General, sir, we have one condition for our surrender. We respectfully request that we be given the same choice offered to the officers and men of the 1st and 2nd brigades."

"And what do you understand that offer to be?"

"A choice between serving you or exile."

I stayed silent for a few moments and watched the major fidget.

"But Major, when I made that offer to the soldiers of those

brigades I needed them."

The major blanched and was visibly shaken by my reply. He had expected my benevolence. It amused me to watch panic rise in him. He controlled it well (better than the captain) but I saw fear in his eyes.

"I offer you a different choice. All those who surrender will live and all those who don't will die."

In truth, I had already decided that I would eventually make the same offer as before. I didn't fool myself. Even with Cottick dead, there would be plenty of other troubles in this world with which I would have to contend. I needed experienced soldiers and, ironically, soldiers that would do anything for their commander—provided of course that I was that commander. However, the second offer could come later and would be seen by the soldiers of the Third as me being magnanimous in victory instead of just making an expedient deal to obtain their surrender. I began to think of the future, now that the end of the war against Cottick was in sight.

I convinced myself I had no vindictive urge to punish the men of the Third any more than I had to. We were all soldiers who once served together in III Corps. We had lived, fought and died together. We had survived through the collapse of our once-glorious civilization and shared a bond which nothing could break—not even Cottick's insanity. His madness had infected us all in different ways—both those who fought with him and those who fought against him. To be whole once again, we had to end this war. And afterwards, I had to re-establish the order that had been lost through the chaos unleashed by Cottick. I would need the willing help of men of the Third to fulfill that task.

The major recovered his voice. "Sir, I'm not authorized to accept different conditions. I must take your offer back to the brigades."

"Then go. And be quick about it. My patience is almost at an end. Your actions and your misguided loyalty to the traitor have cost many lives."

The major and the captain were escorted back to where they had been found.

As the night progressed, my initial benevolent feelings on the matter of the fate of the men of the Third were being slowly eroded by the darkness of the night. My mind told me I would need these experienced soldiers in the future, but something deep in a primitive part of my being wanted these men punished. That something was becoming stronger. The response from the men of the Third had better be quick before I decided to withdraw my offer that they would live after they surrendered.

As it turned out, the men of the Third surrendered unconditionally during the morning. The lengthy process transpired without incident. They were eager to end their fight against me and be free of General Cottick. I decided to honor my part of the agreement and let them live. My dark thoughts of revenge faded with the coming of the dawn.

My army was whole again and Operation SWORD was nearly complete. There was only a small matter of a malignant tumor to be removed.

– Chapter 28 –

Kitchener

I had him! Cottick was trapped. I was tingling with anticipation. The end was in sight.

Between twenty and thirty of Cottick's most fanatical followers were barricaded inside a squat, three-storey, Y-shaped office building. Cottick's followers had hastily prepared a killing zone around the building. All the trees and shrubs near the building had been cut down and cleared away to give the occupants a clear field of fire. Rushed and rudimentary, but effective.

The transfer of the perimeter pickets from the men of the Third (who were now my prisoners) to a mixed force of the 41st and 317th battalions went smoothly. I assigned militiamen to guard the prisoners. This final battle would be no place for inexperienced militia.

The men of the Third had trapped Cottick, and it was now my task to get into his den and kill him. One of my heavy tanks had finally arrived; the other was still miles away stuck in the mud. I could simply have stood off and blasted the building to rubble with the tank's main gun, burying everyone inside. Somehow that wasn't very satisfying. There was no way I was going to fail in my task of personally killing him. Even now I could feel excitement swell in my chest.

I left with Sergeant Kellerman to examine the area surrounding the building, leaving Colonel Sheflin and her staff to pore over a rough sketch of the building which an officer of the Third had made for me. The building was probably close to forty years old and would have once been the office for some business or other. The crux of its 'Y' faced a concrete courtyard with a disused fountain in the center. Some windows had been smashed for gun ports, but most still survived. Two doors opened on to the courtyard. To the left there was a weed-covered parking lot and the main door, where a long time ago employees would have entered, and to the right there was a grassy area covering a man-made oval mound. An emergency exit opened on to the grassy area. At the back, there was a delivery ramp with a large roll-up freight door, and a smaller service door nearby. A hundred yards farther on there was a line of trees—too far away to be of any use to me. On every side, there was a lot of open ground to cross to get to one of the entrances.

"Can you get inside?" I asked Kellerman.

"Maybe, sir, but I would prefer to wait for dark."

"So would I, but I doubt Cottick will give us that time."

"Where can he go?"

"Cottick won't go anywhere. He'll kill himself, Sergeant. He'll kill himself before I can, and that must not happen. Is that clearly understood?

"Yes, sir." Kellerman understood me only too well.

Leaving Kellerman to examine the building and its approaches, I returned to Colonel Sheflin.

"Are you certain the perimeter is secure?" I asked. "I don't want Cottick to escape."

"Yes, sir," replied Sheflin. "My men are in the trees in the back and behind the grassy mound, as well as covering the parking lot and the courtyard."

"How many snipers?"

"Twelve. I have positioned them four to a side. We've already targeted six of Cottick's men. I can have them taken out as soon as you give the order. I can do it now if you like."

It was clear that Sheflin was impatient to get going, and so was I, but first I wanted Kellerman inside.

"Good work, Colonel. Get your men ready. We'll move soon, but not until I give the order."

"Yes, sir."

Kellerman approached. "Sir, I may have found a way inside."

"Go on, Sergeant."

"Do you see the far right corner?" Kellerman asked without pointing, in case we were being watched by someone inside the building, which I thought was very likely.

I nodded.

He continued, "It's less than thirty yards from the top of the mound to the corner of the building. If one of the windows were smashed I could leap in. It's not a blind spot, but its unlikely General Cottick would have put guards there as it is far from any doors. I'll need a diversion though, just to make sure."

"Very well. I'll arrange one. How long will you need to prepare?"

"Five minutes."

I thought for a moment. "Colonel Sheflin, do we have a megaphone?"

"I doubt it," she replied. "It's not something we would've bothered to bring with us, but perhaps the Third Division's stores have one. I'll check."

"Fine, but before you do, assign your best sniper to Sergeant Kellerman. Have the rest of them ready to take out as many of Cottick's men as they can in one volley." I added: "Do you understand, Colonel? One shot from each sniper and then stop. Make sure your men understand that clearly."

"Yes, sir."

"Wait for my orders."

Fifteen minutes later, everyone was in place and ready

to act on my command. However, I was still waiting for a megaphone. I would have to adjust my plan if one couldn't be found. I became more and more impatient as the minutes ticked by, but at last Sheflin appeared. She ran towards me with an engineer from the 41st trailing behind.

"Sir, we had some problems," Sheflin stammered, as she gasped for breath. She waved a hand at the engineer, who held the cone of a megaphone towards me. The electronics had been cut away, leaving just the empty cone.

"Sir, the battery has long since died and corroded away to dust," the engineer reported. "We've no replacements. Even if we had, the corroded battery has damaged the connections. However, the cone alone should adequately project your voice, provided you shout into it."

Not entirely satisfactory, but it would have to do.

I ordered the tank commander to move his tank some fifty yards closer to the building. The tank roared to life and rolled forward. Sheflin and I walked behind it, protected by its armored hull from any snipers Cottick had stationed in the building.

After the tank's noisy engine turned off, I said to Sheflin: "Colonel, you may begin when ready."

I held the megaphone cone and waited.

One minute later, shots ripped from all directions, and then there was silence. Six of Cottick's men lay dead. During the volley, the sniper assigned to Kellerman had blasted open a ground-floor window. Now, I had to distract Cottick so Kellerman could get inside. I put the megaphone's cone to my mouth.

"Cottick, I want to talk to you," I shouted into the cone. "You're trapped and my men can storm the building at any time, but I'm offering you an alternative. If you're interested, talk to me."

I waited. I was gambling that Cottick and his men would be

distracted by the sight of the tank and by what I was going to say. They wouldn't be watching the approach that Kellerman would take.

A top-floor window was smashed out and one of Cottick's senior officers appeared. The wily Cottick wasn't going to expose himself to my snipers, but I never expected that he would. The officer shouted something (I couldn't discern what) and then surprisingly he threw a naked woman out the window. She screamed as she fell, but the sound abruptly stopped when she hit the cement tiles of the courtyard.

I quickly reached for my binoculars. The woman lay still in the courtyard, her arms in an unnatural position. She was likely a prostitute taken into the building as a last amusement for the degenerate general.

Madness! What was the purpose of killing this helpless woman? Did Cottick think that such a display would stop me? He was wrong.

"Cottick," I shouted into the cone, "I'll let you and your men live if you surrender to me now. You're not well. I'll give you whatever medical attention you need." By this, I meant putting a bullet in his brain. I didn't expect Cottick to accept my offer, but maybe one or two of his followers might make a run for safety. None did, however.

The senior officer disappeared from view, but my distraction worked. I saw Kellerman charge across the open ground and vault through the broken window. He had entered the building unseen. He would create mayhem inside as only Kellerman could—and I would help him in that.

As soon as I heard gunfire inside the building, I turned to Colonel Sheflin. "Colonel, order your troops to storm that building. The snipers will cover them. Move!"

There was a flurry of hand signals and radio calls and then my men descended on the building. Assault troops, a hundred strong, stormed it from all directions. Small-arms fire poured into it from my advancing soldiers. The battle, if I can glorify it by that term, was quickly over and with only a few casualties among my forces—none of them fatal.

As soon as the signal for all clear was given, I hastened towards the building. A private held the main door open for me and I entered. I watched as ten prisoners filed past me with their hands high in the air. They would be dealt with later. Right now I had to find Cottick.

Colonel Sheflin appeared from a stairwell.

"General Cottick is under guard on the top floor. We have taken him alive." Sheflin's scarred face beamed as she told me the news.

Following Sheflin, I climbed the stairs to the third floor. At the top, I entered a room once used as a large conference room, although the table had been replaced with a single stained mattress in the middle of the floor. Disgusting.

Sergeant Kellerman stood before me, unharmed after his brief one-man assault. I even imagined that I spied a smile forming at the corners of his narrow mouth.

In the corner of the room, I briefly noticed a woman with messy brunette hair crouched down hugging her crying child. The little blonde girl of about five had her face buried in her mother's chest. Neither appeared hurt. I assumed the woman was another of Cottick's whores, and I didn't care who the child was. My entire focus was riveted on a solitary man sitting on the floor with his back against the far wall. Three of my soldiers were guarding General Cottick. I had him at last.

His jacket was completely unbuttoned, exposing a nasty bullet wound to his stomach. Otherwise, his features were familiar and yet strangely different. He looked old and pale and his powerful frame had diminished. His shaved head no longer gave the illusion of youthful potency. Although he was the same height as me and much broader in the chest, he appeared small to my eyes. Was this the madman who I had sacrificed so much to capture? He didn't seem worthy of my vengeance. However, his eyes betrayed him. They were wide and wild. Yes, insane, but also defiant and challenging.

Kellerman appeared by my side. "Sir, we thought you would like to have the honor."

"Thank you, Sergeant. I would indeed," I replied without taking my eyes from Cottick.

I pulled my pistol from its holster and approached Cottick.

Cottick looked up at me. "Go to Hell!" he snarled.

I paused in my approach.

"Hollis, my dear old friend, we're already there."

It was time to end this. I pointed my pistol at his head.

"You can't kill me, Eastland." He paused. "I am immortality unveiled."

I had no time to reflect on this strange utterance because a sudden commotion occurred behind me.

I turned to see the young woman standing with a pistol leveled at me. She must have hidden it between her body and that of her daughter's.

I stood transfixed as she opened fire. Bullets sprayed wildly across the room. Kellerman slammed into me and we crashed on to the stained mattress. On my way down I saw Colonel Sheflin dive into the path of bullets meant for me. She fell to the floor. I swung my gun towards the crazed woman and fired. The bullet smashed into her chest. She fell against the wall and slowly slumped down. She was dead before she hit the floor.

I pushed Kellerman off me. He mumbled something, but what I couldn't tell. A bullet had grazed his head and another had turned his left hand into a bloody mess.

One of the guards was still and unmoving and another lay moaning. The third guard scrambled to his feet and leveled his rifle at Cottick.

"No!" I shouted. "He's mine! He's mine!"

I stood and approached Colonel Sheflin. A frothy mixture of blood and air oozed from her mouth. I knelt beside her. She attempted to say something, so I leaned closer to hear her feeble voice.

"Are you hurt, sir?" she asked.

"No, Jan. I'm okay."

She frowned. "Victoria. I must—," she started to whisper.

"Shh." I squeezed her hand. "It's not important. Save your strength."

"I love you," she whispered.

Her eyes glazed over and her head rolled to one side. I felt her hand go limp in mine. What might have been was gone.

I leaned over and gently kissed Jan on her cheek.

Why did she have to die? Why did Victoria? Could no one who loved me live? I knew the answer: love couldn't survive in Hell. Hate, however, flourished.

I stood up from beside Jan's body and walked over to General Cottick. I faced my enemy.

"What did you think of my toy, Eastland? She was superb material to work with. The bitch was so easy to twist. She would do anything for the brat. Just a single coded phrase and then … Pity she failed." Cottick began laughing hysterically.

Enough of this insanity.

I placed my pistol against his forehead. He seemed not to notice. I squeezed the trigger and the mad laughter abruptly ceased. Cottick's blood and brains were splattered across the floor and walls. I bent over and ripped one of the stars from his jacket. After putting my pistol back in its holster, I used both hands to pin the last star on to my uniform's shoulder.

My mission was completed.

The door burst open and in rushed my soldiers. The unhurt guard attended to his wounded comrade and I helped Kellerman sit up. Medics arrived and the wounded were taken away, along with the bodies of Colonel Sheflin and the guard. My men returned to remove the bodies of General Cottick and the woman, but I ordered them away. I wanted to first talk in private to the little girl.

The child was crying over the body of her dead mother. I walked over to her and put my hand on her shoulder. She looked up at me with tears streaming down her pretty face. The little girl needed to be cared for and I felt a duty to provide that care for I had killed her mother.

Her mother had been tortured and brainwashed, but Cottick had left this little girl alone. Who was she? A strange thought came to me. Could she be Cottick's daughter? No, not even Cottick would have treated the mother of his child as he had, and he could never have kept the fact that he had a daughter a secret for the past five years. Someone would have found out. There would have been rumors. No, she couldn't be Cottick's.

"It's all right," I reassured her. "I'll look after you."

In a flash, the girl brought her hand out from under her mother's body. I stared in amazement at the barrel of her mother's pistol pointing directly between my eyes. My own gun was back in its holster. I would never be able to draw it in time, and there was no one else in the room to help me.

So this was how it was to end. The great General Eastland, commander of the Army of Threecor and survivor of dozens of battles, was to be killed by a child—a child he had just promised to look after. But how could I blame her? I had shot her mother in front of her. I looked into the girl's eyes; they told me that she was terrified.

So many had died for me to defeat Cottick and I had done so many terrible things. I had hoped to do some good by caring for this child, but so much for my redemption. I would never be given the opportunity to get the stain of so much death off my hands.

The girl's small index finger tightened around the trigger. I felt an overwhelming sense of sadness flood through me.

The trigger moved.

Was this how the people who I had executed felt? Regret for a life unfinished. There was so much left to do. I had promised my soldiers order, but now that promise would be forever unfulfilled. Without me, chaos would consume my army.

I prepared myself for death. I was a soldier and I was not afraid.

The hammer fell.

Click.

There were no more bullets left in the gun. A wave of relief swept through me.

I took a deep breath and held my hand out for the gun. My hand shook slightly.

"I'll look after you now," I promised. "We've so much to do, and I need your help. Will you help me?"

The past and the future looked at each other across an incomprehensible void.

Slowly, the girl relaxed her grip on the pistol and placed it gently in my outstretched hand. No one would ever know what had just occurred between us. In time, I hoped the girl would remember it only as a bad dream—a nightmare which never really happened. The protection and wellbeing of this little girl would provide me with a way of redeeming myself for the many deaths and tragedies that I had caused.

But how was I now to redeem this Hell on Earth that we had created? Where did I go from here? What orders should I give?

Someone had once complained that Hell was murky. True enough, but the path out of Hell, like the one into it, was even murkier.

APPENDIX

ORGANIZATIONAL CHARTS

THE ARMY OF THREECOR
(Established after the recapture of Fort Drum)

Army Headquarters

Commanding General	Lt. Gen. Walter J. Eastland
Army Intelligence Group	Lt. Col. Andrew X. Woo
Army Signals Group	Lt. Col. Mamud Fajia
Military Police Headquarters	Maj. William Beant
1st Engineering Detachment	Maj. Mikel S. Tuti
1st Security Detail & Aviation Support	Maj. Belinda E. Bokuk
Fort Drum Hospital	Maj. Dwayne F. Runciman

Fighting Forces

15th Infantry Battalion.	Col. Juan F.J. Flores
41st Infantry Battalion	Col. Christos N. Petras
88th Armor Battalion	Col. Daniel M. Rourke
132nd Infantry Battalion	Col. Edward C.T. Hunt, Jr.
200th Infantry Battalion	Col. L. Janice King
317th Cavalry Battalion	Col. Jan Sheflin
Naval Detachment (Sackets Hbr)	Maj. Bors D. Barovscu

Supporting Forces

Quartermaster Regiment   Col. Marum Omar

    A Company (fuel procurement)

    B, C and D Companies (foraging)

    E and F Companies (water distribution)

    G Company (stores and motor pool)

    2nd Engineering Detachment

Training Schools   Col. Oliver P.D. Holcomb

    Kingston Military College – 100th Cadet Officers Training Unit

    Light Fighters Infantry School – 101st Advanced Training Unit

Total strength   8,029

Militia Regiments

In northeastern New York:	1st Jefferson	2nd Adirondack
	3rd Syracuse	4th Mohawk Valley
	5th Champlain	6th Seaway
In southeastern Ontario:	7th Frontenac	8th Quinte

Eventual combat strength of militia   approximately 20,000

ORDER OF BATTLE AT SARANAC LAKE

General Eastland's Ad Hoc Forces

Headquarters E1 (Lake Placid)	Lt. Gen. Walter J. Eastland
Task Force R2	Col. Daniel M. Rourke
Task Force H3	Lt. Col. Edward C.T. Hunt, Jr.
Task Force H4	Col. Oliver P.D. Holcomb
Task Force P5	Lt. Col. Christos N. Petras
Task Force K6	Capt. L. Janice King
Task Force S7	Lt. Col. Jan Sheflin

Total strength   993

General Cottick's Forces

Commanding General	Maj. Gen. Hollis Cottick III
1st Brigade of Third Inf. Div.	Brig. Gen. Henry Zwettl
27th Infantry Regiment	
57th Infantry Regiment	
245th Reconnaissance Battalion	
315th Urban Warfare Battalion	
A/3rd Signals Company	
1st and 2nd Transport Groups	
Elements of 32nd Security Brigade	Brig. Gen. Daniel Zhang
9th Mechanized Battalion	
A/1st Heavy Tank Platoon	
C/2nd Urban Tank Platoon	

Total strength	approximately 3,500

ORDER OF BATTLE AT TULLY

Elements of 88th Armored Battalion	
A/2nd Urban Tank Platoon	Lt. Gen. Walter J. Eastland
B/2nd Urban Tank Platoon	Col. Daniel M. Rourke
Elements of 200th Inf. Battalion	Col. L. Janice King
Survivors of 132nd Inf. Battalion	Maj. Vinat Ihrig (a/cdr.)
3rd Syracuse Militia Regiment	Col. (militia) Anthony Sorrento

Total strength	539 regular and 793 militia

El Acero's Marauders

Approximately 3,000 irregular cavalry

UNITS THAT ADVANCED ON KITCHENER

Elements of the Army of Threecor
    Commanding General   Lt. Gen. Walter J. Eastland

Main Forces
    41st Infantry Battalion   Col. Christos N. Petras
    317th Cavalry Battalion   Col. Jan Sheflin
    7th Frontenac Militia Regiment   Col. (militia) Jagdeep V. Ruf
    8th Quinte Militia Regiment   Col. (militia) Wilton M.A. Hiller

Attached Units
    A/1st Heavy Tank Platoon of 88th Armored Battalion
    Ferry detail from 1st Engineering Detachment
    100th and 101st Training Units
    Ad hoc elements from Quartermaster Regiment
    Security detail from 1st and 6th Militia Regiments

Total strength   1,753 regular and 5,108 militia

The Battle of Saranac Lake

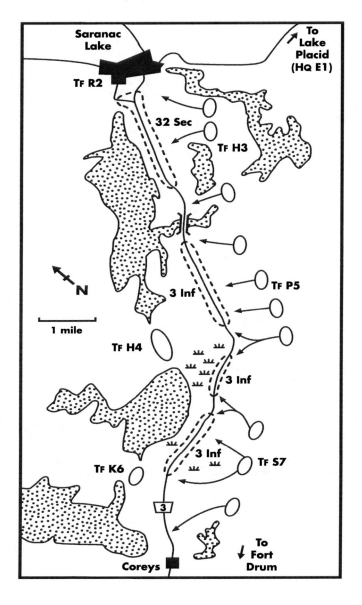

The Battle of Tully

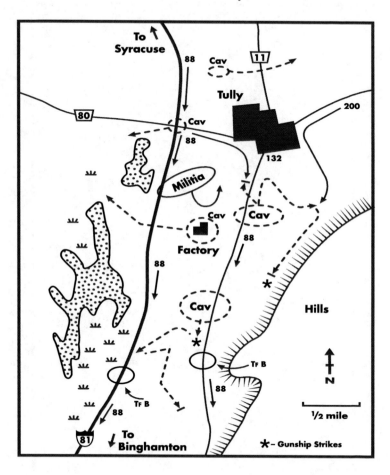

Dr. Mark Tushingham has worked on climate change and other environmental issues since 1981 and continues to do so today. In obtaining his doctorate in 1989, he demonstrated a strong link between climate change and the observed rise in sea level. He has watched the issue of climate change grow from an obscure subject of interest to only a few academics to an issue that today unsettles governments. As a hobby, he has collected a personal library of over eighty books on military matters. Tushingham's first novel, *Hotter than Hell,* was a controversial and brisk-selling cautionary tale of environmental collapse. Tushingham was born in 1962, when the world's population was three billion—half that of today and less than a third of what it will be by the middle of this century.